fireshadow

Anthony Eaton was born in 1972 in a town which later burned to the ground in a volcanic eruption. He has been known to describe this event as "just typical". Generally, though, he is a lot more cheerful and spends his time writing books and occasionally fishing. While he is yet to catch anything larger than a herring, he has high expectations. He has also been known to exercise sporadically ...

In 1997 he met Gary Crew at a writer's workshop, and decided to become a writer. *The Darkness*, his first novel, was published in 2000 and won the West Australian Premier's Award for young adult fiction. His second novel, *A New Kind of Dreaming*, was a Children's Book Council of Australia Notable Australian Book and was also included in the prestigious International Youth Library Selection of Notable Books (White Ravens) catalogue. In 2002 he also released *Nathan Nuttboard Hits the Beach* – his first book for younger readers.

Other books by the same author

Young Adult
The Darkness
A New Kind of Dreaming

Younger Readers
Nathan Nuttboard Hits the Beach
The Girl in the Cave

Anthony Eaton
fireshadow

UQP

First published 2004 by University of Queensland Press
Box 6042, St Lucia, Queensland 4067 Australia

www.uqp.uq.edu.au

Typeset by University of Queensland Press
Printed in Australia by McPherson's Printing Group

Distributed in the USA and Canada by
International Specialized Books Services, Inc.,
5824 N.E. Hassalo Street, Portland, Oregon 97213-3640

Cataloguing in Publication Data
National Library of Australia

Eaton, Anthony, 1972– .
  Fireshadow.

  For young adults

  I. Title.

A823.4

ISBN 0 7022 3381 1

For Imogen

In the bush, we are the only silence.
Always in the background drifts
    the hum of insects,
    distant chirp of tiny birds,
    stir of leaves against warm air,
    raucous cries of cockatoo and kookaburra.

And beneath all, edging subtle
    around the depths of consciousness,
Hidden in the gentle disquiet,
You can feel ghosts,
Spirits of land, fire, sky,
Watching over changing ages,
Standing silent guard over those transients who pass,
Feeling the pain of ravaged trees and scarred earth,
Who know the quiet footsteps of the hunter
    and the jarring scream of white metal.

They are all that remains of time gone before.
They do not judge.
        They do not condemn,
            Merely watch –

And that is how it should be.

PART ONE

One

Vinnie

Old spirits walked here. Ghosts as old as time. Vinnie stepped into the clearing, the leaves of the eucalypts trembled in the midday heat and the occasional insect chirped. Otherwise, the bush stood silent. In the trees behind, the black cockatoos which had been shadowing him through the treetops for the last two hours ceased their cries, and an unusual eeriness descended.

The silence was unsettling. Strange. Not a real quiet, but a kind of gentle restlessness that Vinnie sensed rather than heard. Not since the hospital had he felt so tranquil. And here there was no disinfectant smell, this was no sterile silence – here was not so much absence of sound as lack of noise.

He stood still. During the hike out, he'd become accustomed to the crunch of his footsteps on the gravel path, the gentle labour of his breathing. Now, with a jolt, Vinnie was aware how far he was from other people.

Refreshing, yet at the same time frightening. Walking, his eyes on the path, he had not been touched by the immensity of the forest, the overwhelmingness of it. The trees had closed in, their branches a dim green canopy shutting out all larger perspective. Now though, at the edge of the clearing – because of the clearing – his sense of scale returned and the forest took on new dimensions.

Vinnie moved from the end of the path and took a few steps out into space. The clearing was enormous. It sloped away from where he stood, dropping in rough terraces for about five hundred metres, to where a creek ran hidden through thick brush and scrub.

He glanced back towards the trees. The wall they formed was broken by patches of darkness – undergrowth not yet trodden flat. The path stretching away out of sight, an insignificant curve against the wild.

This would do.

The decision to run had not been difficult. Home was cold and lifeless now, his mother introspective, his father bound up in the hatred of loss. And Vinnie knew that despite their assurances, their empty protestations, his presence there would do nothing to exorcise their grief. Just the opposite. As long as he was around, with their pain etched in the scar tissue on his face, they would look at him and see not their son but their daughter. Would imagine the screams of their eldest child, trapped in her coffin of burning steel, and would resent him.

And what of him? Vinnie wasn't stupid. He knew that his life was never going to be as it was. Not now. The moment he'd made the decision to crawl alone from the flames – to let the monster engulf Katia – he knew he'd changed everything. In many ways it was only fitting – the scarring – so that

4

for the rest of his life he would be reminded, each and every day, of his cowardice.

"You let your sister burn."

Later on, his father had apologised for those words. But why? He was right, wasn't he? The proof was there, in the livid red tissue that covered the right half of Vinnie's face. His own personal mark of Cain. How could he stay in the house knowing that every time he entered a room his dad would think of Katia?

Unconsciously his hand lifted, fingertips tracing gently over the ridges and valleys of his skin, searching for the point where the old met the new.

No, the decision to run had been right. The thought of being in a place without people was appealing. The only difficulty was working out some way of doing it that wouldn't cause his parents any further grief, so they wouldn't search for him. But in the end even that hadn't been too hard.

Vinnie picked his way down the terraces, towards where the creek trickled among thickets of thorn bushes. The day was hot, the pack heavy, and he was out of shape from months spent lying immobile, wrapped in bandages. Still, the sun felt agreeable, and the sweat, and the dirt. After all that time in the clean sterility of the hospital, it was good to feel real again. To be alive once more.

Perhaps that was why he'd ended up here in this place with its dusty colours and persistent sense of restive life, standing alone in the middle of the bush, two hours walk from the nearest town. Perhaps he had needed to come somewhere like this to replenish himself.

Vinnie knelt and examined the water. It was running, seemed clear, but he'd boil it before he drank it. He sluiced some onto his face and tasted the tang of dried sweat mixed with icy creek water. Then he stood again and looked around once more.

The clearing was the site of an old forestry town that had burned in the nineteen-sixties and never been rebuilt – that much was written on his map. But he'd have thought by now the bush would have reclaimed the old townsite – wasn't that what was supposed to happen? Shouldn't there have been a few lumps of concrete and tin and perhaps a stone chimney or two dotted between the trees? But nothing remained, not even ruins, and the forest still stood aloof, leaving the scar of the old town-site as an empty, grassy slope, punctuated only by a few sparse shrubs and a couple of scraggly trees. It seemed almost as though this particular place, once home to loggers and millers and their families, was no longer fit to be forest. Perhaps this land too was being punished.

Even so, it would do. A thick-branched pine stood on higher ground, just a little away from the creek and Vinnie decided to set up camp there, in the deep shade. In his pack he had his sister's hiking tent – no one would even know it was missing – and food for at least a few days. Eventually, he'd have to walk back into town for more supplies, and there was always the risk of him being noticed, but he'd deal with that problem when it arose.

Vinnie sat for a few minutes, letting the unsteady silence of the afternoon settle around him, and, when he felt that the bush was getting used to his presence, he started to quietly set up his camp.

May 1943

The pale light of pre-dawn was filtered by the fog that lay across the clearing. Kangaroos feeding by the fence line were little more than ethereal shadows as they grazed. In the surrounding trees the birds stirred and with the first rays of sunlight the mist began to burn away and kookaburras and magpies launched into strident greeting.

Their cry was answered by the unlikely sound of a bugle, and as the reveille echoed through the trees, wraith-like shapes emerged from the huts, bleary-eyed and stretching, moving automatically towards the latrines and the mess hall, where smoke already drifted from the chimney.

Erich watched the scene dispassionately from the steps in front of Hut Seventeen, German division. His first morning. The cold air bit through the thin material of his desert-issue uniform and he stifled the urge to shiver. No weakness. Not here. Not in the enemy heartland.

"Morning."

The speaker, in a heavy reddish overcoat, emerged from the haze of sleeping men in the hut and stood in the doorway at the top of the steps, lighting a cigarette.

"Want one?" His German was rough and his accent coarse. Nothing like the high language Erich was accustomed to. He shook his head, no, and the man looked him over.

"Get any sleep?"

"A little."

Erich had arrived late, the only German in a shipment of Italians, and the guards who had shepherded them off the truck were disinclined to process a single prisoner at that time of night. Instead, he'd been given some bedding, scrounged together from what was available outside of the store, and escorted to Hut Seventeen. His bunkmates had all been asleep when he'd been shown in. After the long ride, with the truck lurching through the dark along rough gravel roads hewn into the forest, Erich had been exhausted and expected sleep to come easily. Once alone in the darkness though, the night sounds of the surrounding bush, so alien, so foreign, had worked their way into his consciousness, holding sleep at bay. Each distant screech and howl startled him with its primal aggression, until eventually he rose in the first gloom of dawn and crept from the hut to watch the morning slink between the trees.

The other man sat heavily on the step beside him and drew on his cigarette, the smell slightly nauseating in the clean morning air. The stranger took in Erich's brown uniform and high boots.

"*Afrika Korps*, eh? Not a lot of sand here."

No reply was forthcoming and the two sat in silence until the other man stuck out his hand.

"Günter. Günter Bote. *Wehrmacht*."

"Erich Pieters." He shook the offered hand.

"Welcome to Australia."

Erich didn't reply.

"They issue you with a kit yet?"

"Like yours?" Erich nodded at the magenta greatcoat wrapped around the other man's shoulders. It was far too big for him, and the sleeves were rolled up. "I'd rather wear my uniform."

"Suit yourself." Günter shrugged. "You'll freeze in a month or two."

"I'm happy to suffer a little for the Fatherland."

The other man laughed, his mirth striking a blaze of embarrassed anger into Erich's cheeks.

"What's funny?"

"You."

Erich was on his feet, ready to fight, but the other man just laughed harder, until Erich stepped away.

"Your disrespect for your country is a disgrace."

"Settle down, youngster. You might be young, but that's no excuse for being stupid. You want to get thrown into the detention cells before you've even been processed?"

Turning sharply on his heel, Erich stalked off in the direction of what he assumed were the latrines. He could still hear the other man chuckling behind him.

When he returned a few minutes later the hut was empty, all five men up and gone. Erich looked around, confused, until he noticed movement down at the cleared parade ground, a hundred metres away. Rollcall. They'd mentioned it briefly last night. He strolled towards the lines of men.

On the other side of a fence the prisoners in the next section – Italians, he guessed – were also lining up for the morning count. There didn't seem quite so many of them as there were in the German ranks.

"You there! Hurry up!"

The order was barked through a megaphone, the speaker an Australian army guard not much older than Erich himself. Throwing a bored glance in the direction of the guard, Erich continued towards the parade at the same steady pace and joined the end of the back line.

"New bloke, up here. Now!"

There was some sniggering among the gathered men, but no one laughed out loud. Erich fell out and walked to the spot indicated, in the middle of the front row. For the next ten minutes the young one with the megaphone announced the names staccato fashion and the men replied with a simple "here" – most answering in German. Another Australian checked the speaker's identity and a third marked a clipboard. The whole process was quick and efficient, the men cooperative. Erich's name was not called.

At the end of the roll, a German officer, older than most of the others in the compound, stepped forward from where he had been standing beside the Australian officers and spoke in German.

"Another fine day at the office, my friends."

A few men chuckled obligingly. Erich guessed that this was a standard joke.

"Not too much to report this morning. There will be a concert this Saturday evening and the Commandant has generously invited any interested men to attend. Günter will take your names after breakfast. Other than that, have a nice day in the woods. Sick parade in twenty minutes, work parade at seven thirty-five as usual. Enjoy your picnic lunch. New boy" – a nod at Erich – "stay behind for a couple of minutes, please. The rest of you are dismissed."

Again there was some quiet laughter as the men drifted off in the direction of the mess hall. The officer chatted amiably in broken English with the guards for a few moments, before crossing to where Erich still stood at attention.

"Stand easy, young man."

Resentment flared in Erich but he didn't let it show. Hadn't he stood up for himself in Libya when the bastard English had stormed in to their little encampment from all directions? And this man couldn't see past his age.

10

"I'm Heinrich Stutt. Ranking German officer."

"Erich Pieters. *Afrika Korps*."

"Welcome to Marinup."

"Thank you, sir."

The man was middle-aged, wearing a regulation naval uniform beneath his magenta greatcoat. His flashes indicated that he was a first officer.

"I understand that you haven't been processed yet."

"No sir."

"Fine, then. We'll have breakfast and then get you organised with a kit and some supplies. Where did you spend the evening?"

"Hut Seventeen, sir."

"Günter's house. You could do worse. We might leave you there for the moment." A bell sounded from the door of the mess hut. "Come on, breakfast."

Erich followed.

"We organise our own meals and do our own cooking. The Australians keep us supplied with the basics, and we have a vegetable garden for extra nourishment. You won't need to worry about going hungry."

"Thank you, sir."

Stutt stopped mid-stride and turned to him.

"You'll also get along a lot better with everyone, including the guards, if you relax a little. We tend to remain reasonably informal here, within limits, of course. The Australians like it that way, and it certainly makes life a lot more bearable for all concerned."

"Informal, sir?"

"You'll work it out. Hungry?"

A nod, and they entered the mess hut. At one end stood a

rough wooden table where Erich was handed a plate, a boiled egg, and several pieces of bread.

"You can toast the bread through there, if you wish." Stutt nodded in the direction of a small kitchen, built off the main eating area. "And there's coffee in that urn. This mess is also our main recreation area so we keep it tidy. You'll do your own dishes."

The food was good, filling the emptiness that had settled, heavy and insistent, upon him. Throughout the quick meal, Stutt carried on telling him the rules and regulations of camp life.

"This isn't a bad place," he concluded. "Not too bad at all. A bit foreign, but there's not a lot we can do about that."

It was hard to be certain whether the man was trying to be funny.

Outside, a siren shattered the peace and the last remaining men bolted down their coffees and headed for the door. Stutt seemed unconcerned.

"One of the good things about being the ranking officer – no work detail. Come on, let's get you processed."

As they left the mess Stutt pointed out other buildings in the compound:

"Canteen – you can buy supplies and cigarettes there with the credits that they pay you. The latrines you've already found, I imagine. School room and hospital. You have any medical skills?"

"Not really, sir."

"Pity. We need a new orderly. The doctor's having to make do with a stretcher bearer we borrowed from the Italians and he's proving less than satisfactory. You sure you don't know anything about medicine?"

12

"Only what I picked up in the field, sir."

Stutt stopped. "And what was that?"

"When the British took our position we had a lot of dead and injured, sir, including our medical officer. I was one of two who didn't get shot, so it fell to us to tend to the wounded."

"What sort of tending?"

"Fishing out bullets, mainly. Administering morphine, bandaging. At least until we ran out of dressings."

"What then?"

"Made more bandages out of the dead men's uniforms, sir."

"Not a pleasant task."

"They didn't need them any more. In the end it was point-less anyway."

"Why is that?"

"Infection. We were in a fenced compound. Most of the men already had dysentery and there was no way to sterilise the material. The British wouldn't even allow us to boil water, for fear we'd use it to scald the guards. We lost as many men to infection as we did in the initial attack."

Stutt had stopped walking again and was looking the young man over.

"How old are you, Pieters?"

The young man shuffled awkwardly, unconsciously, eyes downcast like a child reluctant to reveal a secret. Talking about Libya, Erich had seemed distant, recalling experiences and sights well beyond his years, leaving Stutt with a fleeting impression of a boy grown old.

"Twenty-two."

"Rubbish. I'm a father of two boys, Pieters, and I know a

twenty-two-year-old when I see one. I'm sure it probably says twenty-two on your enlistment papers, but I'm not interested in what you told the recruiters. How old? And I want the truth – that's an order."

Erich loathed the man for his patronising attitude, for his softness, for his willingness to accept the rules that the Australians – the enemy – imposed.

"Seventeen."

"Seventeen." Stutt shook his head. "So young, so very, young." The implied pity drew no response. Erich stayed mute. If he'd learnt anything in Libya, it was how to remain silent in the face of stupid leadership. Stutt studied him a little longer.

"You'll make a fine orderly, Erich. Come and meet the doctor."

Two

Vinnie

Night settled on Vinnie without its usual baggage of fear and hesitation. Perhaps tonight the dreams would leave him alone – wouldn't be able to find him so far from home. The twilight passed quickly into darkness, and even though he hadn't wanted to light a fire – didn't want to kindle the flames – it was the only way to stave off the cold. He made the camp fire as small as he could – a tiny ring of stones scavenged from the creek bed. A handful of dry brush, one small branch.

His hands trembled as he struck the match and watched the tiny spark take hold, first of paper, then twigs. He held his breath; this was the first time since the accident that he'd been near fire, or even allowed himself to think about it. Already the heat was beginning to radiate and his scars tingled.

With the end of day the bush closed in and outside the small glow cast by the meagre flames Vinnie could hear creatures of the night rustling and foraging. Nearby, a cicada started its incessant ticking. Vinnie started, momentarily surprised. The fire cast leaping shadows against the curtain of trees and Vinnie found himself staring, entranced. The dance of light on darkness was familiar, frighteningly so, and despite himself Vinnie was falling away ...

"Vinnie?"

Everything upside down. After the startling, almost gentle slowness of the slide, and the crushing violence of impact, his world was inverted.

"Vinn ..."

Her voice reached out to him, sloughing into his consciousness. He felt like sleeping. Why wouldn't she let him sleep?

"Vinn. Wake up!"

Awareness. Stillness, darkness, a world upturned. A world of tortured metal. The belt biting into his shoulder, into his waist.

"Kat?"

"Vinn. Are you okay?"

"What?"

"Are you all right?" Her voice scared, insistent.

"I ... I think ... where ..."

Everything so still. So quiet. Only the ticking – the strange, steady, ominous tick of cooling metal.

"Vinn, listen to me. You need to get out. Can you get out?"

Katia. His sister. Always there. Always looking out. Always telling him the right thing to do.

"I ... my belt ..."

Fumbling in darkness, fingers numb with shock and

16

awkward with fear. Finding the button, pressing – stuck – then loose, falling into a heap on the upturned roof.

"Vinn, get out of the car right now. You need to get help. My legs are trapped. I can't move."

The car was a tangle of crushed metal and broken glass, the windscreen crazy with spider patterns that flickered in the firelight …

Fire. Burning.

"Kat, where are you?"

"Here."

Her voice was on the other side, near the door.

"I can't see you."

"I'm here. My feet are caught. Get out and get help."

Light and heat started to fill the space. Beside him the passenger's window was a broken mouth, shards glinting like teeth, the darkness beyond cool and inviting.

"Katia …"

He could see her now. The roof had crumpled between them but her hand wormed through a tiny space and waved him away.

"Vinn, get out. Now."

Hotter. More insistent. Fire licking at the shattered windscreen. The smell. He knew that smell; acrid, bitter.

"What about you?"

"Just get out. Get someone to help me."

Grabbing for her hand. Her skin cold and sweaty. She squeezed back.

"Can you climb through your window?"

"No. My feet are caught. Get out now!"

Hotter. Still hotter. Temperature climbing. Air filled with

angry red light. Crackling, dancing, laughing. Sweat stream-
ing from his brow. Indecision.

"Vinnie, listen to me. I want you out of the car. Can you
smell the fuel? The fuel is going to burn. Get out! Now!"

"Kat …"

"Out, Vinnie."

An explosion. The car shifted, steel groaned.

"Vinn …"

Her grip, icy and vice-like.

"Kat?"

"Don't forget me."

The hand pushed him away. Slipped back though the gap.
Back into the hot steely darkness.

Then he was outside. Bleeding where glass teeth had
bitten into his hands, legs and chest, running around to her
side, reaching, trying to find the handle to try to free her, had
to free her …

But the flames were too hungry, too angry and the car was
burning. Steel and rubber and glass and flesh melting
together, popping and spluttering, and the heat forced him
back, though he pushed himself into it, again and again.
Pain seared on the exposed skin of his face and arms. Her
screaming grew faint and as other arms reached around from
behind, dragging him back into cool darkness, he became
aware for the first time of the flashing lights and the red glow
dancing gleefully through the branches of the trees …

Somewhere in the depths of the forest a creature cried aloud,
and Vinnie, startled, shook himself out of the past. The fire
was nearly dead; glowing embers trapped within the stone

ring. Feeling ill, and wondering what his parents were doing, Vinnie crawled into the tent and slept.

May 1943

"Doctor Alexander, may I introduce your new orderly, Erich Pieters, Afrika Korps, Private. Erich, meet Doctor Alexander, Australian Army Medical Corps."

The elderly man leaning over the bed at the far end of the small infirmary turned.

"Retired now, of course. I'm just helping out for the duration of the war. Does this mean we can send Domenico back to his working party?"

Stutt nodded. His English, Erich noted, was much better than he let on.

"*Ja*. Erich here looked after the wounded and dying in a British camp in North Africa. I suspect you'll find him more useful than the Italian."

The doctor was old, possibly seventy or so. His face, half hidden behind a huge white moustache, was mapped with wrinkles, lending a stern, paternal air. He looked at Erich appraisingly.

"He's not very old."

"Appearances can be deceiving, Doctor. According to his enlistment papers, he's twenty-two."

"Ah, well, that's all right then. If it says so on his papers, it must be true."

The older men shared a smile, which irritated Erich.

"In all seriousness, Doctor, I believe you will find Erich to be a very suitable orderly. The German Afrika Korps are renowned for their discipline."

"You're not a Nazi, are you, Erich?"

"Excuse me?" The question, so blunt and unexpected, caught Erich unaware. He was saved by Stutt.

"Now, Doctor, need I remind you about the screening? Erich is a German, just like the rest of us, who has been caught up in an exceptionally nasty piece of history. If he was an extremist then you know as well as I do that there would be no way he would have been stationed here in Marinup."

There was a long, still silence. The two men regarded one another.

"Very well, Heinrich. I'll take your word for it. When may I send Domenico off?"

"At the end of the day, Doctor. I still need to have Erich issued with kit and provisions, and then he'll be yours from tomorrow."

"Fine. I'll see you then, Erich."

Erich nodded a reply and followed Stutt back out into the morning.

The mist had lifted and for the first time Erich became aware of the immensity of the forest surrounding them. Beyond the barbed wire and no-man's-land of the camp perimeter, trees reared massively into the blue, their smoky green canopy dappling the undergrowth into a thick, dark, hostile world of shadow, pressing in upon the camp. For a moment Erich had the odd impression that the guard towers, some of them perched atop lopped stumps of trees at the corners of the camp, were there to keep the forest at bay, rather than to prevent the prisoners escaping.

They headed towards the mess again, around the side of the canteen.

"So, Erich, was the doctor right about you? Are you a Nazi?"

Stutt asked the question in German, hiding the conversation from Australian ears.

"What do you mean?" The reply was measured, cautious. Everyone knew that the Gestapo had agents everywhere, in every corner of the German army, navy and Luftwaffe.

"Simply that. They screen everyone who is sent here and the extremists never make it as far as Marinup. But every now and then one slips through the net."

Stutt was watching Erich intently.

"Let me make this very clear to you, Erich. There is no room for Nazis here in Camp Sixteen. If your loyalty is to Germany, that's fine. No one here will have a problem with that, not even the Australians. But if you are foolish enough to sprout the philosophies of our self-declared *Führer*, then I'll have no choice but to see you on your way back to one of the less pleasant British camps in India. Do you understand me?"

"Yes, sir."

"Good. This is not a bad place, Erich. My job is to keep things that way. Remember that we'll have no problems. Now, let's get you some provisions."

From a rough storeroom attached to the back of the mess hall Erich was issued with bedding, shaving gear and a set of the heavy magenta clothes that many of the men wore.

"You won't need a lot of this working in the hospital, but take it anyway. You'll probably be glad of it in a month or so when the winter sets in."

The clothes were Australian Army uniforms, dyed bright red especially for the prisoners. If he managed to escape, he'd stand out like a sore thumb.

21

"I'm sure that my own uniform will suffice, sir."

"Take them. The nights are only going to get colder and the days wetter. In a little while you'll thank me."

He took the clothes without further comment. For all he cared they could sit on the floor under his bunk and go mouldy.

"Now, let's get the paperwork out of the way."

Sitting at one of the mess tables, Stutt recorded his details on an official form: name, rank, serial number, where and when he'd served and been captured, next of kin. Each piece of information carried Erich somewhere else – back to the burning sand and dry oppression of the North African desert, back to his first posting on the Italian border, and finally back to his family in Stuttgart. Erich realised with a start that he hadn't thought of them in some time. Not properly. Were they worried for him? Were they even alive?

The paperwork done, he was handed a slim booklet, written in German, and dismissed.

"Take your provisions to your hut. Today I expect you to familiarise yourself with the rules and procedures of the camp. You'll find them written up here. From tomorrow you report at 0735 to the infirmary. If the doctor isn't there, find yourself a broom and start sweeping. Any questions?"

"No, sir."

"Good then. If you have any major concerns, speak to Günter. I'll ask him to keep an eye out for you."

"I'm sure I can manage, *sir*."

Erich spat the final word with a sarcasm that Stutt seemed not to notice.

"I'll see you at evening rollcall then, Pieters."

Three

Vinnie

He woke to a few silent seconds of confused orientation. The morning was cold, and as he shrugged out of the warm cocoon of his sleeping bag, Vinnie shivered. Mist had settled across the clearing, cloaking the trees on the far side. The gurgle of the creek reminded him of the pressure in his bladder and a nearby tree provided relief, his stream steaming slightly in the chill air. A couple of metres away the brush trembled with the passage of some creature startled from its morning feed. Magpies cried in the treetops, the timelessness of their song calling the sun through the fog.

Lighting the fire was easier this time. The flames, stripped of their dancing shadows by pale, growing daylight, were clear and innocuous. Soon a billy of creek water bubbled on its way to boiling. Watching, Vinnie thought of home. By this time his father could be up, boiling the kettle for his mother's first cup of tea. His parents. Had they worried?

The letter should have explained everything. The hours he'd spent on it, trying to put down in writing feelings and ideas he couldn't convey any other way. Rationalising his decision into stark black letters on white paper. He'd left it by the kettle, where his father would discover it first thing.

The letter had been the hardest part. The rest was simple.

Leaving through the back door, retrieving pack, food and tent from the shed, stopping to scratch a silent goodbye behind his dog's ear, the creature dozy at this hour of the night – some guard! Then creeping around the side and out, through the gate into the lane. Sleep hung on the world. Houses, their windows sightless eyes, slumbered either side of him as he walked the few blocks to the all-night deli. There a taxi to the central bus depot. The driver barely looked at him, other than the expected double glance at his scars. Paid for taxi, waited fifteen minutes, sitting on his pack. A little down the platform a couple of drunks slumped, singing unintelligible words at the occasional passing car. Across the road a shopping complex crouched empty amidst its car parks. A security car cruised by, spotlights on the roof, passing both him and the drunks without pause. Bus arrived, driver yawning, drinking coffee from a flask for five minutes before pulling out again into the deserted streets. Ride to outer suburbs, then a forty-five minute hike to the truck stop, the first outside the city limits. A couple of cars rushed past without stopping, lights on high beam, drivers comfortably ensconced in heated cabins, hurrying into the darkness. Nothing for twenty minutes, then the logging truck.

The neon of the roadhouse receded in the mirrors and, after the first bend, he and the driver were left alone in the glow of the moonlight and the faint illumination of the dashboard. The driver, a balding man in his fifties, cast a sideways glance:

"Where you headed?"

"Wherever you can drop me, if that's okay?"

"I'm headed out to a logging stand the other side of Dwellingup. I can let you off there if you want."

"Yeah, thanks. That'd be great."

No further questions. No further conversation. They had driven through the early morning in companionable silence, and Vinnie had been grateful for that.

Dwellingup at sunrise, breakfast in the park, reading until the tourist information place opened at nine. Bought a map of the area, not certain what he was looking for. A little square in the middle of the bush caught his eye. *Marinup. Prisoner of War Camp – Heritage Area.* The idea seemed incongruous – so totally alien. There was a camping symbol next to it, and a hiking path from the town. It would do. A quick walk through the museum, finding out about the timber town, the fire that destroyed it, then into the bush, to here …

Vinnie sipped his steaming coffee and let the morning wash over him, bathing in its quiet warmth. With the growing sun the fog was lifting, shifting, dissolving into blueness. The sounds of night animals surrendered to the more boisterous screeches of those who dwelled in daylight and the diurnal cycle of the forest started again, either unaware of, or ignoring, his presence there. Vinnie found himself filled with a sudden and overwhelming sense of being just another part of something – of somewhere. It was a sensation he'd long missed at home in the city. Hadn't felt since before Katia, and hadn't been alert to even then. As the fire spluttered and hissed, he whistled for the first time in many months.

The day stretched ahead, empty. He had books and his

25

journal but for the moment Vinnie was content to just sit and be.

A few hundred metres away, up at the far end of the clearing, a wooden sign caught his attention. It stood at the mouth of a pathway that disappeared into the shadowy hollows of the forest. A different trail from the one he'd followed yesterday, and with nothing better to do, Vinnie meandered slowly up the terraces, clambering over small piles of rock and crossing the dirt road that ran through the clearing. The words, cut into the timber of the sign and daubed with white paint, stood clear against the greeny brown background:

'POW Camp Trail. 4 kilometres, 1.5 hours return.'

Black cockatoos chortled overhead. Vinnie cast a glance back across the deserted clearing, stepped onto the pathway and into the enclosing, living dimness of the jarrah forest.

Vinnie examined his reflection in the trembling mirror of a small rock pool. The creek intersecting the path gurgled beneath a rough timber footbridge and Vinnie considered his scarred visage. The dull sheen of the water lessoned the impact of the scar, its vivid brightness muted by the mossy rocks below the drifting water. With a little imagination, the old Vinnie could almost be seen there, lurking somewhere in the background, another layer beneath the echo of his face. But the old Vinnie was gone, dead. Burned away at the same time as his sister.

The old Vinnie would have made the walk without stopping to look at a rock pool. The old Vinnie wouldn't have been here in the first place. More likely down at the Galleria, hanging with his mates, eyeing girls and making a lot of noise – drawing attention to himself. He'd be making plans for the weekend with Marie or one of the others. Dancing until the small hours, late night coffee with the gang on the way home …

A water insect swerved its erratic way across the pool, landing here and there on the quicksilver of the water itself, its miniscule weight changing the surface tension just enough to make his reflected face swell and stretch. The old Vinnie didn't have that red welt of shame running from his neck, below his chin, up the right side of his face and nose, under his eye and back to where his ear was a twist of skin and cartilage. The old Vinnie was dead.

This new Vinnie, who stared back from the greeny-grey surface of the water, this was a different person. No, perhaps not person, not even certain of that yet. A different creature. This was something new, something without a place, without friends. A creature whose very image was a reminder of all that the old Vinnie had despised – fear, cowardice, shame. This was a being who could embrace isolation, who chased silence.

A rock eased into his searching hand, and the hated image shattered into a thousand rippling shards. Vinnie turned back to the path.

Here on the other side of the creek the forest seemed to draw in and the path narrowed to a thin trail not much wider than his shoulders, running between a swamp-like clump of ti-trees. The trail was straight, raised slightly off the marshy ground on a causeway of piled earth and lined with decaying railway sleepers. It was firm and easy to walk on.

The end of the trail was only a couple of hundred metres up a slight hill, an arrangement of gates and fences marking the entrance to the old prisoner-of-war camp.

"Erich, would you mind passing the antiseptic?"

The query, like all the doctor's requests, was uttered quietly and Erich took the large brown bottle down from its shelf in the dispensary cupboard and passed it without comment.

"Thank you."

The infirmary fell again into silence, broken only by the soft crackle of the pot-belly stove. Outside, the rain fell in sheets, as it had for three days now, turning the parade ground to mud and soaking anyone caught out in it for more than a couple of seconds. Already the camp hospital was busy with cases of colds and mild influenza.

"Steady now." The doctor's voice was reassuring. The patient, a burly private who had sliced his leg open with an axe, swore in German as the sharp sting of the reddish-brown liquid bit into the wound.

"He doesn't speak English, *Herr Doctor*."

"I know, Erich, but sometimes the actual words aren't important, it's the way that you say them."

Erich didn't reply, just as he didn't respond to most of Doctor Alexander's musings. Instead, he checked the fire, finding it low and the hopper out of logs.

"I will need to get some more wood."

"That's fine, Erich."

Stepping out, Erich shivered as the cold slammed through his thin uniform. Despite the rain and dropping temperature he still refused, even after a week, to wear any of the crimson Australian issue uniform. At first the doctor had tried to persuade him:

"At least wear the coat, Erich, or you'll end up in here as a patient, and I can't afford that."

But Erich knew that his silent resistance sent a message to everyone, Australian and German alike, that despite his age he wasn't the sort who would bow to pressure in the face of the enemy. Never. Unlike some others, he wasn't about to surrender simply because he'd been captured.

During his first couple of days the other men had passed remarks, commenting on his youth and pride, but on each occasion he'd simply fixed them with a cold stare and refused to be drawn by their stirring. The novelty had rapidly worn off and he'd soon been left alone.

The wood pile was under a tarpaulin behind the mess hall. Erich ran through the sleeting rain, enjoying the opportunity to stretch his legs after the claustrophobic fogginess of the hospital. Water sluiced in icy streams down the back of his uniform and shocked him with its touch, but he revelled in the intensity of it, in the living power of the storm. In many ways the orderly position was a good one. The hospital was one of the few camp buildings that was heated and insulated against the invasive cold, and the doctor seemed a reasonable character, if a little staid.

Lightning flickered somewhere a few miles distant and the overcast was lit briefly. It was the middle of the day but so gloomy with thick, low clouds that the perimeter lights had been switched on, and through the rain no-man's-land bathed in the ethereal glow usually reserved for darkness.

At the timber pile he pulled back the tarpaulin and retrieved a couple of large logs, shoving them into the front of his jacket to keep them as dry as possible during the short sprint back.

"You there!"

The day grew suddenly brighter and Erich found himself caught in the sharp glare of one of the tower spotlights. Through the rain a voice floated, tinny and amplified.

"Stay right there."

The light stayed unwaveringly upon him, and a green figure in an Australian uniform detached itself from the gloom near the compound gate and hurried through the mud, rifle held ready.

"Whatcha think you're doing?"

Erich recognised the guard as the young one who called the names through the megaphone at morning roll. He didn't answer, waiting until the guard was standing right before him.

"You speak English?"

"Ja."

"Right. So what are you doing here? Stealing wood?"

"Not stealing. For the stove in the hospital. The doctor sent me."

The guard snorted. A few tufts of red hair sprouted from under the brim of his slouch hat. Erich could see a smattering of pimples dotting his chin.

"Not likely, mate. He always sends Domenico for this sort of thing."

"I am his new orderly. Domenico is back in the forest chopping wood, and has been for a week."

The guard's eyes narrowed.

"You better watch how you speak to me, Fritz."

The insult drew no response and the two stood eying one another in the rain, Erich acutely aware of the Australian fingering the trigger-guard of his rifle. He drew upon all of his self-control. No fear. Not in the face of the enemy.

"Come on." The guard waved his rifle at the hospital. "Let's check your story out, and you better not try anything. Understand?"

Erich trudged back through the mud, up the steps, and into the infirmary. The guard, rifle levelled at the middle of his back, followed.

If the doctor was at all surprised to have an armed guard follow Erich into the room, he didn't show it.

"Thomas. To what do we owe the pleasure?"

"This bloke was nicking wood from the pile."

"Not at all, Thomas. This is Erich, my new orderly."

The boy threw a sullen look at the far end of the room, where Erich had dumped the timber into the hopper and was busying himself re-stoking the fire.

"Wasn't informed about no new orderly."

"I'm sure the paperwork has been held up somewhere in administration, Thomas. You know how things are around here. You can take my word for it, though. Erich is simply doing as I asked."

"If you say." Thomas seemed reluctant to let it go.

"I do say."

The boy turned to leave, but the doctor stopped him. "And Thomas ..."

"What?"

"I'd consider it a personal favour if you wouldn't bring a loaded rifle into the hospital in future."

"Can't leave it outside. Regulations."

"Then I imagine that next time you'll simply have to stay outside with it. Have a nice day, Thomas."

31

The door slammed and the guard was gone.

"I'm terribly sorry about that, Erich. Thomas is only young, and at times can tend to be a little ... enthusiastic. He's really not a bad boy, for all that."

Erich shrugged.

The man on the bed moaned again and Doctor Alexander returned his attention to his patient. Standing by the fire to dry out and warm up, Erich considered the look in the young guard's eyes and wasn't so certain.

Four

Vinnie

The morning heat grew strangely muted as Vinnie weaved between the crumbling remnants of the old prison camp. Very little remained, just some concrete foundations and a few low stone walls. Grass covered the clear areas of ground, but much was already tangled and overgrown. The old townsite, where he had camped, seemed shunned by the forest, but the same was not true here. Jarrah saplings, already well on the way to two-hundred-year adulthood, were interspersed among the ruins, bringing with them clumps of dappled shade and undergrowth and attendant wildlife. Tiny birds picked and hopped, and the buzz and drone of insects played a constant background to the morning.

A quiet unease edged into his mind as he walked. This place had a sense about it. Once he wouldn't have been aware of it, but now there it was, a fluttering awareness, unsettling the calm he was chasing.

At one corner of the camp the stump of a jarrah that had once served as a guard tower stood alone in a clearing. The tree itself was long dead, its life severed when its crown was cut off to leave a base for a platform, years since removed. Still, the trunk had endured, had kept solemn vigil over the departure and decay of the camp. Its wood was marked in the places where iron rungs had once been hammered into the living timber.

Men lived here, thought Vinnie, studying the tower. Lived and worked and died here, in the bush, and the real prison wasn't the rows of wire and the spotlights and the armed guards. The real prison was the forest itself. He studied it; pressing in, always there, beyond the perimeter, alive, dark and threatening.

A cloud drifted across the face of the sun, and the sharp relief of the morning faded into haziness. In Vinnie's imagination young men, soldiers of foreign armies, marched through the muddy trails of the Australian forest, cowed and startled by its brooding atmosphere.

Under a clump of scrub at the far end of the camp a blackened, unnatural mass caught his attention, almost missed in the quiet of the morning. Coils and coils of rusted barbed wire, lay exactly where they had been cast years ago, entwined and entangled now with native thorn creepers. The years had dulled the shine of the steel, pitted it with oxidised craters, but the knotted spikes still looked sharp, vicious.

Crouching, Vinnie stretched a hesitant finger. The skin of his fingertips was still soft and pink and the spike left a small impression, a gentle dimple in the tender new flesh, and briefly Vinnie was a modern sleeping beauty, pricked by a spindle of darkness and falling into a cavern of sleep – descending through layers of thought and feeling into a dark

34

cell of night – waiting for someone who would wake him and bring him back into the world, into a proper life, out from this half-world of shadows.

It took some seconds for Vinnie to shake off the despair, to return to the world of the real. There were no fairytale spirits here. All that lingered in this place were the passing hopes of the men who had been brought here, lived for a while, and, in the way of things, moved on.

Making his way back towards the trail, a patch of mossy ground stood out from the surrounding brush. A carpet in a small, shaded clearing that the forest had still not reclaimed, right at the edge of the site. Something about the velvety smudge of dark green was incongruous and Vinnie tried to work out exactly what.

The sun emerged, the shallow contours of the ground fell again into perspective and Vinnie saw it clearly. The moss grew in the shape of a large heart – perfect in form and symmetry. It was not natural. The earth here had been shaped by human hands, and now that the image was clear Vinnie could see the remains of the rock border that had once bounded it.

Strange to think that in this secluded corner of the bush someone had laboured to create this shape. For what purpose? As a symbol of lost love? Someone left behind, or killed in the war? Or was it just an attempt to introduce something recognisable into this alien landscape – some reminder of the familiar shapes and sights of a European homeland? Walking back along the trail to his camp site, Vinnie turned this mystery over in his mind.

The end of the trail loomed with unexpected speed, like the end of a long green tunnel. Reaching it, Vinnie was startled again by the unusual silence that pervaded here, but he was alarmed when that silence was broken, suddenly and harshly, by the lilt of disembodied voices, floating across the clearing like smoke in the morning air.

August 1943

"Doctor, what is this word?"

Erich carried the ageing medical textbook to the desk, indicating with his finger the unfamiliar term.

"*Cauterise*, Erich. It is when you use a hot iron or flames to literally burn the infection out of a wound. It's something we have to do occasionally, and also when we desperately need to stop some bleeding."

For the last few days, at the doctor's suggestion, Erich had been spending his spare time reading from the old medical texts that were kept on a small shelf behind the doctor's desk.

"It sounds primitive."

"Much of modern surgery is based on primitive techniques, don't forget that. In any case, you should remember that fire can be a strikingly effective antiseptic measure, if nothing else is available. Very few diseases can survive extreme temperature. Sometimes burning is all you can do."

Erich offered no further comment as he returned to his seat by the fire. The rain had lifted and the sun glistened wet on smoky green leaves. After a week of constant drumming on tin roofs the world seemed silent, the morning still, cold and crisp. There were no patients at the moment, and Erich found himself falling into contentment, which he knew he must resist.

"I suspect we will be busy later, Erich."

Doctor Alexander spoke without looking up.

"Why?"

"The change in the weather. It often brings accidents with it. Men get careless, distracted. Axes are swung haphazardly, footing lost in the mud. Rarely does a change like this herald good news for you and me."

"Should I do anything to prepare?"

The doctor considered.

"That's a very good suggestion. Can you prepare a tray of bandages and mix some more antiseptic?"

Erich set to the task without reply. As he rolled bandages and mixed the brown Condy's crystals with boiling water, he could feel the old man's eyes on his back.

"Is something wrong, Doctor?"

"No, not at all, Erich. I was just thinking to myself what a great deal of aptitude you show for this kind of work."

"Thank you, Doctor."

"Not at all. What do you plan to do after the war?"

"After the war?"

"It can't last forever, you know."

Erich stopped, mid-bandage, considering, reminding himself that the old man behind the desk was still his captor, the enemy.

"I think I will wait and see who wins first, Doctor."

"A wise answer, Erich. But may I offer a suggestion?"

Erich said nothing.

"Regardless of who wins, you should consider most carefully joining the medical profession. A young man with your intelligence and ability could do a great deal for the world."

"I don't think so, Doctor."

Thoughts of after the war, of home, were dangerous.

Already, after only a few weeks of camp life, Erich had seen what happened to men who let themselves become caught up in dreams of home and of peace. They became complacent, domesticated, sacrificing their pride for a quiet life. They stopped fighting. Men like Stutt and Günter were now little more than lapdogs for the Australians and English. Men with no honour.

"And why not?"

Erich considered the best reply. "Because I suspect that my father would not approve."

"Why on earth not? It is a very respectable profession for a young man, I would have thought."

"My father has other plans for me."

Erich pictured the stern figure of his father, striking and severe in his brown *Wehrmacht* uniform. He recalled the pride that had tempered his father's anger at the discovery that his eldest son had lied his way into the military, deceived his way into his father's and grandfather's footsteps. For generations, Erich's family had supplied officers to the Kaisers, and Erich was certain that it would be impossible for his father to consider any path but a military one for his only son.

"And what plans are they?"

"He will want me to follow his path."

"What does he do?"

"He ..." Erich stopped himself just in time. In the companionable warmth of the hospital he had almost allowed himself to be lulled into giving information, important information, to this man, this enemy.

"... he is in business."

The explanation sounded weak, suspicious even to Erich,

but the doctor, twisting at his moustache, seemed to accept it.

"That is a pity, Erich, because I believe you would make a fine doctor someday."

"Thank you, Doctor."

"In the meantime, however, I would still like you to study these books. For purely selfish reasons, I'm afraid, because the more you know of anatomy and medicine, the more use you will be to me."

Erich nodded and, returned to his pages. Now, however, he found it difficult to concentrate on words and diagrams. His mind returned again and again to their conversation. The truth was he was enjoying the study, the challenge of learning, and in a foreign language. His English, which had already been passable, was improving by the day. And his medical skills, the feeling of seeing infection vanish, wounds healing, of watching the patients, *his* patients …

Erich dragged himself from reverie, from daydreaming.

In some cases, (see appendix 1.5) cauterisation is the only effective method of both infection control and …

The door slammed open, admitting a rush of cold air. A guard rushed in, agitated.

"There's been an accident."

Doctor Alexander rose from behind the desk, calm and unflustered in the face of the man's anxiety.

"What has happened?"

"They're bringing him in now, they'll only be a couple of minutes."

"Good. What happened?"

"I didn't see it, only his leg, it …"

The door swung again and Stutt entered, followed by two

German prisoners bearing a stretcher between them. On the stretcher the prone figure of Günter groaned in agony, at the very edge of consciousness, his right leg a bloody twisted pulp.

Five

Vinnie

The campervan, its sides smeared with a fine coat of reddish-brown dust, had parked near some low scrub on the terrace about fifty or sixty metres from Vinnie's camp. He watched from the shadows of the trees as two figures went about the business of setting up their own camp site. One, a girl, was engaged in the process of putting up a small dome tent nearby, while the other, older, more ponderous in movement, unfolded chairs and a table, installing them under a brightly striped canopy which extended from the side of the vehicle.

What were they doing? Vinnie knew that the camp site was public, but still he felt invaded, violated, by their bustling presence. He knew they would see him, look at him, notice the scarring and wonder to themselves, or worse, ask questions.

He toyed with the idea of packing up his own camp and moving, but as he lurked indecisively the intruders finished their setting up and settled into the two chairs. Vinnie skirted down the terraces choosing a path that would keep him as far as possible from the campervan and its occupants.

Back under the deep shade of the pine tree, he felt more comfortable. Already his camp site had acquired the easy familiarity of 'home' and belonging. He rekindled the fire, boiled some water, and made himself strong black tea with his lunch. The morning's walk had left him feeling hungry, and the taste of the tinned fish and dry biscuits seemed somehow intense. After rinsing his knife and plate in the creek, he crawled into his tent and lay on his sleeping bag.

Through the open flap he could see the other campers clearly. The girl, perhaps a little older than himself, the man elderly. They seemed at ease in one another's company and the quiet noise of their conversation, the words indistinct, floated across the clearing. The girl was more active, climbing into the campervan on several occasions to fetch things for her companion. At one point she remained inside for some minutes, before Vinnie saw her bring out a steaming cup, placing it on the table beside the old man. As she did so, he reached out and touched her arm lightly in a gesture which, even from this distance, Vinnie could read as affection. He felt a sudden stab as he tried to recall the last time his father had reached to him in that way.

Katia had always been the favoured child. The loved one. His dad made no secret of that. The eldest, the first born, the focus of his love. She had always been the smartest, and the brightest. When she received the letter inviting her to study medicine, his dad had cried. Actually wept. His father the bricklayer, who for his entire life had espoused manliness and toughness as though they were the only virtues a man could hope for, had tears in his eyes like an old woman.

42

"I always knew you were the one who'd make this family something." He had held her at arms-length, looking into her face. "Knew you'd lift us up."

There'd been no such discussion when Vinnie had been accepted for the apprenticeship program at the nursery.

"Plants? Why waste your time on fucking plants, mate? Set yourself some real goals. Look at your sister, for God's sake. You've had the same opportunities as she has, and you're not stupid. Why don't you want to go to uni?"

And the old Vinnie had looked at the floor, crimson with anger, and not said anything. Not to his father, not to Katia. His rage wasn't directed at them, but at himself. At the weak little part of him that was unable to stand up, and be counted for who he was, who he wanted to be.

Then the accident and that dark little seed had opened. Self-doubt, self-loathing was given months and months to grow and flower and had blossomed across the side of his face, killing the old Vinnie. In its place now this new one. This creature born in the flames of cowardice. It was no wonder his father couldn't bear the sight of him. No surprise at all that whenever they were alone in a room together the conversation would wither and die into awkward silence. The gap which had always been between them was an ocean now, or a wall. Enormous. Impenetrable.

"You let your sister burn."

The words had been uttered only a couple of nights ago. Three months home from the hospital. Three months back in the house. Three months of being a shadow, dead, detached, watching his parents torn apart from both him and one another by unshared grief and agony. Something inside him had snapped. The plate had shattered where he hurled it, leaving a smear down the wall, and he'd screamed at them, both of them, and at the world:

"Fuck! Why won't you *talk* to me? Why?"

And for a brief period time had stopped, stood still and listened with grave attention, while his father had looked him in the eyes.

"You let your sister burn."

His mother released a small gasp of … what? Shock? Fear? Consent? Her fork dropped from slack fingers, clattered onto the china. And his father, in an uncharacteristic moment of weakness, had lifted a hand to his mouth, biting hard on a thick, calloused knuckle. A trickle of crimson ran across his hand and arm and slowly dripped, mixing with the bloody red of the sauce on his plate.

And Vinnie had not replied. He was not angry or hot or mad, but in a moment of cold clarity he knew that tonight was the night. He would leave – run. He could not stay here any longer. And later, when his father had crept silent into the darkness, Vinnie had feigned sleep and listened to the shambling apology with deaf ears. And a few hours later he was in the cabin of a logging truck, driven by a silent Samaritan into the solitude that he craved.

"You let your sister burn."

Those words. The calm, sad, almost wistful tone in which they had been pronounced didn't hide the anger behind them and they were seared indelibly into his memory. Vinnie knew that even as the vivid welt on his face slowly faded and healed, the scar of that quietly spoken sentence never would.

August 1943

"Erich, I'd like you to meet my grand-daughter, Alice."

The girl stepped from where she had been standing by the fire. At first Erich hadn't noticed her. He'd run through the door into the warm dimness of the hospital, shaking droplets from the back of his uniform jacket.

"Hello."

Her voice was soft, clearly shy. Erich stared.

"She'll be here with us for a while. My son-in-law is away overseas, and my daughter, her mother, is quite ill at the moment, so Alice will be staying with me while her mother recuperates."

"Good morning."

His accented English surprised her, his voice so much deeper than his youth implied. The greeting hung in the air until the doctor spoke again.

"We should have a fairly quiet day today, Erich. This might be a good opportunity for you to catch up on your study. Alice might be able to help you with some of the more difficult English."

Erich considered the girl. She was sixteen or seventeen, no older. Her dress was simple and her dark hair hung to the middle of her back, tied with ribbon. He had to remind himself that she was the enemy, this child, despite her pretty eyes and smile. As much a part of the enemy as that guard, Thomas.

"I am sure I can manage, Doctor."

"If you say so. I can find other things to keep Alice busy."

From his bed, Günter moaned. Erich nodded.

"How is he?"

"Still not at all good, I'm afraid. If by some miracle he

45

stabilises today then we'll move him to Perth, but I'm thinking we'll have to remove the leg here."

The big German had been caught and mangled beneath a falling tree. For two days they had kept him dosed on morphine, bathing the misshapen limb with massive amounts of antiseptic.

"We cannot save it?"

Doctor Alexander shook his head sadly.

"No. The infection is wreaking havoc. I'm certain that gangrene is already setting in."

Erich had noticed the sick, sweet stink of infected flesh the moment he'd entered the room. It took him back to Africa, to the camp where he'd watched men rotting alive until finally, mercifully, the shock killed them.

"What can we do?"

"Very little. The rain has potholed all the roads to the point where trying to truck him out would almost certainly kill him, but at the rate infection is setting in, if he hasn't stabilised by this evening the leg will have to go."

"How?"

The doctor handed him a thick textbook.

"It won't be pleasant, I'm afraid. I'd like you to familiarise yourself with chapter twelve of this today. It will tell you everything you will need to know about rough amputation."

"Rough?"

"We have only morphine and basic tools. This morning I'm going to find a suitable saw to cut cleanly through bone. I imagine that one of the small timber saws will do the job. I'll ensure that it's sharpened, and you'll need to sterilise it this afternoon."

"How?"

"Start by putting it in the fire for half an hour, in the coals, then into boiling water. No point in starting a new bout of infection when we try to cut out the old one."

"Does he know?"

Doctor Alexander shook his head.

"I haven't let him regain consciousness enough to tell him."

"What about Stutt?"

"He knows." The old man's voice was flat.

Erich crossed to where Günter lay, sunk in morphine. His leg beneath the sheet was flattened, misshapen. What must he be dreaming? Erich wondered. Günter had spoken several times about a young wife back home and a farm owned by his parents. What dreams had died with that falling tree?

"There is no other choice, Erich." The doctor observed the young man closely. "If we want to save his life, the leg needs to go."

"Of course, Doctor."

"I'm going to find that saw. Keep an eye on Günter."

Erich nodded, and the doctor eased himself up.

"If there are any problems, shout from the door – don't leave the patient. I'll be sure to stay within earshot."

He crossed to the bed, rested his hand on the soldier's forehead, his voice a whisper: "Hold on there, Günter, hold on."

Erich wondered if the soldier could even hear the words, let alone comprehend them.

The door closed, and without the doctor's presence the hut seemed strange, different. This was, Erich realised, the first time that he'd been left alone there.

"Have you been in Australia long?"

47

The girl. He'd forgotten her. Through his conversation with the doctor, she'd stood silent, watching. He shrugged.

"Nine or ten weeks, I think."

"Where were you before?"

"Africa."

"Were you in Egypt?"

"No."

"My uncle went to Egypt during the Great War. He did his training there."

"I have never been there. I was in Libya."

"What was it like?"

"Please, I would rather not discuss it."

"Oh. I'm sorry."

A heavy silence followed. Günter murmured, and Erich moved silently to the bedside.

"What happened to him?"

"A tree fell on his leg."

Why would she not stop these questions?

"It must be hard for you."

She also moved to the bed, standing opposite, the fevered figure of Günter between them.

"I beg your pardon?"

"Living here, I mean. So far from home."

Erich remained silent.

"Paul, that was my uncle, used to say that the worst thing about the war was the distance. He wrote that it was like being on the moon or a star, being so far from familiar places. Do you find that?"

A shrug. "I do not let myself think of such things."

"What things?"

"Home. Family things. There is a war and I am a fighting man, that is all there is."

"You must think of your family. Paul used to carry a photograph of my grandparents. They sent it home after ..." She turned towards the spluttering stove.

"Yes?"

"After he was killed."

"I'm sorry."

"It's not your fault."

"Where did he die?"

"France. A place called Flanders."

"And he was your uncle?"

"I never met him. It was before I was born. Mother told me about him. Paul was her older brother, her only brother. Grandad John's eldest son."

"Grandad John?"

She looked at Erich as though something was wrong with him.

"The doctor, silly."

"Oh."

The incongruity stunned him. The doctor's son, killed fighting for his country, against Erich and Günter's, over twenty years ago, before he or this girl even existed. And now, here was this old man, in the middle of the bush, himself fighting to save the lives of those who'd been – who still were – the enemy. His enemy.

Alice watched him closely.

"He must hate us."

"No." She shook her head at him. "Grandad's not like that. He doesn't hate. Just feels ... I don't know ... sad. He doesn't like to talk about Paul. You shouldn't mention it."

Outside, gentle splatters on the roof heralded more rain. The steps creaked and the old man returned clutching a vicious looking handsaw.

"Right, Erich. Let's get to work."

Six

Vinnie

Twilight, the sky a blaze of crimson, stars winking into nightly existence between the branches with an intensity he'd never experienced in the city. Springy pine-litter soft and dry beneath him, Vinnie concentrated on one of the pinpoints. The immensity of distance was a distraction from dangerous, hypnotic memories stirred by the fireshadow.

Even with eyes and mind on the void above, part of him was still aware, still feeling the presence of the flames trapped beside him in their stone prison, the ring of rocks containing the licking fire much as a magic circle or pentagram might hold some primal power at bay. In the chill night the fingers of heat that stretched and caressed the tender skin of his face lent warmth but no comfort – the touch of a devil, he thought.

Crunch of footsteps on gravel. Sitting up.

"Hi there."

The girl from the campervan stood uncertainly a few feet away, outside the dancing ring cast by his fire.

"Hi."

51

"Do you mind if I join you? My grandfather goes to bed early, I'm afraid."

She loomed into his space, into his thoughts. Even in darkness, with only the flickering red and yellow glow for illumination, Vinnie was uncomfortably aware of her eyes – piercing, blue, probing, taking in his face, the scar.

He didn't want this. Didn't want the intrusion, or the judgment which he knew must follow. Didn't want to be called to explain his presence in this haunted clearing. But could he refuse? Hers was the first voice he'd heard since the previous morning, and despite himself Vinnie was drawn to it, taken suddenly and unexpectedly by the idea of conversation – any conversation – with a stranger, with someone who didn't know. Didn't know him, didn't know his family. Someone with no interest in the state of his mental health or his ability to "let go".

The girl stood expectant, her weight nervous on one hip.

"Sure, take a seat."

A smile, hesitant. Should he be smiling?

"I'm Vinnie."

"Helen."

Pine needles crackled as she settled beside him, firelight skittering across her face, throwing half of it into deep shadow. Her handshake was so different from the sterile, professional touch of the nurses or the perfunctory contact of his parents.

"I hope I'm not intruding. I'd finished cleaning up from dinner and really didn't feel like reading – we've been doing that all afternoon – and I saw you sitting over here so I thought ..."

"Nah, that's okay."

The forest woke around them and a chorus of insects screeched at the night, bringing with it the rustle of predators and prey alike.

"You getting away from it all for a while?"

"Something like that." *Drop the subject*, his tone implied, but gently, and she did. "What about you?"

"I volunteered to bring my grandfather here. He's visiting from Germany."

"And he wanted to come here?"

"He's got his reasons."

Now it was her voice carrying a quiet warning. Both sat in silence, listening to the night.

"Would you like a cup of coffee?"

"If you're having one. I'd love a tea."

"I've only got one mug."

"I can get mine from the campervan."

"Beaut."

Vinnie watched her receding figure – a nice one, he noted – slipping through the shadows to the dark, crouching shape of the campervan, then busied himself filling the billy. When he returned from the creek, she was already by the fire, poking at the coals with a long twig, a packet of biscuits and a stainless steel mug on the ground.

"So, Vinnie, what do you do?"

What do you do? The question brought with it a surge of panic, nauseating in its unexpectedness. Vinnie fought it down, struggled for an answer.

"Dunno. Not a lot."

"Unemployed?"

"Been in hospital."

Silence again. The awkwardness of strangers feeling their way around barriers.

"What about you?"

"I'm at uni. First year."

The billy bubbled and Vinnie poured, the two mugs throwing ghost-plumes into the night air.

"That's good. It's colder here than I thought it would be."

"Yeah. You got plenty of blankets in that van?"

"Grandad's in the van, I'm camping out. A man his age needs a little privacy. So do I, for that matter."

"Right."

"What about you? You warm in your little tent?"

"Yeah. Got a good sleeping bag."

"Have a biscuit."

The crackle of cellophane sounded foreign in the forest darkness.

They munched. Her company was good. He was enjoying it. That admission, and all that it implied, came as a surprise. He didn't voice it, didn't want to, and knew instinctively that he didn't need to. Sitting in silence, companionable and pleasant, came the realisation that tomorrow he would find himself reassessing some things, some aspects of the person he'd become.

Dregs of tea thrown into flames, the fire hissing an angry retort.

"I'd better get off to bed."

"Yeah, me too."

"You going to be around tomorrow?"

"Guess so. No other plans, anyway."

"I might see you then. Nice meeting you, Vinnie."

And she was gone into the night, leaving Vinnie alone

with the quiet skitter of nocturnal business, and his thoughts.

August 1943

Erich stood in the rain, the driving, icy rain, willing it to dissolve him, wash him away, take from him all the buzzing madness he could feel building up and up inside himself. A couple of hundred metres down the hill the lights of the perimeter glowed through the sleet-hazed night and the occasional searchlight probed the gloom lethargically. If one caught him in its gaze there'd be problems, questions, but Erich didn't care. All he was aware of was his need for the rain to pound from his head the memory of Günter writhing in agony on the bed, four guards holding him in place while the doctor sawed.

It had taken a little over half an hour. A bloody, horrible thirty minutes of frantic activity. The doctor, calm and controlled, hacking steadily at the shattered limb, severing tendons, muscle and bone and issuing calm instructions to Erich, who daubed antiseptic onto raw tissue. Then the cauterising, the sizzling stink of flesh and hot iron, and then, finally – mercifully – silence.

Now Günter lay quiet again, lost in morphined sleep. The sheet fell flat on the mattress where his leg had been, gradually staining with blood that seeped from the bandage-swathed stump. The hospital was a muggy fog, a stinking combination of wood-smoke, blood and antiseptic, and Erich needed to get outside, into the rain, into the clean, pure, storm-charged air. The doctor slouched exhausted on a chair beside the bed, his shirt-front stained crimson, barely even aware of the door slamming.

The rain drove harder, lightning crashed somewhere out in the forest, and Erich turned his face to the driving streams, savouring the delicate sting on the skin of his eyes and lips. He let them sweep him away, take him off to familiar places, smells, sounds, voices.

"Erich?"

Someone called from the hospital verandah – a person disembodied by the darkness and the driving power of the storm.

"Erich?" The voice became his sister's, looking at him in his uniform, half-brother, half-man, leaving forever to catch a train to the Italian front.

"Erich!" His mother's quiet sobs in the midnight darkness, unaware of her son – her soldier boy – listening silently at the door.

"Erich." A hand came to rest lightly on the shoulder of his sodden uniform. Something wrapped itself around him, warm, enclosing, pushing away the freezing power of the night and the rain and bringing him back through time, through space, into the icy present of an Australian forest winter.

"Grandfather says you need to come in now."

She'd been sent to the guard's mess during the amputation, and had returned afterwards, alerted by the four guards returning, bloody and shocked, to their own quarters. They'd tried to persuade her to remain a little longer, to have another cup of tea, not wanting her to return so soon to the blood-stained stink of the tiny hospital, but there was something in their eyes, in their manner, that made her frightened – not for herself but for her grandfather and the boy – so she'd half run, half stumbled back through the compound gates, over the mud and into the hospital.

"Erich, come on."

Alice tugged gently at Erich's shoulder. Earlier in the day, standing proud in his thin brown uniform, he had tried to carry himself like a warrior, like a man. Now she felt her touch raise goose flesh on his chilled skin and the warrior was gone. Now she saw only a lost boy in a foreign thunderstorm, his fear and grief not quite fully swept away by the rain.

"Come inside."

Hugging the lapels of the magenta greatcoat, drowning in its warmth, Erich allowed himself to be led back up the stairs and into the hospital.

Seven

Vinnie

Vinnie slept late, emerging bleary-eyed into a world already well awake. Kangaroos, their morning feeding over, had long retreated from the clearing into the forest to wait out the day. The campervan and tent were silent, their occupants either still asleep or off somewhere else. Keeping a hopeful eye in the direction of the other campsite, Vinnie prepared his breakfast.

He had enjoyed her company. No question about it. Her lack of curiosity, her willingness to simply accept the moment of companionship by the fire had appealed. It was nice just to be himself again.

He needed to go into town. The couple of days in the bush had exhausted his supplies faster than he'd expected. There were also things he needed and hadn't thought of, items like string and pegs.

The walk out took him past the campervan, its interior silent, its windows shuttered. Almost as soon as he stepped onto the trail and into the forest he was aware of movement in the treetops. Bush cockatoos, picking up his path and flitting in his wake, occasionally heralded his approach to the rest of the world with loud, grating screeches. His pack, free of tent and food, was light on his shoulders. It seemed no time at all until he was on the outskirts of town.

The small supermarket was open and a couple of old blokes were sitting and smoking on a park bench out the front. Vinnie could sense their eyes tracing across his face, absorbing the livid welt, making their own silent conclusions.

"Poor bugger," one remarked when they thought he was out of earshot.

The shop was cool, dark, the shelves cluttered with the usual cans and groceries but also the necessities of small-town life: hardware, fishing tackle, four-wheel drive accessories, tennis balls. A hand-painted mural covered the wall above a row of refrigerators. The artist had painted the whole region – rivers, roads, forests, camp grounds. Vinnie found the old town site where he had pitched his tent. Nearby, the remains of the prison camp were represented by a barbed wire fence and guard towers. The scale made it look much closer to Dwellingup than it seemed when walking the trail.

"Can I help you?"

The speaker, a woman in a green apron, stood a couple of metres away, filling a freezer with boxes of fish fingers. Vinnie turned to face her and she visibly stifled a gasp.

"No, thanks." A muttered response. He retreated back from the lights of the fridges into the protective shadows of the aisles.

Tinned meat. Tinned fish. Tomatoes. Oil. Washing detergent. Tea towel. Pegs. String. Vinnie worked his way along

59

the four rows of shelves, filling a small wire hand basket. At the checkout counter, a teenage girl rang up his purchases, her eyes locked on the scanner, or the till, or above his head, or anywhere but his face.

Cheeks burning, Vinnie emerged into the day. The light was fierce, scalding. It was close to midday. He found himself craving the solitude of the bush, the company of the cockatoos. On the way out of town he stopped at the pub, an old building with grubby lino floors and walls festooned with logging implements – saws and axes reminiscent of medieval torture. He bought a six-pack of beer and the man behind the bar sold it to him without question. He had always been big, and the scarring made it difficult to guess his exact age. That's one advantage, he thought.

While the barman was sliding the beer into a brown paper bag, the door swung open and a man in uniform entered. Vinnie started, at first glance thinking it was a cop. Closer inspection revealed the man's garb to be that of a forestry official.

"Morning, Ernie."

The man behind the bar nodded.

"Morning, Jim."

"Busy day?"

"Not so far. That'll be twelve-fifty, thanks. How about you?"

Vinnie paid the man and took his purchase, loading it into his pack.

"Pretty quiet. Heading out to the old POW site this afternoon. A couple of people camping there at the moment, I'm told."

"Trouble?"

60

"Nah, just want to have a look, make sure they're doing the right thing. Got a missing kid that the cops have asked me to look out for."

"Runaway?"

"Yeah, something like that. Don't have all the details, just need to keep an eye out. A logger dropped him off here the other day ..."

Vinnie hurried outside.

A telephone box stood on the other side of the road outside the tourist information centre. His mind racing, his pack in the dirt, Vinnie dropped a coin into the slot, listening to the hum through the earpiece. The phone gave thirteen rings and then the machine cut in, the greeting light and cheerful.

"Hi, this is the Santianis'. No one's home so please leave a message."

Katia's voice. Redolent with memory. Unchanged, happy, outgoing. He remembered the day his father made her record the message, and his refusal now to erase it, unable to bear the thought of wiping that last trace of her from the house. So now callers were greeted from the grave. Messages left for a ghost – except she was still alive, wasn't she? Kept in some kind of half-existence by his father in the thirteen words on that tape. Kept alive in the pocked and scarlet skin on Vinnie's face and neck.

The beep prompted him. His voice suddenly scratchy and hoarse.

"Hi. Mum, Dad. It's me. Uhm ... I just wanted to tell you not to worry, I'm ..."

"Vinnie?"

The machine clicked into silence, his father cutting across the recording.

"Yeah."

The line hummed. Linking them while at the same time holding them separate.

"Where the fuck are you, boy?"

"Listen, Dad ..."

"Your mother's going bloody insane worrying about you."

"Dad, let me explain ..."

"I'm not interested. Tell me where you are."

Vinnie took a deep breath, his heart echoing.

"I'm okay. Tell Mum."

The earpiece clunked back into its cradle.

Shouldering his pack again, Vinnie drew a couple of ragged breaths, steadied himself against the weight and walked towards the bush.

August 1943

"Here, you must eat."

Günter lay, pallid and somehow empty, staring out the mud-streaked window and ignoring the bowl of porridge that Alice proffered.

"He doesn't speak English." Erich looked up briefly from his book.

"He doesn't need to." The girl reached out, rested her hand lightly on the soldier's arm, easing his attention back into the real world.

The murmur of rain was muted by the walls of the hospital. A dim, grey light filtered into the room and a couple of hundred yards away on the other side of the camp wire the dark tree line crouched, solemn and forbidding. Now and again large black birds, similar to crows or ravens, would flap silently through the rain, flitting ghost-like between the treetops.

Distracted by her touch, the soldier looked from Alice's face to the enamelled bowl and back again, managing a thin smile and a nod of refusal before returning to his brooding.

In the week since the operation Günter, who had been kept more or less unconscious for the first few days, hadn't eaten or spoken. Even after he had woken to discover the loss of his leg, he hadn't said a single word. Just lay staring into space or out of the window. When the doctor wasn't around he smoked cigarettes smuggled in by Erich but refused to talk, in German or otherwise.

The starvation was destroying him – the once fit and muscled body already shrinking and wasting before their eyes.

"Please, Günter."

"Let me try." Putting down his textbook, Erich crossed to the bedside and took the bowl from her.

"Günter," he said in German, "you are making this pretty lady worried. You, of all people, know that when a beautiful woman offers you food, you must eat."

The man gave no sign that he had even heard Erich's voice, let alone understood the attempt at humour. He just lay and stared, seemingly lost in a world a long way from the wire and tree enclosed prison. Erich shook his head in frustrated anger and turned from the bed.

"What is the point of eating now, young one?"

Günter's guttural accent, which on his first morning had struck Erich as both common and strong, now rang weak and empty. The voice of someone who already considered himself dead.

"If you don't eat, you won't heal."

Erich turned again to the sallow face which regarded him from the pillows.

"This won't heal." Günter rested his hand lightly on his stump. The sound of his laboured breathing filled the room, the rise and fall of his chest beneath the bedclothes seeming forced. "This scratch will be with me forever."

"What is he saying?" The doctor, who had been working at his desk, had risen at the first words of the conversation and crossed to stand beside Erich.

"He doesn't want to heal."

"Tell him that he must eat."

"He knows. He doesn't want to."

"Does he know that Stutt has ordered me to force-feed him if necessary?"

"I'll tell him."

Erich translated the news and to his surprise Günter laughed – a hollow empty chuckle.

"Tell the good doctor that I would like to see him try. Even without a leg I can still stand up for myself."

Erich couldn't help but smile a little at the joke.

"Not even you, Günter, could stand up to this man once he sets his mind to something."

"No?"

"No. Besides, you owe him your life, so you should do what he says."

The soldier turned his head back to the window. "Did you know that I have a wife back home?"

"I did."

64

"What use will I be to her now? Better I think that the doctor here had not wasted his time on me."

Erich allowed the words to hang in the air while he considered his response.

"Does she love you?"

Günter shrugged. "She says she does."

"And you believe her?"

"Of course."

"Then your question is stupid. Of course you will be of use to her. More than you will be if you become a skeleton, force fed on baby food."

"What would you know of love, youngster?"

Suddenly the man in the bed was sitting up as best he could, propping himself up on one thin arm, his breathing more ragged with the effort.

"What did you say?" The doctor interrupted, alarmed by the sudden flash of anger. Erich gestured him to silence.

"I know enough from listening to the men in my division to understand that when someone loves, then a little thing like a missing leg is nothing. I know that when a man is facing a machine-gun-nest then some things, like the woman he will be leaving behind, are a lot more important to him than whether he has big ears or a missing tooth. And I know enough to realise that if a little wood-chopping accident is enough to make you useless in her eyes, then she probably doesn't love you at all."

The words had poured themselves from him in an unexpected torrent and Erich's hand flew to his mouth, steeling himself for Günter's anger as what he had said sunk in. But the soldier stayed still, half propped on one elbow, regarding the boy not with anger but with quizzical amusement.

"And you know all these things, do you? At the tender age of twenty-two?"

"Actually, I'm seventeen. And yes, I do."

"Ah. Well then."

Without further comment, Günter sunk back onto the pillows and nodded his consent to Alice, who began to spoon the congealing porridge.

"What was all that about?" Doctor Alexander regarded Erich curiously.

"Nothing important, Herr Doctor."

"You must have said something significant. I thought for a minute there that he was going to launch himself at you."

"We discussed his wife."

"His wife?"

"Yes, sir. I told him that she probably didn't love him, and that he was most likely right to starve himself."

"You didn't, did you?"

"Yes, sir."

The doctor smiled. "Erich, sometimes I really do think that you would make a better doctor than me."

"Thank you, Doctor."

"Only some of the time, though. So don't go getting ideas. Now, how about going up to the mess and seeing about getting some tea?"

"Yes, Doctor."

Eight

Vinnie

As the protective envelope of forest closed around him again, Vinnie began to shiver. The phone call had frightened him. He was back in the months of pain he was trying to put behind him.

Waking in the hospital had been the worst moment. The impersonal click and quiet beep of the machines had been the first sensations to worm their way into his consciousness. Then the light, the subdued glow of a night lamp, and the harsher glare of the fluorescent-lit passageway outside, all muted by thin, blue privacy curtains. Finally the grunting snore of his father, slumped in a nursing chair at the foot of the bed. Sleeping and waiting.

Then the pain. Rolling across him in waves somehow both distant and immediate. Awareness of sheets held aloft by frames, of raw skin constricted by thick, tight pressure, of fuzziness, of one eye and half his head swathed in slimy bandages, of not being able to think through the fog, to see, to breathe ...

Sleep again. Then daylight, oozing in through a narrow,

wall-length window. Through it, the distant clock tower of the university was framed against an overcast sky. And his mother by the bedside, reading a magazine with the distracted air of someone looking at words and pictures on a page but not seeing anything. He'd studied her, then, for a couple of moments, confused and disoriented, but at the same time, for the last time, secure.

Finally, speaking, his voice croaky after a week unconscious. Tears. Nurses. Doctors. Dad. Noise and bustle. Temperatures and readings. Injections and pills. And then the moment when the world fell apart ...

"What happened? Where's Katia?"

Now, though, crunching along the track, shadowed again by the black cockatoos, memories of that other world grew slowly remote, and Vinnie could feel his perspective changing with every step. Of course they weren't missing him. That was impossible. The house, his home, had been dead from the moment Katia drove the car off the road. His presence served only to remind his parents of what they had lost.

He knew he'd have to go back eventually, of course, but when he did it would be on his terms, not theirs. Just as he'd left. And it wouldn't be Vinnie who returned. Not old Vinnie, anyway. It would be ... someone else.

The afternoon grew warmer; his t-shirt became damp against his skin, especially where the straps from his pack rubbed. He stopped by the edge of the path and removed it, stuffing it into an outside pocket, liberated by the sensation of warm air on his exposed body. A couple of flies buzzed at him as he re-shouldered the pack, one landing on a wrinkle of grafted skin that ran horizontal across his chest. Vinnie flicked at it, stirring it into a gentle frenzy. He knew that his body was becoming healthy and fit below the patterned discoloration of scars and grafts. As he walked, he toyed with the idea that his markings were a camouflage, allowing him to blend like a lizard or a snake into the surrounding bush, helping him to hide from the world, from the predators.

It was a false hope, of course. The marks set him apart, made him different, and would never be anything but scars of isolation. Who would accept or care for someone damaged like he was? He'd heard the men outside the shop, had seen the look in the woman's eyes at the refrigerator.

Swinging through the early afternoon, though, with the faintest stirrings of a breeze cooling him and his load bumping gently at his back, Vinnie allowed himself to drift away into a reverie of better times lost.

The clearing stood still and silent, much as on the afternoon he'd first arrived. As usual, the world seemed to hesitate for a couple of seconds when he entered the scarred landscape and began to pick his way down the terraces. In the gentle warmth, with his sweat cooling on his naked chest as he walked, Vinnie meandered towards his camp.

Drawing near to the silent campervan with its attendant dome tent, Vinnie pondered for a moment the whereabouts of its occupants. He'd seen not a sign of them that morning, and the camp still seemed deserted now. The memory of the girl – Helen – sitting with him by the fire stirred something in him, and veering his course slightly carried him closer to her campsite.

As he drew parallel to the tent his calm was paralysingly shattered as the zippered opening drew itself upwards, and

Helen emerged, blinking, into the afternoon light, not two metres from where he stood, exposed.

For a moment everything seemed far away, as though he was viewing the scene through a mirror of distance. Filtered, hazy objectivity removed him from the sensation of the girl's stare, the almost physical itch of her gaze as she examined his ravaged torso, bare of hair, etched with healing scar tissue and tracked with the remains of sutures. For long moments, she allowed her eyes to travel across him as he stood, livid in the sunlight.

"Vinnie, hi."

His mind was numb, a fog of naked discomfort and embarrassment.

"Been into town?"

God! Why didn't she say something about it? Why wouldn't she comment?

"Good walk?"

It was as though she didn't see him. See what he was. He could feel colour rising in his cheeks and neck.

"There was a ranger here about half an hour ago, checking up on the place, making sure we're doing the right thing."

"Huh?"

"He wanted to know about you, and I told him that you were just a bloke camping. Nothing unusual."

Something in the way she spoke, the way she chose the words, managed to penetrate the haze of embarrassment.

"Unusual?"

"Yeah." For the first time the girl looked askance, not meeting his eyes. "He was pretty interested in whether I'd had a close look at you. If you had any … distinguishing features."

70

Vinnie lifted a hand to his face, unconsiously.

"I told him I hadn't seen you close up, but that you seemed fine to me."

She was looking directly at him now. Her hair glinted a reddish hue in the sun, her head tilted slightly to one side and a small wrinkle of concern creasing between her eyebrows.

"I did the right thing, didn't I, Vinnie? I mean, you're not on the run from prison or anything like that, are you?"

"No. I ..." Words abandoned him.

"Didn't think so. You look like you just need some time away from the world. That's right, isn't it?"

"I gotta go ..."

He pushed past, stepping off the path to get by her, and his shoulder and upper arm, still moist with sweat, brushed lightly against hers. The echo of contact coursed along his nervous system; his toes and fingers tingled with brief adrenalin. Then he was clear, walking, stumbling, almost running back to his tent, to the safe, tenuous privacy of those flimsy canvas walls.

September 1943

In summer, before the madness of war, his family would picnic in the nearby forest. Father, Mother, Mathilde and himself. Mother would pack food and they'd carry it deep into the woods, sometimes near a lake, and spend the afternoon there.

Erich studied the gnarled, reddish trunks that surrounded the camp. The forest was so different. Here, trees grew twisted and misshapen, prowling through undergrowth so thick and spiny that to venture into it without protective

71

leggings was madness. Plants here would leap at you, snagging your clothes and hair, opening seams already ragged with wear. And the animals – the birds – it was as though they were laughing at you the whole while, screaming from the green shadows, mocking these strangers in all their alien hopelessness. Sitting on the hospital steps and looking out through the fence line, Erich longed for those warm summer afternoons in the forest, for trees that shed their leaves with the onset of cold, for the moist crackle of leaf litter below his feet.

"How's the reading?"

Alice emerged from inside and gestured at the book which lay, ignored, on his lap.

"Fine, thank you."

She sat on the step beside him.

"Grandfather says that Günter is getting much better now."

"Good."

"You should be proud of yourself."

Erich shrugged. "I did what was necessary."

Laughter echoed across the compound from the guardhouse by the gate. The girl's constant presence and chatter were irritating. It was as though she didn't realise the gap between them – that they were enemies.

"Are you all right?"

"Excuse me?"

"You. Are you all right? You've hardly spoken to anyone since the night we" – she hesitated – "since the night of Günter's operation."

"I am not the talking to people type."

72

The girl stifled a small giggle and Erich threw her a sharp look.

"I'm sorry. You sound so formal sometimes."

"I am sorry my English is not so good."

"No, it's not that at all. You speak beautifully. I just wish you'd relax a little. It would make everyone so much more comfortable."

"There is a war on. Comfort is not important."

She was still smiling. "It's silly, don't you think?"

"Silly?"

"This war. Pretending that you're still fighting it, right out here in the bush. Don't you think it's a waste of energy?"

He stiffened. "Not at all."

"Well, I think it is."

Erich stood, careful as he did so to keep his stance military and correct.

"If you will excuse me, I should see if the doctor requires me."

The door swung hard into its frame behind him.

Inside, Günter and the doctor were playing some sort of card game that they had managed to work out despite the language barrier. They were silent, yet communicating clearly through the slap of the cards on the table rigged beside the bed.

"Erich." Doctor Alexander looked up from his hand. "Join us?"

"No, thank you, Herr Doctor. I will continue my study in here" – a disdainful glance back in the direction of the door – "where it is a little more silent."

"Something is bothering you out there?"

"No, sir. It is just that I ... just too noisy."

73

Settling by the stove, Erich opened his book and made as if to read.

"You know, Erich, it would be good for you to talk to Alice sometimes."

"Excuse me, Doctor?"

"She would be a good friend for you here. Especially given the similarity in your ages."

"I am afraid that apart from that we have very little in common, sir."

"You might be surprised."

Günter, lying and listening, asked in German, "You have found a sweetheart, no?"

Erich stared coldly at the man. "No."

"Why not?"

"Because she is the enemy."

"Ah, yes, that." Günter shook his head in mock sadness. "And this from the boy who told me that he knew so much about love."

"That was just to make you eat."

"Well, it worked, so what you said must have been correct. If a woman can look past something like a missing limb, do you really think a little thing like being her enemy will be a problem?"

"What is he saying?" interrupted the doctor.

"Nothing. He is being stupid." Then he added in German, to make sure that Günter understood, "*Ein dumkopf!*"

"Doctor ..." Günter's English was halting and broken. "I tell boy to open his eyes, see past ..." He paused, searching for the word.

"See past?" Doctor Alexander prompted.

"To see past war. See real people." Erich thought he caught

74

a wink pass between the amputee soldier and the old doctor. Günter was grinning.

"That's good advice, Günter." The doctor was smiling slightly himself. "Very good advice indeed. And he could start with my granddaughter."

"May I be excused, sir. To the latrine."

"Of course."

Alice was still sitting on the step, reading. Erich stormed past without a word.

In the latrine, he considered his anger. Why did they all insist on unsettling him like this? And Günter, who should have been his ally, was the worst - he'd forgotten about national pride, about the future of the greater Germany, everything taught at school and in the *Hitlerjugend*. What was the point? If his father were here ...

Erich shook his head, stifling that line of thought before it had a chance to germinate. His father was half the problem. If Erich closed his eyes for a second his father was there before him, as clear as day, his uniform shirt, neatly pressed jacket dripping with decorations and commendations, the iron cross at his throat. How many times had Erich listened to his father speak of their family, and the pride in his voice as he told his son of the bravery of his grandfather, and of his own adventures during the first world war, and of the importance of being loyal to your country, of always being a soldier, even in peacetime.

This was his problem. This was what made him angry. If his father and all that he stood for was right, then why was he, Erich, so easily captured? Why was he in the middle of this ugly foreign forest, waiting for nothing and surrounded by weak men like Stutt and Günter? Worst of all, why was it their words sounded like they made sense?

Nine

Vinnie

The beer, cooled for a couple of hours in a plastic bag in the creek, was bitter and at the same time sweet as it trickled down the back of Vinnie's throat. Around him the night buzzed and he sat, listening, going over his meeting with Helen outside her tent a few hours ago.

She had startled him, true. He'd thought the tent empty, the camp site deserted, and if he'd known she was there he would have replaced his shirt and covered the scars before setting out across the clearing. But all the same, he hadn't expected, to feel so ... so naked.

And he liked her. There was no denying it. She was the first person in a long time to make him feel complete again. She didn't seem to see the scars, didn't seem to notice, but he was pretty sure that was an act. Some people are good at that sort of thing. No, it was something else as well, something about the way she spoke to him. There was no bullshit, no pretence. Just conversation. That was the attraction.

He stirred the coals and sipped at his beer. The taste, familiar and yet distant, called up memories of the party, the music, people being thrown in the pool, Katia chatting to some guy in the corner, laughing, drink in hand. Vinnie could tell by the way she was standing, even from across the room, that she wasn't really interested, just making small talk.

His mate Johnno was trying to get him pissed, kept handing him bourbon and cokes which he didn't drink, leaving plastic cups half full of the sickly brown liquid on various window ledges around the house, pouring them into pot plants when no one was paying attention. He didn't feel like getting wrecked, not that night.

And later, when it started raining, everyone had come inside and couples were getting together in dark corners, and he'd watched the bloke who'd been chatting her up earlier lean in to his sister's ear and whisper. She'd thrown her drink on him and everyone had laughed. Then she'd flounced over to him and Johnno, wriggling her bum and putting on a show, but still angry, burning inside. If you didn't know her, you'd never spot it. Katia all over.

"Let's go, Vin. We're out of here."

"Ah, come on, Kat, the night's still young."

"Bullshit, Vinnie. I'm going. You can walk home if you want."

"Nah."

And then, in the car, trees and darkness whipping by the slick road, she was driving hard, but in control, like always.

"Kat?"

"What?"

"That bloke, at the party ..."

"Asshole."

"What did he say?"

"None of your business."

Night-car-silence. The hum of the road. Silent swish of tyres on wet asphalt. Rush of slicing through the night. Accelerating into the corners.

"You okay, Kat?"

She never answered. The cat, black and white and feral and caught in the glaring cone of the headlights, darted from the shoulder onto the black tarmac. Katia jerked the wheel, an instinctive, uncontrolled spasm of movement and then the car was sliding, slowly, so slowly…

"Vinnie?"

Helen stood a few feet away. He hadn't heard her approach.

He climbed to his feet, awkward and shambling, limbs moving independent of brain.

"I won't stay. I just wanted to apologise for this afternoon. I …"

"Nah, listen, I'm the one who should say sorry."

Firelight sparked reflections in her eyes.

"You sort of caught me by surprise, that's all. I didn't think you were in your tent, so I wasn't really ready to, well, you know, to bump into you like that. I'm sorry for runnin' off."

"Don't worry about it. Happens all the time."

"Really?"

"Actually, no." She laughed softly and for a moment they faced each other across the flames, then she moved to go. "Anyway, I wanted to come over and clear the air. I'll leave you in peace."

"You don't have to. Stay a while. You want a beer?"

"You have beer?"

Vinnie nodded towards where the creek burbled in the darkness.

"Chilled by nature."

"In that case, as long as you're offering ..."

Helen eased herself down beside the fire, and Vinnie clambered through the shadows, retrieving another two cans from the cold, black water.

"Here you go."

"Thanks. You look after yourself okay. Do you do this a lot?"

"This?"

"Camping. You seem to have it all under control."

Vinnie shrugged. "Don't have a lot of choice. I've always been pretty good at lookin' after myself, though."

"So why here?"

Vinnie looked at her. Her face, half turned to the fire, picked up the red hue of firelight, and the blackness of the shadows.

"It's ... a bit personal."

"You run away?"

"Yeah. But that's not my worry. Mum and Dad never gave a shit about me before ..."

The silence of the night fell between them, until Helen spoke "Before?"

"I was in a car accident. With my sister. She was killed. That's how I got ... all this. I guess I'm just trying to get myself a bit straightened out, you know? I'm pretty messed up."

"Do you miss her?"

"Yeah. Of course. She was always lookin' out for me. But that's not why I'm here."

"It isn't?"

"Nah. I ran 'cause, well ..." A branch in the fire burst into popping sparks, interrupting him. Vinnie shook his head slightly. "Shit, I'm carrying on like an idiot."

"No, you're not."

"Whatever. What about you?"

"Me?"

"Yeah. What brings you and Grandad all the way out here to the middle of the bloody bush? You can't leave me wondering, you know. I'll suspect the worst."

"Nothing too sinister. A history project."

"History?"

"Yeah. My grandfather spent some time in the POW camp here during the Second World War and he wanted to see the place again."

"Is that where you were this morning?"

"Yeah. It took ages to get there and back again – he moves pretty slowly."

"What did he think of it all?"

"Don't know. He doesn't say too much. He spent about an hour sitting on an old foundation and then we left again."

"He didn't look around?"

"No. Didn't seem interested."

"Weird."

"Not really. He's not a young man. I think he just wanted to see the place. He wants to go back again tomorrow."

"I'd like to meet him."

"Come across in the morning and I'll introduce you, I should warn you though, he can be a bit bad-tempered, especially with strangers."

"Ah, well then, we'll see tomorrow, eh?"

"Sounds like a date."

"Probably the only one I'm likely to get in the near future."

Helen threw a strange look in his direction. "Why?"

"Look at me. I'm not exactly Mr Universe."

"So?"

"So, what girl's gonna be interested in me now? Looking like this."

"Plenty of them. You seem like a nice bloke."

"Yeah, with a face like half a prune."

"That shouldn't matter."

"Come on, you telling me you'd go for a guy with this sort of damage all over him?"

"If I knew him and I liked him, yeah, I think I probably would."

"I reckon you're lying. People aren't like that. Women especially."

"I don't know what type of girls you've been hanging out with, Vinnie, but you should give some others a chance."

"Whatever."

"No, not whatever. You can't simply write yourself off to the rest of the world just because you've had some bad breaks lately."

"Bad breaks? Look at my bloody face, will you?"

"I've seen your face. I don't mind it."

Vinnie stared hard at her, trying to make up his mind whether she was making fun of him. "In that case, how about dinner?"

Helen laughed, breaking the tension. "Sorry, you'll have to work a bit harder than that to get a date with me."

"See? Told you. You're just like the rest of them."

"No, Vinnie, I'm not." She drained the rest of her can and

stood to leave. "But I reckon you are. See you tomorrow." Walking away, she seemed to melt from firelight into darkness.

September 1943

The signal for evening rollcall echoed between the buildings and back into the camp from the tree line. Erich, excused by the doctor's brief nod, stepped out into drizzle. It was almost dark and the parade area was lit in the pale glow of overhead lamps. The dispersed light turned the men into rows of ghosts, their features sunk into skeletal hollows and pools of darkness. Sodden greatcoats hung limply and disguised bodies.

In these conditions, rollcall always took longer. One of the guards would move along the lines, from man to man, double-checking the identity of each prisoner against the name called by Thomas – a precaution against a substitution, covering for an escape.

Not that escape seemed to be a huge consideration. In Erich's third week, the sirens had sounded and search parties dispersed, hunting for two men who had failed to return from their work assignment. Within a couple of hours the two had appeared at the camp gates, wet, cold, muddy and miserable. They had become disoriented in the forest on their way home and walked in the wrong direction for several hours until they came across a familiar track. Stutt had given them each a week in detention.

None of Erich's camp-mates seemed interested in the idea of escape, and Erich was too nervous to broach the subject. In any case, from what he remembered of his geography, Australia was a long way from anywhere.

"Pieters."

It was so unfair. So wrong that he should have ended up here, where there was not so much as an opportunity to return home, even if he managed to find a way out from the enclosure.

"Pieters!"

On the other side of the fence, the forest still pressed in, thick and black, on the camp. If he were able to get to the other side of it, he still wouldn't know in which direction to head off. The roads would be too dangerous, too exposed for a man in a German army uniform.

"Pieters!"

A hard slap stung across his face, cracking wetly in the silence, dragging Erich from his musings. Guard Thomas, young, pimpled and angry, stood directly in front of him, one hand holding the clipboard loose at his side, the other still raised to strike.

"You bloody answer me the first time I call your name, understand, Fritz?"

Several of the men stiffened at the taunt, but none moved. Erich stared into the straw-coloured eyes and held silent.

"I've got better things to be doing than wasting my time chasin' up and down just 'cause you're havin' a bloody day-dream. You get me?"

When Erich didn't answer, the young guard's hand flew again and Erich felt the salt tang of blood tickling his mouth.

"I asked you a question. Do you understand?"

"That will do, Thomas." Stutt, having broken from his place at the front, stepped across and seized the guard's hand before he could strike Erich again. "I think that you have made your point quite clear. Erich will apologise. Erich?"

84

Meeting the senior officer's eye, it was clear that the request was really an order.

"I apologise for inconveniencing you."

"Sir!" snarled the guard.

"Excuse me?"

"I apologise for inconveniencing you, *sir*." The guard's eyes narrowed to dangerous slits.

"I don't believe you have been commissioned quite yet, Thomas." Stutt's quiet interruption raised a gentle snigger from the men standing nearby. "I think Erich's apology will be sufficient for us not to have to report this incident to the camp commander, don't you?"

Thomas refused to back down.

"If he tries this again, I'll assume that he's covering some type of escape attempt and ..."

"If you strike one of my men again, Thomas, I'll assume that you are not familiar with the terms of the Red Cross guidelines for the treatment of prisoners of war."

For a long moment the young guard and the older German officer stared at one another through the drizzle before Thomas wheeled and stalked back to the front of the parade, consulting his soggy list as he did so.

"Reichman!"

"*Ja!*"

Five minutes later the parade was completed and the men dismissed. Erich made to head straight towards his hut, but was intercepted by Stutt.

"What was that all about?"

"Sir?"

"Why didn't you answer him?"

"It was a mistake, sir. I was not paying attention."

Stutt regarded him for a long moment.

"And what were you thinking about that is so interesting it makes you fall asleep during rollcall?"

"Home, sir. Of my family in Stuttgart."

The lie seemed to satisfy the commanding officer. He relaxed a little.

"That kind of thinking is fine for when you are in your bunk at night, Pieters, but the rest of the time you will need to remember that there is still a war on."

Pathetic, thought Erich. Couldn't the man see how ironic it was? That kind of advice coming from a man who had made himself into nothing more than an Australian lap dog?

"You need to be a little careful around Thomas, Erich."

"Why is that, sir?"

Stutt glanced quickly about.

"He is not the most stable of young men." He reverted to German. "Even the other guards keep him at a distance."

This was true. Most of the other guards were either veterans of the first war, serving out their time here in the bush, or were recently returned from the fronts in Europe and Africa to recover their nerves somewhat before they were demobilised. Most were old and war-weary. Among them, Thomas clearly stood apart.

"He didn't serve overseas, Erich. Not actively, anyway."

"Sir?"

Again, the nervous glance around.

"I shouldn't tell you this, Erich, but after tonight you probably need to know. He was injured before he completed his training."

"What kind of injury, sir?"

86

For the first time during the conversation, the hint of a smile creased the commanding officer's face.

"A gunshot wound. To the foot."

Erich fought back the urge to laugh. Everyone knew what that meant.

"So he is a coward?"

In his own division, several men had shot themselves deliberately in the feet and legs during training, in attempts to escape the war. They had been tried as traitors. Stutt made a non-committal gesture with both hands.

"Possibly, but from what the other guards tell me, it was a genuine injury. This is why he was not drummed out of the army."

"So then he is just incompetent." The idea that Thomas might have shot himself in the foot accidentally was even better than that of him as a coward.

"Also possible. In either case, you need to remember one thing, Erich."

"What is that, sir?"

"This young man could well be very dangerous if he decides to. There's no bully worse than a coward, and no man more dangerous than one with damaged pride. You should steer clear of him if you can, because I get the impression he doesn't like you much. Now get yourself across to the hospital and, if the doctor hasn't gone back to his hut for the night, have that cut on your lip seen to."

Stutt made his way off towards the mess, where boisterous laughter probably marked a retelling of the evening's parade, and Erich, wiping at his face, trudged back towards the hospital.

And from the deep shadows cast by the far wall of the mess
hut, Guard Thomas watched him go.

Ten

Vinnie

For some unaccountable reason Vinnie's gut churned as he picked his way up the terraces to where Helen and her grandfather waited. A few moments earlier, when he'd noticed them making their slow way out for the day, he'd not hesitated in raising his arm and calling. Now, climbing towards them, he could see impatience in the old man's stance and wondered if the invitation from the night before was still open.

"Vinnie. Hi."

Helen also seemed ill at ease. Something in the way she glanced nervously at her grandfather, and the nervous moistening of her lips suggested thinly-masked apprehension.

"Are you going to join us?"

"Yeah. Thought I might. If that's okay?"

Vinnie shuffled his feet, acutely aware of the gaze searching him. The old man's body was gnarled with age, but his eyes, blue and unwavering, suggested none of the watery senility Vinnie had seen in other old men.

"This is my grandfather. Doctor Pieters."

"G'day."

No hand was offered, none expected. All that filled the silence was a continuing appraisal. For long seconds, even the constant restlessness of the bush seemed to fade. Scar tissue itched as it felt itself scrutinised, and Vinnie tried not to scratch at phantom nerve-endings.

"Shall we go, then?" The man's voice; deep, strong and accented, held none of the tremolo of age. He didn't wait for the consent of the two younger people but wheeled on his heel in a slow, military turn and started into the dim forest.

Behind his back, Helen offered a wan smile before following. Vinnie hesitated. At the bottom of the slope the security of his camp site called. It would be easy to slip back down and spend the morning in quiet, secure solitude, unconcerned about the judgment of an old man. A few steps along, Helen stopped and turned, and with another smile and a shake of her head she drew Vinnie onto the path and into the darkness of the bush.

Progress was slow, set by the pace of the retired doctor. On occasion they would arrive at some small obstruction, a tree or branch fallen across the path, and would have to wait for Helen's grandfather to negotiate the difficulty. At first Vinnie reached to assist, an instinctive gesture, but Helen had caught his eye and gestured *don't*.

"Did you sleep all right?"

"Fine, thanks. A little restless in the middle of the night, but I've been finding it pretty easy to sleep out here."

"It's sort of hypnotic, isn't it? Lying at night and just listening. The first night freaked me out, but I'm used to it now."

90

The old man made no attempt to join the conversation and Vinnie and Helen restricted themselves to inconsequential chat. They stopped to rest at the bridge beside the pool where Vinnie had considered his reflection. Sitting, Vinnie was again uncomfortably aware of Helen's grandfather examining him.

"What happened to your face?"

The bluntness stung more than the question. Helen frowned but said nothing, leaving Vinnie to respond.

"I was in an accident."

"Did you burn?" The German accent revealed only detached curiosity.

"I ..." Words deserted him. Vinnie stood, trembled, prepared to flee.

"Grandfather," Helen gently chastised, "it's not a question you should ask."

The old man shrugged. "Why not? I am a doctor. It seems clear to me that the boy has been burned. I am curious, that is all."

"It's not something that he likes to discuss."

Through this Vinnie stood, acutely aware of the instinct calling him back into the tree-closed protection of the path behind. There was something else, though. A tiny spark of ingrained knowledge that kept him rooted. If he left now, if he ran, then part of him would always be running.

"It's okay." His voice rang strange in his own ears. "I'll be right."

Even through the conversation with his granddaughter the old man's gaze hadn't wavered, but remained steady on Vinnie. Now, for the first time, Vinnie returned it, meeting the doctor's stare directly.

"Yeah," he replied, "I burned."

"Ah, then." The old man looked away, up the path towards the old prison camp. "We shall continue onwards?"

Helen fell into step alongside and touched Vinnie on the forearm, her voice low.

"I'm sorry about that. He tends to confront people when he first meets them."

"It's okay."

And, in a moment of startling revelation, Vinnie realised that it was.

"People are gonna want to know about it, aren't they? I guess someone had to ask sooner or later."

"Exactly my point." The old man didn't even glance back towards them. "It is far better to have these things out in the open from the beginning, I am thinking."

Vinnie threw a brief grin at Helen.

"His hearing's pretty good too."

"As good as ever."

Emerging from the trees, the trio followed the slight uphill path to the gate arrangement at the edge of the old prison camp site. Vinnie was aware of a strange new lightness within, of having faced and beaten a demon, perhaps one of many. A couple of black cockatoos flitted towards the tree line, oblivious to the three people below.

A thin breeze quivered and again Vinnie was struck by the different stillness that pervaded here.

"It's a strange place."

Abruptly, Helen's grandfather stopped.

"What do you mean?"

"Can't you feel it? There's an atmosphere here that's, I dunno, something different from the camp site, anyway."

A bushy white eyebrow lifted itself on the old man's forehead.

"Do you think? Ghosts, perhaps?"

"No idea. Just something I felt the other day when I came here the first time."

"Do you believe in ghosts, Vincent?"

"Nah."

"Good. That sort of thinking defies rationality. Still, I am thinking that you are right about this place."

Turning, the doctor murmured, "Let me remember ..."

The blue eyes closed and the old body relaxed. Vinnie tried to imagine the prison camp rebuilt in the old man's mind – wire and guard towers, lights and wooden buildings.

"Over here, I think."

The old man led off again, shuffling up a gentle incline towards some decaying foundations a few hundred metres away.

"Mess hall, guards quarters ..." Each landmark, now no more than grey, mouldering blocks, was indicated with small, impatient gestures.

"There," he continued, indicating a small square foundation set some way apart from the others. "There was the German detention compound – the isolation cells. Boiling hot in the summer, freezing cold in the winter, and tiny. I only visited it once, for a week."

"Why?"

He smiled.

"A little matter of a disagreement with a guard. Silly to think about now."

The matter clearly closed, the tour continued. Making slow progress between the ruins, Vinnie was struck by the change in the old man's demeanour. It was clear that memories and visions of a lost place were transporting him not only out of time, but also out of place and body.

"How different it all seems," the old man said, almost as if reading Vinnie's thoughts.

"It's the same forest, though, surely?"

"In some ways, yes, in many others, no. Ah. Here …" A shallow ditch scored the mossy ground, running off towards a clump of trees several hundred metres away. "The German fence line. That means …"

With no further remark, the old doctor led the two young people up the slope towards a rectangular foundation a little way off. There he eased himself down, settling on the cold concrete. A smile hinted at the corners of his mouth as he gazed around, left and right.

"There. Just so … familiar."

"What is it?"

"Excuse me?"

"This building."

"This, Vincent, is all that remains of the place where everything changed."

September 1943

"What happened to your face?"

Doctor Alexander crossed the room quickly, concern in his expression.

"Nothing, Doctor, a little mishap at rollcall last evening."

Arriving at the hospital after his run-in with Thomas the night before, Erich had found the little hut deserted, apart from the sleeping form of Günter, and not wanting to disturb the patient he had retreated again to his own bunk.

Now, in the light of day, his lower lip was swollen and crusted with dried blood.

"Let me take a look at that."

"I'm certain that it will be fine, Doctor."

"Nonetheless, I'm going to make sure."

"You have been fighting, youngster?" Günter looked up from the old woman's magazine he had been flicking through.

"No. Go back to your knitting."

The soldier grinned. In the last few days his spirits had been rising steadily and he was almost back to his old self.

"Your lip should have been stitched right away. How did you do this?"

"An accident, Doctor. Nothing serious."

"Erich, either you tell me yourself or I'll get Commander Stutt in here and he can inform me."

Erich considered the doctor. Behind his moustache his eyes were hard, a flinty quality reflecting in the dull light.

"I had a run-in with one of the guards, sir. Commander Stutt has already dealt with the issue."

"Which guard?"

"I do not know his name, sir."

It was clear that Doctor Alexander knew he was lying, but there was little he could do unless he was prepared to push the point.

"If something like this happens again, Erich, you are to inform me immediately, do you understand?"

"I will try to, sir."

"No, not try, *immediately*. If I am not around you ask one of the gate-guards to get me. All right?"

"Yes sir." It was an empty promise. Both knew that there was no way the doctor would ever be able to enforce it.

"In the meantime, I think I will speak to Stutt about this."

"I would rather you didn't, Doctor."

"Why not?"

"It has already been dealt with."

For long seconds the doctor regarded his young orderly, tugging thoughtfully at his left moustache.

"I will think about it, Erich. That is all I can promise. Now come here and let me see if there is anything we can do for your lip."

With the swelling, there was little to be done, so when Alice entered the hospital a few moments later the doctor was daubing brown antiseptic onto the cut.

"What happened?" Alice crossed to them.

"It appears Erich had a run-in with one of the guards last night."

"Are you all right? Who did this?" Her concern seemed genuine, and for the first time Erich regarded the girl through different eyes.

"I am fine – just a little cut."

"Now that you're here, Alice, would you mind finishing this for me while I see to Günter's dressings?"

Erich was only faintly aware of the feather-light touch of the cotton wool against his lips. Involuntarily, his tongue flicked out at the irritation, and the acrid taste of the antiseptic caused him to start.

"Careful!" The girl smiled. "You're not supposed to eat it."

"I am sorry." Erich's voice seemed thick through his swollen lip, but he made an attempt to return the smile. "I have not yet had breakfast."

"Well, that's all right, then." She finished applying the rest of the antiseptic. "There. You'll probably need to put some more on in a little while, when this lot wears off. Now, who'd like a cup of tea?" The girl crossed to the wood stove, stoked the flames and placed the kettle on the top.

"That would be nice, my dear." The doctor didn't look up from his work. "This is healing nicely, Günter."

Günter, understanding roughly what the doctor had said, replied in German, which Erich translated.

"He says that he can still feel his toes, Doctor."

"A quite normal response, I'm afraid. The nerves are still alive, even though they're no longer connected to anything. Poor Günter here is going to get the occasional itch and have nothing to scratch."

Erich translated again and to his surprise Günter laughed.

"At least he can see the funny side."

"I cannot understand how he does so."

"Perhaps you need to go through a tragedy in order to really understand one, Erich."

"Excuse me, Doctor?"

"I am saying that it is a matter of perspective, which you cannot realise until you are actually faced with the prospect of dealing with a changed life. You and Alice would both be too young to know what it is to face a life different from the one you had envisaged for yourself."

"I have seen many tragedies." A trace of the old anger blossomed inside Erich. "In Africa and Italy."

"I'm certain that you did, Erich. And I'm not for a minute suggesting that you are any less of a man or a soldier. All I am saying is that at this point in your life your foundations haven't yet been shaken, and you should be glad of that."

Erich still wasn't quite certain what the doctor was trying to imply, but the conversation was getting dangerously personal so he stayed silent. After a couple of minutes the doctor finished Günter's bandaging.

"There. Perhaps, Alice, you could make a cup for Günter as well?"

"Of course, Grandfather." She fetched another cup from the sideboard.

"And Erich, if you don't want a cup of tea, you could deal with these for me."

The doctor gestured at the bloody bandages which he had removed from Günter's leg.

"Yes, sir." Taking the bowl, Erich made his way over to the laundry hut, where a copper full of boiling water steamed in the cold morning air. Franz, the private assigned to laundry duty, greeted him cheerfully.

"Youngster! How's the mouth?"

Despite himself, Erich had stopped responding to baits about his age, and now 'Youngster' was his accepted nickname.

"Fine. Looks worse than it feels."

"He's a swine that one."

"Who?"

"That guard, Thomas." Franz lowered his voice. "They say he's a little mad."

Erich shrugged. Franz was a notorious gossip and the less he said the better.

"Whatever. I have these bandages to clean."

"Of course." Franz emptied the dirty bandages into a trough and ladled cold water over them. "You know he is in love, don't you?"

"The guard?"

"*Ja.*" Franz touched the side of his nose in a gesture of conspiracy. "You should be careful not to get between him and his girlfriend."

"Me?"

"Of course, Youngster."

"How could I get between him and his girlfriend?"

"You might not mean to. From what I hear, the affection is very much from him to her and not the other way around, if you know what I mean."

"She doesn't like him?"

"From what I'm told."

"But what has that to do with me?"

Franz winked as he fished the bandages from the water. "There, we will boil these up now, I think." He wrung the water from them and dropped them in the copper. "Think about it, Youngster, there are not too many attractive young ladies here in the forest, are there?"

"So?"

"So who do you think our friend has his eye upon?"

Erich realised what the other soldier was saying. "Do you mean ...?"

"*Ja.* And the handsome young orderly who spends his days working in the hospital with her might be seen as competition, don't you think?"

Eleven

Vinnie

"So you're heading back to town tomorrow?"

The afternoon sun dropped below the tree line, throwing long shadows and sinking the clearing into premature twilight. Vinnie and Helen sat at a picnic table beside the creek.

"I imagine so. I can't see him wanting to make that walk a third time."

The journey back from the prison camp site had been arduous. Helen's grandfather, already tired, had lost his footing a couple of times, and on one occasion Vinnie had leapt forward and caught him before he toppled onto the rough gravel path. The old man had snapped at him, then not spoken again for the rest of the walk.

"I'm sorry about Grandad this afternoon."

"Nah, it's okay. He's a proud old bloke."

"Too proud, I'm afraid."

"Eh?"

Helen looked at him. "He's dying, Vinnie. Cancer."

"Ah." Vinnie struggled for something to say. "I'm sorry."

He reached down, picked up a small handful of red gravel pebbles from the ground, and lobbed one into the creek.

"Me too. Until this trip, I'd never seen much of him, living in Germany as he did. He'd phone at Christmas and on my birthday and send presents, but that's not the same. I've never had him around as a grandfather and now I'm going to lose him, and he won't let anyone help."

"He's letting you look after him out here, isn't he?"

"Not willingly. Mum had to insist. He was planning to come alone."

"Seriously?"

"Yeah. It's strange. He's spent most of his life healing other people, and now that it's his turn to be looked after he won't do a thing to help himself."

"He can't be treated, then?"

Helen shook her head.

"No. Perhaps six months ago, when he first noticed the symptoms, but not any more."

"Didn't he do anything at the time?"

"My grandmother, his wife, she died a couple of years ago, and he's been wanting to join her ever since."

"Ah." It was hard to imagine that tough old body riddled from the inside. "So why the trip here, then?"

"Not sure. He hasn't really told anyone, only that he wanted to come here one last time. I guess it's just some kind of farewell. I can't understand how he's so accepting."

"Accepting?"

"Of the cancer. It's a death sentence, and yet he just seems to take each day as if it were any other. If it were me, I'd …" She stopped.

"You'd what?"

"I don't know. I wouldn't just accept it, that's for sure."

Vinnie glanced back up the slope to the campervan. The old doctor sat under the awning, reading. Before him, spread out on the table, were all manner of documents: maps of the old camp, forestry surveys, an old notebook. Through a pair of thick half-frame glasses, Doctor Pieters studied the documents intently.

"He looks okay."

"He does at the moment." Helen picked up a couple of pebbles and threw them, watching the concentric circles of their splash waver slowly towards the banks. "He won't in a month or so."

"Is he going to stay here?"

"No. Mum'll go back to Germany with him. That's where Grandma is buried, and he'll want to die there."

"Will you go too?"

"Don't know. It'll depend on my study. This trip is sort of my goodbye, I guess."

They lapsed into silence while evening settled over the clearing. Above, the sky faded red into purple, against which the first few stars winked into being. Somewhere nearby a frog chirped lazily in the mud.

"You got grandparents, Vinnie?"

"Not in Perth. Dad's folks still live in Italy, and Mum's people are interstate."

"You miss them?"

Vinnie thought for a minute.

"I do nowdays."

"What do you mean?"

"Before the accident, well, family wasn't so important to me, you know? But now ..." He paused. "I dunno, things are just different at home, and sometimes it'd be nice to have them around."

"Them?"

"Grandparents. Just for somewhere to escape to. For a bit of support."

"But what about your parents? They must be giving you heaps of help."

Vinnie threw another stone.

"Vinnie?"

"They don't even know where I am."

Helen's brow creased. "You mean right now?"

"Yeah. I took off. Couldn't take it any more."

"Take what?"

He shrugged. "Home. Mum and Dad can't handle it without Katia around. Dad blames me."

"Blames you?"

"For the accident. For not getting her out. It's fair enough. I mean I did get out, after the crash, and she couldn't, and if I'd been a bit quicker, listened to her earlier or somethin', I dunno ..." Vinnie's voice trailed into silence.

"Are you certain that's how he feels? I mean ..."

"Yeah, I'm certain. He told me as much on the night I ran off."

"He told you it was your fault?"

Vinnie nodded.

"Shit, Vinnie."

"He apologised later, but at the time he said it, he meant it."

"How could he?"

"You don't know my dad. He's a tough bloke. All his life

103

he's worked his arse off so that Kat and I would have the opportunities that he didn't have."

"But I don't see how that makes everything your fault."

"Kat was the smart one, she was gonna be a doctor, but I was more interested in having a good time with my mates and stuff. Anyway, I didn't want to spend my whole life in a library, I wanted to be out, actually doin' stuff. That's why I dropped out and got a job in a nursery."

"You mean with babies?"

"Babies?" Vinnie looked at Helen as though she'd gone mad.

"The nursery."

"Ah, no." He laughed. "Plants. Natives, mainly. A plant nursery."

Now Helen laughed too.

"So you work with plants. What's wrong with that?"

"Nothin', far as I'm concerned. I love it – getting my hands dirty, workin' in the sun. You know where you are with plants. Dad didn't like it though. Thought I was chucking my life away. He reckoned that he'd slaved to make sure that Kat and I would never have to do something like work in a nursery. That was what he said. So when Kat died, and he was left with me, well ..."

For a long time the two sat still and silent. Helen shot small glances at the boy hunched beside her, wondering how much of the damage from that accident was on the inside.

"Vinnie?"

"Yeah?"

"We'll probably be heading back to town tomorrow. You want a lift?"

He looked at her. "Nah. I think I'll hang here for a little longer. Thanks."

"You can't hide forever, you know."

"I know. But I can't go back, either. Not yet."

"It is not mattering anyway, I am afraid." Both turned, startled to see the old doctor standing in the shadows only a few metres away. "The only place we will be going tomorrow is back up the hill to the camp."

"Grandad ..." Helen started to interrupt, but he silenced her with a wave.

"We will be paying one more visit, and Vincent" – he focused his stare again on Vinnie – "we will be needing your assistance, if that is possible."

PART TWO

1943-1946

Twelve

October 1943

"Tell me about your family."

Erich looked sharply at Alice. "Why?"

"I'm interested, that's all. I want to know if you're really all that different."

"Different?"

"From me. From the rest of us."

"Who is 'us'?"

"Australians."

A few metres away on the other side of the fence the forest steamed gently in the warmth of the sunshine. For three days spring rains had soaked the tangled undergrowth, and earlier that afternoon the sun had finally broken through. At the doctor's suggestion Erich had grabbed the opportunity to escape the confines of the hospital and to go for a quick walk to stretch his legs. To his discomfort, Alice had immediately volunteered to join him.

"It is not necessary, I will only be a short time."

"Don't be silly. I want to get some fresh air as well."

"I'm sure it won't kill you to have a little company, Erich."

Doctor Alexander hadn't even looked up from his notes. "Be back in fifteen minutes, please, both of you."

But Erich was uncomfortable. In the fortnight since his discussion with Franz, he'd been avoiding the girl as much as possible. He'd met men like that guard Thomas before, and for once he agreed with Stutt. The man was unstable – dangerous. And Thomas had a gun.

"Well?"

"Excuse me?"

"Your family?"

Erich looked away, into the forest. "They are not a subject I like to discuss."

"Why not?"

"Because" – he paused, considering his answer carefully – "it is easier not to think about them."

Alice stopped walking, a thought-crease wrinkling her forehead.

"How can not thinking about your family be easier? Easier than what?"

"Look at some of the pathetic men in here. They have no pride left, no hope of returning home with any honour as Germans. That is because all they do is mope about things that are impossible for them at the moment. Wives, lovers ..."

Alice interrupted. "Are you saying that Günter is any less a soldier because he thinks about his wife?"

"No, I am saying that ..."

"Because if you are, then you're sillier than I thought. Thinking about his wife – after you reminded him, I might add – was the only thing that saved his life. You of all people should realise that."

"That is different."

"How?"

"Because Günter, he …"

The sentence trailed to silence. For a time the two stood in the pale afternoon, the muted scrapings and whisperings of the wet forest the only sounds.

"I'm right, aren't I?"

Erich shrugged. "Perhaps."

"I am, you know."

"How can you be so certain?"

Alice started to walk again. "Grandfather let me read the letters that my Uncle Paul sent back from the last war. Letters to my grandmother, and to him."

"So?"

"So when I read them there was something there, something between the words and the descriptions. I could tell that, even though he was so far away, every time he wrote down his thoughts, every time he told my grandmother how much he missed her cooking, every time he sent one of those letters, it seemed like a little bit of him came home with it, and after he was killed those little bits of him were all that my grandparents had to hold on to."

Erich said nothing, uncomfortable at the emotion.

"That's why you need to think of your family. That's why you need to keep yourself human. Because otherwise, if you don't, then you really are a soldier, nothing more, and I think that would be terrible. You might as well be a slave."

For a long time the two young people continued their way in silence, accompanied only by the steady dripping off leaves onto undergrowth.

"I have a sister."

111

Alice looked at him. "Do you miss her?"

"Of course. She didn't want me to join the army."

"So why did you still join?"

Erich considered the question carefully. "Because of my father. I wanted to prove to him ..."

Erich stopped himself suddenly, almost caught. The relief of remembering had almost erased the need for caution.

"Prove what?"

"I am sorry. I cannot talk about him."

"Why ever not?"

The girl reached out and rested her hand lightly on Erich's arm. With the tingle of his flesh, he briefly recalled her touch when she had led him inside from the storm after Günter's operation.

"You can tell me. You know that."

Indecision flickered. He wanted to tell her. Every part of his mind was screaming out to him that he needed to tell her. Needed to let her in. He realised with shocking, sudden clarity just how lonely he was.

"Whatever it is, it can't be that bad." Alice watched him carefully.

"It is not bad at all. It's different to bad."

"Different?"

"*Ja*. My father is an honorable man. One of the most brave and intelligent I know."

"That's good, isn't it?"

Erich didn't answer, refusing to be drawn any further.

"I think perhaps we should be getting back to the hospital. The doctor will be wondering what has happened to us."

Erich started to turn, but Alice stopped him, increasing

her grip on his arm. "You really don't like to talk about him, do you?"

"I do not mean to be impolite, it is just that …"

"Don't worry," she interrupted, "you don't have to tell me anything."

Suddenly angry, she pulled her hand back and strode away, ahead of him.

"Alice …" It was the first time he had spoken her name, and he paused, tasting it, liking the way it came off his tongue. The girl turned.

"Yes?"

"I …" His English deserted him. She waited briefly for him to find the words and then as the rain started and the first drops splattered into the mud around them she turned again.

"Come on, Erich. Let's get back to Grandfather."

"Alice, Erich. You were gone a little longer than I'd expected. It's almost time for us to go, but before we do, Erich, would you mind changing the dressings on Günter's leg for me?"

"Of course, Doctor."

Erich crossed to the bed and applied himself to the task silently and efficiently, his mind wandering.

"What have you said to the lady, Youngster?" Günter's heavy German broke into Erich's thoughts.

"Excuse me?" he replied, also in German.

"The young lady, if I am not mistaken, is rather upset about something."

"You are mistaken."

"I do not think so." Günter smiled and touched the side of

113

his nose. "I am very good at spotting such things, you will find."

At the far end of the hospital, Alice was seemingly engrossed in a novel.

"I do not know what you are talking about."

"She is not reading that book."

"How would you know?"

"From the way she is glaring at it. And by the fact that every time you look away she glares at you. Have you been upsetting the locals?"

"Not at all. Now hold still." Erich tugged at the loose end of the bandage, tightening it perhaps a little more than was strictly necessary. Günter didn't even flinch.

"You should not take your bad temper out on a poor crippled soldier, young one."

"And you should mind your own business, or I will organise to take the other leg off also."

Günter grinned. "At least then I will be a little more balanced. There was a visitor while you were on your walk."

"Who?"

"A friend of yours. That guard." Günter avoided saying the name, and Erich realised he was hiding the conversation from the two Australians.

"What did he want? Trying to make more trouble for me?"

"My English is not so good, as you know." Günter winked. Over the last couple of weeks it had become apparent to Erich that Günter understood a great deal more than he let on. "But it seemed to me that he was not interested in you at all until he found out that you were out walking with your little friend over there."

"She is not my friend."

"The guard seems to think she is."

"What did he want with her?"

"Who can tell?" Günter gestured with open palms. "The good doctor told him that the two of you were out for a few minutes, and then sent him to take paperwork over to the camp commandant's office. He was not too happy about that."

"What did he do?"

"Tried to get out of it. He suggested that the job was below him, but, as you know, the doctor can be very persuasive."

"Nearly finished, Erich?" Doctor Alexander had locked the heavy cupboard at the end of the room that contained all the medicine and surgical implements. He shrugged on his coat and crossed to the bed. The old man bent to examine the freshly swathed stump. "A fine job, as usual. Alice and I will be off now. Will you be all right to finish cleaning up?"

Erich answered with a nod.

"Fine, then. We'll see you in the morning. Goodnight, Günter."

"*Auf wiedêrshien, Herr Doctor.*"

Alice passed Erich without saying a word, or even so much as a sideways glance, and as the door swung closed behind her Günter gave a low whistle.

"You really have upset that girl, Youngster. What did she do to you?"

"Nothing. She was just prying."

"Prying?"

"Into things that are none of her business."

Günter shook his head. "Youngster, where women are concerned, everything is their business. How about a cigarette?"

Erich went to a small sideboard near the stove, reached under it and extracted a crumpled packet from a small ledge hidden beneath. Removing a single cigarette, he handed it to Günter, who wrinkled his nose in distaste.

"These pre-rolled ones are terrible. Are you sure you can't get me my tobacco?"

"No. Doctor's orders."

Günter smiled.

"The old man is right, you know. You would make a very good physician. You have the demeanour for it." The lit cigarette glowed in the dimness, and Erich set about sweeping the floor.

"I have other plans."

"So I understand. You intend to follow your father up through the *Wehrmacht*, no?"

Erich froze. The words hung in the air.

"What did you say?"

"You heard me clearly enough, didn't you? You military types are all the same. How high up is your father? A general?"

"I don't know what you are talking about."

"Don't fool yourself, Youngster. You carry your family with you everywhere. It's in the way you speak and walk, and Stutt is no idiot. He and every German in this camp knows who you really are, and you can bet that most of the Australians probably do too."

Erich crossed to where Günter was lying back, one hand behind his head, exhaling thick smoke into the gloom. His eyes narrowed.

"I think you need to be careful what rumours you spread

116

about people, Günter. Some around here might think they are true."

"And I think it is time you were a little more honest with yourself, Youngster. Everyone here knows that the Nazis are losing their power, and they'll drag the army with them, even the careerists, the old military families like yours. Germany is suffering, Erich, and people like your father don't have a lot of time left."

"What would you know, cripple? My father is a patriot, a true German." Erich's voice was low, anger underlying his words.

"Probably. A lot of good soldiers are. But when the British win do you think that will make any difference?"

"The British will be defeated in the end. Germany is winning the war."

"That is the official Nazi party line, true, but have you had any letters from home recently?"

Erich stared. "You know I haven't."

Günter nodded. "*Ja*. Well, some of the men have and the Australians like to talk also, and let me tell you, Youngster, the war is going far from well for our *Fuhrer*. It is only a matter of time until he and all who support him, and probably many who don't, fall by the wayside, and then we can all go home again."

There was no anger in Günter's voice, only an indefinable sadness that set Erich on edge.

"What are you saying?"

The old soldier took another long draw on the cigarette and shook his head, exhaling slowly.

"Nothing, Youngster. I am just rambling."

"No." Erich pressed him. "You are trying to tell me something. What is it?"

Günter looked him directly in the eyes and the contact – not physical but emotional – was frightening.

"Many things will be very different for a lot of us when we return home, Erich, but also for you." He hesitated. "Especially for you. You would be wise, I think, to prepare yourself."

"For what?"

"Your father will be dead, for one thing. There is a good chance that he already is, I imagine."

"How can you know that from all the way out here in this ugly forest?"

"Common sense. The tide of the war has turned and we here, you and I, we are the lucky ones. It is only a matter of time until this whole sorry episode is consigned to history for us. But for men like your father, Erich, there can be little hope. Think about it. Hitler is going mad, that's what all the letters say. Launching insane campaigns, regardless of the cost in lives, and that's only going to get worse as the war progresses. And even if your father does, somehow, manage to survive the collapse, how long do you think it will be before the allies start to look for scapegoats? Someone to blame for the war? Career men, like your father, officers, will be the first targets. Can't you see that?"

Erich, his sweeping abandoned, sat heavily in the chair beside the bed, the throbbing of rain on tin the only counterpoint to his breathing.

"Erich?" Günter's voice was gentle.

From somewhere deep within him a wave of pure, raw emotion started to grow, and sensing it, aware of its potential to tear him apart and destroy everything he had been so careful to build here – the safety, the security of superiority – Erich rallied himself against it, squashing it. He forced the wave down and down again until it settled once more, a dull ache in the pit of his stomach and the back of his mind. Finally, he stood on shaking legs to tower above the man in the bed.

"I think you are wrong."

For a long moment the two regarded one another through the haze of tobacco smoke, until Günter shook his head, resignedly.

"Perhaps I am, Youngster, perhaps I am. In any case, how about one more cigarette? To help me sleep."

Crossing in silence to the sideboard, Erich bent to retrieve the hidden cigarettes and was holding them, getting to his feet again, when the door slammed open.

"Well, well." Guard Thomas removed his slouch hat, flicking droplets of moisture onto the bare floorboards. "Look what we have here."

"Be careful, youngster."

Erich barely heard Günter's whispered warning. His eyes were locked on the figure standing in the doorway framed against the darkening sky outside. Thomas's rifle hung sloppily from its strap, slung under his right shoulder. Runnels of water streamed off his greatcoat, forming dark pools. His flaming red hair was heavy with moisture and his face twisted in a crooked half-smile.

"Speak English, or don't speak at all," he snapped at Günter, not once taking his eyes off Erich.

"Can I help you?"

Thomas didn't answer, but started to prowl around the

119

room, touching this and that, running his fingers lightly over the surfaces of the desks and beds.

"What are you doing in here on your own?"

"I am finishing the cleaning up for the evening." Erich gestured at the broom, abandoned by Günter's bed. "Then I will be leaving."

"Is that right?" The guard's eyes glittered.

"Yes."

"Yes what?"

Erich knew that the guard expected him to say 'sir', and knew that the safest course would be not to antagonise the young man, but pride wouldn't allow him.

"Yes, it is right. You are correct."

"Be clever, Erich." Günter whispered again in German.

"I said, speak *English*." By this point Thomas was beside the bed, and he made as if to hit Günter's bandaged stump. Günter jumped in involuntary readiness for an impact that never came, the guard's hand stopping to hover just milli-metres above the wounded leg. Thomas laughed.

"Don't worry. I'm not about to touch *that*." He spat the word. "Who knows what sort of diseases I'd pick up from you *krauts*, eh?"

He was being provoked. Erich deliberately calmed him-self.

"Do you need something?"

"I told you." Thomas's gaze returned to meet his. "I want to know what you're really doing here on your own, talking German to him at this time of night. It looks suspicious to me. What's in here?" He had reached the locked cupboard behind the desk.

"That is the medication cabinet. Also where the doctor keeps the surgical implements."

"Locked, eh?" Thomas jiggled the sturdy lock and tested the door. "Makes sense, I guess. No trusting you lot, is there?"

"I should be leaving now." Erich stepped towards the door.

"Don't move." In a fluid motion the rifle swung into firing position, aimed directly at Erich's stomach. "You still haven't given me a decent explanation for what you're doing in here without the doctor. Giving contraband to the patients, by the look of it."

He nodded at the cigarettes which Erich still clasped, forgotten, in his right hand.

"It is not contraband. It is cigarettes."

"Yeah? I thought the old bloke didn't allow smoking in here? So you must be goin' behind his back."

"I do not understand."

"Don't play stupid. I know what's goin' on. You keep the cripple here supplied with ciggies, but what do you get in return, eh? That's what I'd like to know."

"I am sorry, but you are not making sense."

The guard's eyes became thin, dark slits.

"Not making sense, aren't I?" He took a step towards Erich, the muzzle of his rifle glinting metallic around the black opening of the barrel. "I've told you before to be careful how you speak to me."

"I am sorry. I meant no offence."

The apology floated as Guard Thomas continued across the room until the rifle hovered just millimetres from Erich's body. Erich stared, mesmorised by the circle of darkness hovering in front of him. He considered the consequences if Thomas's finger twitched against the trigger. The safety catch was off – he had noticed that immediately. Erich imagined the sensation, the bullet snaking its way into his body, shredding and destroying organs, tearing flesh, scorching its way through him.

"Listen to me carefully, Fritz." The boy's voice was little more than a guttural hiss, barely audible. "If I find out that you've been sniffing around my girl, if I see the two of you wandering around together again, or if I hear another word out of your mouth apart from 'here' at rollcall, then there's going to be a little 'accident' around here. You understand?"

For several seconds they held one another's stares until the guard leaned closer, pressing the end of the barrel hard into Erich's stomach.

"And just in case you're thinking of reporting this little conversation, have a think about who's going to be believed, eh? 'Cause I reckon you're a bit of a troublemaker, you Nazi."

Some insane impulse, the need to make some kind of stand, welled up inside Erich. He remembered standing up to the bastard English in Libya. Acutely aware of the cold, round circle of steel pressing into the flesh of his belly, Erich spoke softly and calmly, keeping his voice steady: "You are not a very good soldier, no?"

"What?"

"If you pull that trigger now, I will die, yes, but probably you will also blow your hand off. You do not hold a rifle hard against the target. Any good soldier knows that."

Somewhere in the forest a bird screeched raucously into the night, the sound unearthly as it slid into the gloom of the hospital, and Erich held his breath, listening to the racing

122

thud of his heartbeat – feeling it at his temples. Then slowly the barrel withdrew and Thomas stepped back, not dropping his eyes for a moment.

"You watch yourself, mate. You just watch out."

But he'd backed down, and both of them knew it.

"You better keep an eye on your back."

The young man stopped briefly to replace his hat and then the door slammed behind him as he vanished, his exit admitting a burst of icy wind.

"You have made an enemy there, Youngster." Günter was propping himself on one elbow.

"He was already my enemy." Erich slumped into the chair beside the bed.

"Nonetheless, I think you need to let Commander Stutt know about this immediately."

"No need. It is in the past."

"He needs to know. For your safety."

"The boy is all talk. You saw him back away."

"Only because he had no choice."

"Still, I would rather not make a scene about this."

Günter shook his head. "You are making a mistake."

"We'll see."

For some minutes the two remained silent, each alone with his thoughts, until Erich stood up.

"I should go. It's almost time for rollcall. Will you be all right for the evening?"

"*Ja*. But think about talking to the commander."

"I'll consider it."

Erich slipped quickly out into the rain.

Thirteen

October 1943

The desert night was almost over, the velvety darkness thinning to pink. At his post, Erich glanced up, watching the foreign stars beginning to twinkle into obscurity.

"It is cold, yes?"

"Yes." His companion was talkative. A private named Janz. Twenty-two or three years old but still wet behind the ears, as far as Erich was concerned.

"You think they will come today?"

Erich shrugged a noncommittal reply. Who knew? Perhaps today, perhaps tomorrow. Sometime soon, that was certain.

"They say there are reinforcements on their way from the north." His companion reached for a cigarette.

"Put that away, idiot! Do you want to bring the whole British army down on us?"

"Sorry." Janz's fingers, numb with cold, fumbled the cigarettes back into his shirt pocket and the silence of the desert settled again.

Erich stared into the growing dawn, watching the light

slowly ooze along the landscape and across the rolling dunes towards them as the invisible sun climbed towards the horizon.

"At least it will warm up soon, yes?"

"Yes. And then we will burn all day."

It was the worst thing about this cursed desert – when it wasn't freezing, it was boiling. During the day the sun would blaze down on the little encampment, scorching pale Germanic skin into angry red welts easily inflamed by the sand which seeped its way into every crack and cranny of the body. It was bad enough that they were there, worse because none of them had any idea why.

"We will be moving soon, do you think?"

"Who knows." Erich hoped so. Their encampment was weak, nestled on low ground between dunes for protection from air attack, but to his eye clearly vulnerable. That was no surprise, though, given their commanding officer's incompetence.

"Do you think …"

"Shh." Erich waved the man to silence. "Did you hear something?"

Janz wrinkled his brow in concentration, listening to the desert for long seconds before shaking his head.

But Erich, alert now, was peering intently at the crest of the nearest dune. It had just been a whisper, the faintest hint of a human voice echoing on the slight breeze. He glanced behind at the tents a few metres from their watch post. Their sand-coloured camouflage nets fluttered slightly, but otherwise no sound emanated from them, the men all still in deep, exhausted sleep.

There it was again. A muted whisper, right at the limits of

his hearing. He reached for his rifle and gestured his companion close.

"Go and wake the captain. Quietly."

Nodding, Janz slung his rifle under his arm and set off, running low and silent towards the nearest tent. In the gloom beyond the encampment Erich could make out the barrels of the two mobile artillery cannons they carried with them, glinting dully in the growing light.

The desert fell silent again. Hunkered low in his post, Erich again scanned the crests of the dunes surrounding the camp. As soon as the sun broke the horizon he'd feel a lot happier. This pre-dawn light played tricks on the eyes – shadows slinked around the edges of the tents and between undulations in the sand, drawing his eyes left and right. Where the hell was Janz? The seconds ticked away with agonising, silent sluggishness.

Behind, light footsteps slid towards him and Janz was there again.

"He'll be right along."

"What's keeping him?"

"He's just getting dressed."

Erich cursed inwardly. What sort of commander didn't sleep battle-ready?

Above them the sky took on the first hints of indigo. Apart from the whisper of the wind across the sand, Erich hadn't heard another sound.

"There he is."

Their captain was slipping from behind the flap of his tent to stand outside. He was helmetless.

"Fool."

For a couple of seconds the man stood still and erect and

then, yawning, stretched his arms out. At that moment the sun burst into full light, sliding with unexpected rapidity above the crest of the dune right ahead of them.

Erich blinked and felt his skin tingle, welcoming the warmth. Their captain started towards them, still yawning, but made only two steps when a shot rang out and his chest exploded into bloody fragments.

"Captain!" Janz was on his feet and running.

"Janz! Get ..."

The guard's head snapped back and he too fell, face first.

Erich turned his attention back to the dune ahead of him, but the glare of the sun, still low to the horizon, blinded and dazzled him, forcing him to crouch below the parapet of the guard post, aware only of bullets hissing down out of the sunrise and thumping into the other side of the sandbags. One penetrated with a 'whump' and buried itself in the sand beside him.

Men were emerging from tents now, yelling and firing wildly into the dunes, hitting nothing. Then came the staccato chatter of a machine-gun and they too began to fall, clutching at limbs, stomachs and chests. The artillery cannons exploded, first one, then the other, shattering into fiery fragments, hot metal tearing through the fabric of nearby tents, adding new screams to the noise of the battle.

Crouched low, Erich waited for his opportunity, checking the breech of his rifle, making certain it had a bullet in it, slipping off the safety catch. Patience. The worst thing he could do now would be to put his head up and start firing wildly into that dazzling sun. Wait.

Footsteps thudded heavily down the dune behind him, accompanied by shouted orders. British. English. He tensed, finger at the trigger, prepared. Heart pounding ready to burst. In a moment the British soldiers would come past his parapet, down into the camp, into his line of fire, and then he would kill them. The wooden stock pressed against his cheek, and he had to push it harder to stop his hands trembling. A rush of blood ran salty down the back of his throat, and he realised that he'd bitten the inside of his mouth. Breathing in gasps, Erich tried to summon the willpower to steady his index finger against the trigger. Why wouldn't it stop shaking?

Then, with a yell, a figure vaulted over the parapet, almost landing on him and knocking his rifle from his trembling grasp. The infantryman spun, rifle levelled, and in the moment of eye contact, of connection, Erich realised with shock that he knew the man, knew him well. He found himself staring into cold, blue eyes as familiar as his own, and reaching towards the soldier, calling to him: "Father!"

But there was no return of the recognition. Only hard distaste in those blue eyes, and when he thought he was about to drown in them, his father's rifle butt swung up towards Erich's head ...

Sweating, gasping, Erich sat upright, his cot creaking under him. Outside, the forest slept in the pre-dawn fog. Reaching out in the darkness he found his clothes and, trembling, pulled them on silently before stumbling outside.

One of the other men stirred but no one woke and Erich sat heavily on the top step, shaking. So real. He'd not thought about the battle in North Africa in all the time since he'd been captured and now here it was, haunting him in his sleep. He breathed the sharp air deep into himself, trying

128

to throw off the effects of the dream. And that last vision, his father as an enemy, clubbing and attacking him. The thought disturbed him far more than he dared to admit.

Behind the huts, a spotlight snapped on from one of the guard towers, raking along the tree line, the powerful lantern struggling to throw a beam through the fog. Erich could see droplets drifting nonchalantly through the white light. A couple of grey kangaroos looked up as the beam captured them, their startled eyes glinting red before they bounded away into the dark safety of the forest. A man emerged from one of the huts a little further down the row and stumbled off in the direction of the latrines.

Slowly, he felt the icy touch of the dream lifting and his heart steadying. As the man returned from his early morning ablution, Erich settled himself back into the reality of the Western Australian forest, forcing the sands of Libya down into the depths of his memory, until he felt some sort of calm again.

But it wasn't real calm; there was no contentment. There hadn't been since the moment he'd arrived here at Camp Sixteen, or even before that. Now he thought about it, Erich found it difficult – no, impossible – to remember life without the cold weight of fear, suppressed and controlled but ever present, guarding every thought. The only time it had lifted, even a little, had been the previous afternoon, walking with the girl. Allowing himself back into his life, to remember things deliberately left unacknowledged ...

Standing, Erich crept around into the shadows behind the raised hut and relieved himself on the ground. It was forbidden not to use the latrines, but all the men did it at one time or another. Sometimes it was just too cold or wet to make the walk down the hill, and anyway there was a strange feeling of liberation about it. Once finished, he climbed the steps, collapsed fully clothed onto his cot and fell immediately into a heavy, dreamless sleep.

Fourteen

October 1943

"Pieters, a word, please!"

Stutt stood expectantly, waiting, as the rest of the men, dismissed for the morning, wandered idly off to sleep the day away or play cards in the mess.

It was Sunday, a day for recreation and no work parties. Later some of the men would be allowed to walk under guard into Marinup, the nearby logging town, to play football on the town oval or just to watch the passers-by. It also meant that, unless something urgent happened in the hospital, Erich too had the day off.

"Yes, sir?"

"Walk with me."

To Erich's surprise, Stutt proceeded not towards the mess as he usually would, but in the other direction, towards the gates.

"I visited Günter in the infirmary this morning."

So that was it.

"Yes, sir."

"He filled me in on the details of your little incident with Thomas last night."

Meddling fool.

"Why was I not informed about this immediately, Pieters?"

"I did not think the incident sufficiently important to bother you with, sir."

"No? What did Günter think?"

Stutt clearly knew the answer already.

"He was of the opinion that I should let you know, sir."

"And you decided otherwise?"

"Yes, sir."

"Can I ask your reasoning, Erich?"

"Excuse me, sir?"

"Your reasoning. A guard threatens an unarmed prisoner going about the course of his allocated duties, with a loaded weapon – safety off, I'm told – and you don't think that the incident is serious enough to warrant a report to your commanding officer? Did you read the regulations handbook I gave you on arrival, Erich? Are you familiar with the Red Cross guidelines?"

Erich could never have imagined Stutt this angry. He didn't seem the type.

They reached the double gates to the compound and Erich followed Stutt through the first one, across no-man's-land, and over to the external gate, where a guard stood waiting.

"Well?" Stutt looked expectantly while the guard fiddled with the lock.

"I do not wish to antagonise the man further, sir, as you advised me after parade the other night."

"So you think he'll just go away, is that it, Pieters?"

Erich didn't answer, uncertain what to say.

"Listen carefully to me, Pieters. These camps have rules and procedures that everyone – guards and prisoners alike – are expected to follow, for good reasons. You're the one who is always so pious about still fighting a war, so you'd be well advised to think about the rules of warfare. If you're prepared to allow this guard to make life difficult for you, then that's your funeral, but as the ranking German officer in this compound I am *not* going to allow this, this *child,* to think that he has the right to bully German prisoners of war. Do you understand me?"

"Yes, sir."

Erich retreated into sullen silence. Accompanied by a guard they started towards the camp commandant's office. As they passed by the small German detention compound, Stutt nodded at it.

"By rights, Erich, I should have you thrown in there for a week or so, as much for your own safety as for ignoring my rules, but I won't, for one reason only and that's that the doctor and Günter can't manage without you at the moment. But you can rest assured that if there is one more incident of this type then I won't have the slightest hesitation in putting you in there."

Erich considered the small compound. This was the first time he'd been close enough to see it, though there wasn't much to look at. It was a small yard and building, contained within a solid fence topped by razor wire. Stutt noticed him studying it.

"The fences are concrete, so you can't see anything outside. The cells are either too cold or too hot, depending on the season, and the roof leaks during the winter. You can trust me, Erich, it is not a pleasant place to spend time."

Nothing more was said until they reached the commandant's building, which stood in a grove of gum trees on the other side of the guards' and officer's hut lines. Somewhere in the bush beyond, Erich could hear the faint hum of generators. Stutt stopped at the bottom of the two steps that led up to the front door.

"I will do the talking in here. You do not speak unless spoken to, and answer questions asked of you as fully and formally as required. You will also stand to attention when speaking. Do you understand?"

"Yes, sir."

"Good. Come on."

The guard waited outside, lighting a cigarette and rubbing his hands against the cold, while Erich followed the officer through the door.

It was quiet inside. Stutt led him through a small, unattended reception area to an open door off to one side, and knocked quietly.

"Enter."

The camp commandant sat at his desk, which was covered by small, neat piles of paperwork. Erich hadn't seen him closely before and was surprised at the man's age. He was younger than the doctor, but clearly older than Stutt, probably nearing retirement. His uniform was neatly pressed and ironed, and he carried himself with a military bearing that reminded Erich uncomfortably of his own father. Like the doctor, the commandant wore a groomed and waxed moustache on his top lip. He looked up from his paperwork as the two men entered.

"Heinrich, come in."

"Good morning, sir. I am sorry to disturb you on a Sunday."

"Not at all. I was just wading through paperwork. A distraction will be welcomed."

"It is not a pleasant one, I am afraid."

"That's unfortunate. Please take a seat." He gestured at the one wooden seat in front of the desk and Stutt made himself comfortable while Erich remained at attention slightly behind him. "What seems to be the problem?"

"This is Private Erich Pieters, Doctor Alexander's orderly ..."

Stutt proceeded to outline the story of Erich's two run-ins with the guard, at rollcall and in the hospital. He made no mention of the doctor's granddaughter though, which was strange. Perhaps Günter had not told him the story in its entirety. When Stutt had finished, the commander turned and considered Erich, seemingly for the first time.

"Do you speak English, son?"

"Yes, sir."

"Is all this true?"

"Yes, sir."

"You don't have anything to add?"

"No, sir."

"One thing puzzles me, Commander." He turned his attention back to Stutt. "Why exactly has Thomas taken such a dislike to your young soldier here? Do you have any explanation?" The question, though asked of Stutt, was directed at Erich.

For a second Erich considered telling him about the girl, but if Stutt had deliberately failed to mention it, he must have had his reasons. Beside, if her name came up, then the easiest solution would be for the commandant to prevent her assisting in the hospital, and that wasn't what Erich wanted either.

"I really do not know, sir. Perhaps I have inadvertently offended him at some point. He would be able to inform you, I am sure."

"Perhaps. I shall certainly speak to him. If it is true, then this is a very serious allegation indeed, Commander, and you can rest assured that I will do something about it."

With a brief nod, Stutt stood and walked towards the door, gesturing Erich to follow. Not another word was spoken until the two were back inside the German compound.

"You didn't mention the girl, Erich, why?"

"Neither did you, sir. I was simply following your example."

"And I was leaving you the opportunity to tell the commandant everything relevant to this case."

Erich shrugged. "In any case, this is really nothing to do with her, sir. The doctor enjoys having his grand-daughter's company, and I would not like to be the one to deprive him of it."

"Commendable. But you will need to be very careful around her, because, as I told you, further incidents of this nature will reflect badly upon you and quite possibly on her as well."

"I understand, sir."

"Good. You are dismissed."

Stutt turned and headed towards the mess. Erich watched him go, angry at the lot of them. Stutt, for interfering in events that were clearly none of his business, Günter, Alice, Thomas. All of them were making it difficult for Erich to concentrate on the important business of fighting the war, any way he could, of remaining a German soldier.

A group of men was assembling near the gates and one of them, seeing Erich standing alone, called, "Youngster! Coming into town?"

"*Nein!*" Erich waved a polite thank you. "You have fun without me."

"*Ja*. We will."

Erich turned away and, after a moment's hesitation, walked towards the hospital.

"Good morning, Youngster, what brings you to work on a Sunday?"

Günter, his leg still swathed, was sitting in the sun on the front steps of the hospital. Erich wondered for a moment how he'd managed to get himself out there, but concentrated on the more important business at hand.

"Why did you tell him?"

"Him?" Günter feigned ignorance.

"Stutt. I told you I'd see him myself if I thought it necessary."

"I know you did. But as a prisoner and a patient I have every right not to be threatened by a guard while lying injured in hospital."

"He was threatening me, *dumkopf*."

"And in doing so, every one of us. Listen to me, Erich; these men in here, they have enough to worry about having to go out into the forest every day; cuts, injuries, falling trees" – Erich's eyes flicked involuntarily to Günter's stumpy leg – "and they miss their families, and they're cold and wet, and in short the last thing that we need in here is some young guard on a vendetta against the Germans."

"He's only interested in me."

"Don't be naive! Do you think for a moment that this is really about the girl? Come along, Youngster, you claim to be perceptive. What do you think is the real reason you've become his number one victim?"

Erich considered for a moment. He didn't get an opportunity to respond. Günter answered his own question.

"I told you last night. It's your family history. This is a young man who never got the opportunity to prove himself against any real Nazis, and between you and me, it's made him the butt of almost every joke in the guardroom. He's angry and shamed, and now here you are, young, arrogant and German, the ideal target. The rest of us are all too tired to fight any more, but not you – and that makes him angry."

"You talk rubbish."

"Not at all. Stutt told you on your first morning, I imagine, that you'd passed a screening process to get posted to Australia. If they really considered you to be a dangerous Nazi threat, then you'd be elsewhere. I guarantee it. No, this boy hates you because of what you represent, more than for any other reason."

"So you are saying that I should ignore my pride in my country and my family?"

Erich waited for him to respond but Günter had fallen silent. At length he leaned back, turned his face to the sky and sighed.

"It is good to be out again, after all these weeks. Good to feel the sun on tired old bones."

"How old are you?"

Günter turned away from the sun and stared at him. "Why do you wish to know?"

"Just curious."

The older soldier looked away, back into the sunlight, closing his eyes as he answered. "I am twenty-eight."

Erich had no reply and after a few moments settled on the step alongside Günter where they sat in silence until Günter spoke again.

"Youngster?"

"*Ja?*"

"Do me a favour and get my tobacco for me. It is back in my hut, in a pouch beneath my cot."

Erich looked again at the man beside him. Twenty-eight. And somehow he had always seemed so old, even before his accident.

"I will be right back."

Jogging lightly across the parade ground Erich thought about what Günter had been telling him. The tobacco pouch was where it was supposed to be and on the way back Erich stopped in at the mess where a group of sailors was engaged in a card game.

"Youngster! Want to play a hand?"

"No. Just getting some fruit."

There were apples in a bucket near the kitchen and Erich grabbed a couple, one each for Günter and himself, before heading back towards the hospital. Coming around the far end of the mess he looked down to where Günter was still sitting on the steps. He wasn't alone any longer, though. Thomas was also there, at the base of the steps, standing with his back to Erich and his rifle slung under his arm, sloppily as usual. Erich slowed to a halt, staying as quiet as possible. Fragments of the conversation floated to him.

"... need to be certain you don't decide to make trouble for me," Thomas was saying.

Günter shrugged a gesture of not understanding. The guard continued, regardless.

"And you reckon you haven't seen him, eh? Well, I might take a look inside, just to be sure."

He shoved past Günter and up the steps, deliberately bumping the stump of Günter's leg as he did so. Even from a distance Erich could see the man tense with pain. Thomas vanished into the hospital and Günter spotted Erich. He gestured Erich to disappear and, not needing a second warning, Erich ran back around the side of the mess hall.

After twenty minutes waiting, trying to ignore the increasingly boisterous catcalls from the card game, Erich cautiously checked outside and, finding the yard clear, bolted back across to the hospital. Günter was still on the step.

"What was that about?"

"Nothing to worry about, I think, Youngster."

"Nothing to worry about?" The sudden change in Günter's attitude was unexpected.

"*Nein*. I don't think our little friend will bother us again for a while."

"Why not?"

"Because just after you vanished, while he was still inside the hospital poking around, the doctor came by to see how I was going."

"Ah. I wish I'd stayed to watch."

Günter grinned. "*Ja*. It was quite a performance."

140

"Where is he now?"

"The commandant's office, with the doctor. Somehow I don't imagine he'll receive a very warm welcome."

Erich joined him on the step and fished the tobacco pouch out from his pocket.

"Here, but you didn't get it from me."

"Of course not, Youngster." The crippled soldier set immediately about the process of rolling himself a slim cigarette.

From the mess hall, the shouts of the card game drifted across the clearing, and on the other side of the fence two guards patrolled lazily along the perimeter, on their way towards the Italian compound.

"Günter?"

"*Ja*?"

"What is waiting for you at home?"

The other man shrugged. "Who knows, Youngster. Life will be different for all of us, eh?"

"*Ja*."

A large black bird, red markings below its wings and throat, flitted high above the compound. Erich followed its progress over the huts and into the forest on the other side.

"Do you ever wish you could be like that bird?"

"In what way?"

"You know. Just take to the sky and fly out of here."

"And go where? Home is a long way from here, you know."

"*Ja*. But still, if I could fly ..."

Sitting in the sunlight, Erich thought about home and his mother and sister and for the first time in many weeks allowed himself to picture them clearly, to drift back to the

141

day, well over a year ago now, when he'd told them he'd joined up.

His mother hadn't responded, simply wept gentle, silent tears. Mathilde remained composed. She'd at least had some warning.

"Erich …" Her gaze caught him straight in the face. She shook her head slightly but held his eyes. "I told you not to."

"I know, but it is something I must do. This country needs soldiers."

And later, after their mother had left the room and he had taken her place at the table, his sister reached out and took his hand in hers.

"You will leave her with nothing, you know."

"What do you mean?"

"If you get killed in some foreign battle, what will she have left? Not even a grave to visit."

"You and Father will still be here."

"Father is never here."

This was true. Since the war had escalated, their father spent more and more time in Berlin. Often it would be months between visits, and with the state of the post, weeks between letters.

"I will not get killed. I promise."

Her grip tightened. "I will hold you to that promise. See that you don't."

Erich kissed her lightly on the forehead.

"I will look in on you in the morning, before I leave."

But the following morning he'd risen early, eager to get on with the rest of his life, and when he'd looked though the door of her room she was still asleep. Not wanting to wake her, he'd crept away.

142

From the treetops the bird called to its mates, a grating screech that seemed to shudder right to the core of Erich's thoughts, calling him back from home.

"Do you know, youngster, it is actually a beautiful place." Günter too had been following the bird's progress.

"What?"

"This country. Beautiful. Rough, it is true, and very different to what we are used to, you and I, but beautiful none the less."

"*Ja*. And full of poisonous animals and rotten weather."

"But look at those trees, Erich. How old must they be?"

Erich studied the brooding wall of timber beyond the wire but found himself unable to see it as anything other than alien. There was no beauty in those dark green hollows and tangles, only danger and fear. Günter was also studying the tree line, though with a far more gentle, reflective expression.

"I think a man could be happy in this country, Youngster, do you know that?"

"It is enemy territory, don't forget."

But even as the words came out, they sounded false. Hollow. He didn't really believe it any more. Günter seemed to be aware of the same thought.

"Only at the moment. In a little while it will be just another piece of this world that we live in. Like those trees – they have been watching over here since long before this war and will stand guard for many years yet. I think I would like to be a part of that."

"What about your wife?"

"We will see, Youngster, we will see."

After a couple more seconds Günter reached across and

took his shoulder, his grip firm for the first time in many weeks.

"And now, I am tired from all this thinking and excitement. How about assisting a cripple back to his sick bed?"

Fifteen

November 1943

The worst part about the camp, Erich discovered, wasn't the captivity, nor the people, but the boredom. Despite the doctor's best efforts to keep him engaged, there was only so much to do in a compound in the middle of the bush, and as the weather continued to improve and the days grew warmer and longer, so too the workload in the hospital grew lighter, and Erich found himself with more and more time on his hands.

"You know, Erich, I have a colleague at the university in Melbourne who teaches in the medical school there."

Doctor Alexander stepped from the cool darkness of the hospital and sat slowly on the verandah beside Erich, who had been idly drawing. He stopped his sketch and listened as the doctor continued, "I think I might write to him and ask him to send across new textbooks and perhaps some basic exam papers."

"Examinations, Doctor?"

"Nothing that would count for any official qualifications,

145

of course, but it would give you something to focus on and would certainly assist your work for me."

Erich considered. He'd finished working through all of the medical books the doctor had available to him in the small hospital, and his medical skills, which had been developing so rapidly before, seemed to have reached a plateau. Besides, it would be something to do.

"If you think it would be a good idea, sir, then I am happy to try."

"I do, Erich. I'll try to get some more advanced anatomy and surgical procedural lessons."

"That would be good."

"And how is Günter going? I haven't seen him this week."

A couple of the men had fashioned crutches from forest timber and, mobile again, Günter had bounded out of the hospital and back into the thick of camp life. His new assignment in the camp kitchen had captured his imagination and during the days he was to be found ordering the gardeners around or propped against one of the rough wooden benches chopping vegetables. Erich suspected that the doctor missed his company.

"Fine, Doctor. He tells me there is no longer any pain at all."

"When you see him next, remind him to come and let me examine the healing, will you?"

"*Ja*, I will."

"Have you had any problems with Thomas lately?"

"No, sir."

Not problems as such. Since being disciplined over the incident in the hospital, both Erich and Thomas had been at pains to avoid a direct confrontation. This didn't mean that

146

there was no longer enmity. Thomas still had the task of checking the roll each morning and evening, and he would spit Erich's name with a degree of venom absent from the others on the list. It was also clear from the way Thomas watched him, closely with narrowed eyes, that the bad feeling between the two was far from forgotten.

"That's good news. He was punished quite severely, you know?"

"I had gathered. What happened?"

"His pay was docked and his weekend privileges cancelled for three months."

Erich smiled. Günter had also heard from one of the Australian guards that Thomas was now so much of a joke in the guard's mess that the boy almost never appeared there except for meal times. This was a mixed blessing, though. While Thomas was now too nervous of the repercussions to pursue his animosity, he was an almost constant presence around the camp. Erich often felt a strange sensation, and a glance around the perimeter would reveal Thomas in one of the towers or on foot patrol outside the wire, watching. Always watching. And waiting, Erich suspected.

"I don't imagine he'll give you any more trouble." The doctor changed the subject. "The war is not going too well for your country, I understand."

A shrug was all the reply Erich could muster. In truth, despite his best efforts, nowdays he was finding it increasingly difficult to maintain his interest in such far-off matters.

"Some are saying that it will all be over before Christmas."

"Do you believe them?"

"It is possible, Erich, certainly possible. Have you heard from your family at all?"

The question, asked casually, was nonetheless a deliberate probe. It was a subject Erich still studiously avoided and the doctor was well aware of the fact.

"No. The mail is not working well. I think that things at home must be very confused at the moment." Just last week Herman in Hut Twenty-six had received a letter from his sweetheart, dated over a year earlier.

"Well, I'm sure that things will be fine. They usually manage to get bad news through, so it is probably good that you don't hear anything."

The doctor stood up.

"As there doesn't appear to be anything for me to do here, I might wander back to my hut for a little rest, Erich. If anything comes up, will you please have the guards summon me?"

"Certainly, Doctor."

"Good. I'll pop back across later in the afternoon, just to check in before you go off duty."

Erich watched him as he picked his way across the compound towards the gate. The last six months and the cold, wet winter had taken their toll on the old man and even in the short time that Erich had known him he'd become more frail. He needed his afternoon rests now.

Bored, Erich wandered back inside hoping to find something, anything, that needed doing. As soon as he walked through the door, he had the feeling that something was wrong, out of place. He couldn't work out exactly what and for a few minutes he wandered the room, checking that everything was where it belonged.

Then he noticed it. At the far end, behind the doctor's

desk, the supply cupboard, full of drugs and equipment, was unlocked. The doctor had forgotten to secure it.

In all his months in the hospital, not once had the cupboard been open and unattended. It was far too dangerous. When there were patients in the beds, the doctor would be careful even to the point of positioning himself to shield the contents of the cupboard from their eyes when he opened it.

"If they don't know what's in there, Erich," he would say, "they won't be tempted to explore it further."

And Erich agreed. The routine of camp life made items like morphine and rubbing alcohol attractive forms of recreation.

But now the cupboard was unlocked and there was nobody around. Crossing to the hospital door, Erich checked outside. The camp was all but deserted. Most of the men were in the forest and would be for hours. Erich quickly snapped the lock on the door to keep others out.

He'd been in the cupboard many times, but always under the watchful eye of the doctor, getting only what he'd been asked for. Now, swinging the heavy wooden door fully open, Erich's heart pounded. He knew what he was looking for.

The scalpels were in a tin box on the top shelf, and with trembling hands Erich eased the box down, placing it on the doctor's desk. Camp regulations meant that all sharpened or cutting implements needed to be accounted for daily and kept locked away when not in use. Everything, from the cutlery in the mess to the axes used in the forest, was strictly inventoried and tracked. Snap inspections and counts of equipment would take place, and if anything went missing, thorough searches followed immediately. The Australian guards, though relaxed, took no chances with the possibility of the prisoners arming themselves.

But here, in padded slots in the tin, were six pearl-handled surgical knives. Their blades, wrapped in little cardboard sleeves, nestled in a separate compartment. In all the months he'd been here, the only time that the scalpels had been used was during Günter's leg operation. Other than that, there'd been no call for them.

Lifting one of the slim-handled implements from its slot and clipping a blade into place Erich hefted it lightly, appreciating its balance. The knife was weighted perfectly for delicate cutting and slicing. In the pale hospital light, the mother of pearl handle took on a lustre that gave it a slightly iridescent appearance and made it seem to glow from within. Without stopping to think, Erich slid the protective cardboard sleeve back over the blade and slipped the whole thing into the inside pocket of his uniform jacket.

Closing the tin, a beam of light angling in from one of the dusty windows caught the lid, and in its gleam Erich noticed some fine engraving etched into the metal. He had to strain his eyes to read it: *To my darling husband on the occasion of his graduation. With fondest love, Emmaline.*

He stopped, guilty, realising with a sudden, sickening jolt the enormity of what he was doing. This wasn't simply theft, certainly not war. Taking that scalpel would mean much more; it would mean a betrayal of trust, of friendship. An act without honour.

The excitement that had so briefly clouded his judgment lifted and, feeling shamed, Erich was reaching back into his pocket to remove and replace the scalpel when the door behind him was kicked open with enough force to shatter the lock.

Sixteen

November 1943

"Stand right where you are, Fritz. Don't move a muscle."

Turning slowly, Erich stared once again along the barrel of Guard Thomas's rifle.

"You didn't think this was over, now, did you?"

The only thing Erich could think of doing was staying mute. In his inside pocket, the weight of the scalpel was heavy and accusing.

"You seem to make a habit of poking around in here on your own, eh? Step away from the desk, nice and slowly."

The rifle twitched and, obeying, Erich moved to the middle of the floor.

"I knew if I watched you for long enough you'd throw an opportunity like this my way." He was moving towards the desk himself now, all the while keeping the gun level.

"Now, let's see what you're up to." Holding the rifle with one hand, his finger still hovering at the trigger, he reached down with the other and flipped the tin open. From where Erich stood, the empty slot for the missing scalpel seemed dark and enormous.

"Right," said the guard, "where is it?"

"Where is what?"

Thomas's eyes narrowed. "I'm very glad you chose to say that, mate."

Thomas snapped the tin closed and slipped it into his pocket, then, levelling his rifle with both hands once more, he gestured in the direction of the door.

"Move."

At gunpoint, Erich was forced out and into the sunlight. At Thomas's direction he headed towards the parade ground. They were halfway there when Stutt, stunned at the sight of one of his men being so openly marched under threat, came bolting from the mess towards them. Close behind him, Günter hopped on his crutches. Seeing them, Thomas stopped.

"Wait!"

It took only seconds for Stutt to arrive.

"May I ask what is going on here?"

"Yes, *sir*." Thomas smirked and emphasised the "Sir". "I have just detained this prisoner for theft of contraband items."

"Don't be ridiculous."

"If you wouldn't mind, *sir*, I would request that you search the prisoner."

For a long moment the German officer and the Australian guard held eye contact. Thomas was grinning, clearly enjoying the moment. From the nearest gates, two of the senior guards, noticing the confrontation, were running towards the group. Stutt looked at Erich, his expression impossible to read. Both knew that he had no choice.

"Very well. Erich, would you empty your pockets, please."

153

Resignedly, Erich reached into his jacket and drew out the scalpel, handing it to his commanding officer.

"What is this?"

"A scalpel, sir."

"I can see that, Pieters. What are you doing with it in your possession?"

"I ..." There was no explanation he could give. Thomas pulled the tin from his pocket.

"It belongs in here, sir. I found the prisoner in the process of removing it from a locked cupboard in the hospital."

"Is this true, Pieters?"

"No, sir, I was about to return it."

"Ha!" Thomas snorted. "With respect, sir, I don't think this prisoner suitably trustworthy."

"The commandant'll decide that, Thomas." The guard captain on duty arrived and took charge. "Stand at ease!" he ordered Thomas, who reluctantly lowered his rifle.

"Heinrich, what do you think?"

Stutt shrugged. "It would seem that we have little choice but to take Pieters here across to the commandant's office for disciplinary action."

"Fair enough. Come on, son."

The older of the two guards took Erich's arm and led him towards the gate, Stutt and the other two guards following. As they exited the outer gate the captain turned to Thomas.

"That'll do for the moment, Thomas. Return to your duty and I'll send someone to get you if you're needed."

"But sir ..."

"Don't give me that!" he roared. "Get back to your bloody post and later on we'll discuss the reasons for you not being there in the first place."

Chagrined, but still smirking, Thomas slouched away along the perimeter wire, and Erich headed under escort towards the administration office.

Seventeen

November 1943

The detention cells were in their own enclosure, just a few metres from the German fence line. There were four in all, cubicles containing a wooden bunk and straw pallet, each with a tiny window high in the wall, offering only a barred glimpse of the sky beyond. The cells opened onto a narrow yard and shared a single lavatory and cold shower. Apart from Erich's all were empty.

If Erich had been bored by the daily routine of the camp, two weeks in the cell drove him to distraction. Time there passed with interminable sluggishness. Most days were spent sitting in the shade of the small building, staring at the narrow rectangle of sky visible above. Bland meals were delivered by the guards, and Erich spent the hours in frustrated contemplation.

There was nothing to see or do, so inevitably his mind drifted back to home, to his sister and mother, and of course his father. At nights the dream of the desert continued to haunt him, but now, in the cell, the dream seemed even more real, more intense and harder to shake off afterwards.

After the first few days, time seemed to float into a continuous cycle of waking and sleeping, and by the end of the first week he'd completely lost track of the days. Apart from the guards, who were under strict orders not to speak to him, he saw no one. It was a surprise, then, when on the second to last day he heard the scraping of the lock in the middle of the day.

Erich sat up as one of the guards put his head through the door.

"Special visitor for you. Commandant's permission."

Doctor Alexander entered the small yard, wrinkling his nose in distaste at the smell from the latrine, which didn't always drain properly.

Erich lowered his eyes to the floor. For two weeks he'd been playing this moment out again and again in his mind, and now shame and guilt seized him in equal proportions. The doctor sat heavily on the cot beside him. Erich thought he looked even older than he had two weeks ago. For some time the two sat in uncomfortable silence, until the old doctor spoke.

"I didn't believe them at first, Erich. But it is true, isn't it?"

Aware of the heat rushing to his face, Erich offered a mute nod.

"I want to hear you say it to me."

"*Ja*, Doctor. It is true."

Doctor Alexander shook his head sadly.

"That is what I can't understand, Erich. Why you would do this thing?"

"It was not ..." Erich stopped. Despite everything, he wasn't prepared to inflict further dishonour upon himself by offering excuses.

157

"I cannot tell you, Doctor. I have no explanation."

"That's what I thought."

Once more, silence filled the small cell. Sighing, the doctor looked up through the narrow barred window.

"You know something, Erich?" he continued. "I didn't want to take on this job. When the War Department first approached me, I refused it. Too old, too tired. And in all honesty, the thought of having to tend to Germans repelled me."

Erich kept his eyes locked on the concrete floor.

"You know about my son, I presume. I imagine that Alice will have told you. It was only after the minister appealed to me personally, told me how desperate the army was to find a qualified camp physician, that I agreed, with much reservation, to come out of retirement. But once I started, do you know ..." He paused. "It was good for me. Good to meet men like Heinrich Stutt and Günter, good for me to see your comrades not as the soldiers who'd killed Paul but as men like me. Men with families, men with love. That was why I was happy for Alice to come down here. Because she, like you, is of a generation who would otherwise grow up believing without question the same prejudices I've spent the last twenty-four years harbouring."

For the first time, Erich turned to face the doctor. The old man's breathing was laboured, but he met Erich's gaze directly.

"And do you know something else, Erich? It was especially good when Henrich assigned you to work with me in the hospital, because you remind me very much of my son. He also lied about his age to get into the army – did Alice tell you that? No. You are like him in so many ways, and I think I needed to see that, to comprehend for myself, so that I could begin to understand why he felt he had to leave us. It killed my wife, you know, his death. She died of a broken heart and for a long time I blamed everyone – the Germans, the English, even Paul, for that. I blamed him for the war, for running away, for the fact that he'd never follow in my footsteps. And then Heinrich brought you into the hospital that morning ..."

The old man's voice trailed away, and Erich found himself suddenly and strangely aware of the minutiae of sounds surrounding them: the tick of the tin roof expanding in the midday sun, the delicate rustle and chirp of insects in the low grass outside the walls, the distant cackle of birds in the forest.

"I think I know why you took the scalpel, Erich. I can understand it. I can imagine my Paul doing something similar, because sometimes young men do foolish, impulsive things they later regret. Heinrich tells me you claim that you were about to replace it when you were caught, and I believe that, also."

And for the first time since that now distant afternoon when he'd been caught, Erich was aware of the faintest glimmerings of hope inside himself. The doctor continued.

"But of course, things are different now. They have to be. Heinrich and the commandant are both in agreement that you can no longer be trusted to work in the hospital, despite my appeals."

"What shall I do, then?"

The doctor shrugged, the movement slow, dispirited.

"I really do not know, Erich. That is for Commander Stutt to decide. I imagine that with Thomas still around he will assign you to one of the working parties, so that you are out in the forest during the days. Whatever he allocates to you, I hope that you will apply yourself with the same diligence and care that you took for me. In the meantime" – he touched Erich's arm – "I would appreciate it if you would continue to look into the hospital regularly. Both Alice and I would welcome you."

At the mention of the girl's name Erich felt his stomach sink again.

"What does she think?"

The doctor went quiet for a few moments, and answered without meeting Erich's eye.

"She refused to believe it, at first. She blamed everything on Thomas. Now, I am not sure what she thinks. You will need to discuss that with her yourself. Like a man."

The doctor stood.

"They will release you back into the general camp population tomorrow, Erich. I will need to look you over before you are assigned to your new duties. Camp policy, I'm afraid. I'll see you then."

He made to leave and Erich also stood.

"Doctor" – the old man turned – "I am sorry."

The apology sounded pitifully inadequate, but to his surprise the doctor's eyes moistened and he reached out and squeezed the younger man's shoulder with a strange intensity.

"I know you are, Erich, I know you are. I'll see you tomorrow."

And the door closed, leaving Erich to contemplate his final day in isolation.

Eighteen

February 1944

The morning air was already warm as the canopy of branches and leaves closed overhead and the number three working party made its way into the green dimness of the forest. The darkness in the shadows created a false impression of coolness and Erich looked up, as he did every morning, acutely aware of the claustrophobic pressure of the trees pressing in upon them. His axe jogged at his shoulder and apart from the crunch of men's boots on the rough gravel trail the morning was silent.

It was the same every day – the sensation of close confinement during those first moments in the forest. Often the men would sing bawdy German marching songs to shake off the unsettling strangeness, but this morning, for whatever reason, they marched in subdued silence.

As usual, the black birds – cockatoos, the Australian guards called them – picked up their trail almost immediately and shadowed the working party, flapping between the treetops with awkward grace. Occasionally one would issue a strident, harsh shriek to the rest of the forest, but otherwise

161

they trailed above almost in silence. Somehow, Erich felt, it added to the oppressiveness of the morning.

A fly buzzed at his head, and with his free hand Erich swung at it, the gesture almost subconscious after two months with the work crew. Even this early in the day the heat of the Australian summer was stifling, baking the land, coating both trees and men in a constant layer of dust, which kicked up from their boots and settled quickly over everything, lending a feeling of constant grittiness.

Slowly, lulled by the rhythmic swing of the walk and the gentle pace of the morning, Erich drifted into reverie, as he always did, replaying the last couple of months in his mind.

At first, he'd hated being in the working party. He'd quickly realised what a favour Stutt had done him by allocating him to the hospital. Work in the forest was back-breaking and difficult. There was the incessant marching to and from the logging stands, the heat and the flies, and of course the forest with its brooding presence, its constant threat hanging over him.

He thought about Alice. Their first meeting after his release from the detention cells was still clear in his mind. He'd reported, filthy and unshaven, to the hospital for his mandatory check-up. The doctor had not been there and they'd stood in discomfited silence until she spoke.

"What were you thinking?"

And he'd looked at her, strangely aware for the first time of how pretty she was. Not in a conventional way, not like the girls he'd known back in Germany, but pretty none the less. He noticed the way that light seemed to gleam in her dark hair and fall across her face.

"Do you know how much you hurt him, Erich? Do you?"

162

She was flushed with anger, colour rising in her cheeks, and she tossed her long hair back over her shoulder angrily. Erich felt within him a growing bubble of quiet despair at what he had thrown away.

"Well? Say something."

His voice was scratchy and hoarse. "I do not know what I can say."

"Anything. I don't care. Just tell me why you did it."

He could not look at her any longer. Her face was crimson with anger and disappointment, so he looked out the window.

"I do not know. It was just … just a moment. I cannot explain."

And she turned and walked away, crossing to the far end of the room before facing him again.

"That's what grandfather says, but I don't believe him. And I don't believe you. I think you were still trying to fight this bloody war. Weren't you?"

Erich took a step in her direction, desperate. "No! Not at all. I was only, I was …" She cut him off.

"Don't even start. How many times did you tell me that you, no *us* – that we were still at war? That we were all enemies? Well, I hope you're happy now, Erich. I hope you're pleased with your little battle."

Tears ran freely down her cheeks and Erich wanted nothing more than to go to her and wipe them away. But he stood still, mute and ashamed, pride tearing him in two directions.

"Alice, I … I think that …"

"Do you want to know something else, Erich? All the time you were carrying on about the war and being a soldier, all that time I didn't believe you were serious. I thought you

163

were just covering for something, just lonely. I thought you had more to you than that. That you were more than just some" – she hesitated – "some *German*."

She hissed the word and it rang around the empty hospital like a gunshot. Erich felt it tear into him with a force almost physical. He struggled again to speak.

"I ..." But there were no words. Alice stared at him through tear-hazed eyes and, as their gazes locked, both shuddered at the confusion of feelings which echoed around them. For an age there was nothing at all in the world but the sad dark eyes of the girl across the room.

Then footsteps sounded and the doctor entered, instantly aware of the charged atmosphere.

"Alice, Erich ..."

But the girl stormed past and out. Barely aware of himself or the doctor, Erich took a couple of involuntary steps to follow and then stopped, his eyes still locked on the spot where the door had shut behind her. He scarcely felt the doctor's gentle pressure on his shoulder.

"Come on then, Erich, let's have a look at you."

Through the examination the boy stayed quiet, and the doctor allowed him his silence. Then when the check-up was over and it was time for Erich to leave, the old man led him gently to the door.

"She will come around, Erich. Have faith, Youngster."

And Erich had nodded, said nothing and stumbled to his bunk through a fog with her words still echoing in his mind.

That had been weeks, no, months ago. And still the numbness stayed with him. Each day in the forest Erich swung his axe, hauled timber to the cart, ate and laughed and joked with the other men, but all the time part of him stayed in the hospital, listening with silent, unexpected despair as her trembling voice accused him, over and over – "some *German*."

If the other men in the working party were aware of what he was going through, they gave no sign, and as the weeks passed his hands grew the thick calluses of the timber worker. His shoulders and back filled out, stretching at the fabric of his uniform, and the men would include him more and more in their jokes and ribaldry.

"Come on, son, swing the thing!"

"You're not in the hospital now, Youngster!"

Even the hated nickname, 'Youngster', had somehow taken on a new meaning. Now they called it with affection, even a kind of respect, which was something Erich had never experienced before, not from men. Time passed and he began to feel more accepted, a part of the crew, and a little of the fog faded and lifted.

"Here we are then, quick drinks!"

Stopping at the end of the trail, the men flopped to the ground and drank deeply from their canteens. Their crew leader was a 32-year-old known to everyone simply as 'Kaiser'. He'd been a tank commander before he was taken prisoner, while hauling the rest of his men from their burning vehicle. Before they formally captured him the British had allowed him to continue while they'd sat and watched. In the process he'd been badly burned and his skin was wrinkled and pock-marked.

"Right then, usual jobs. I want to get that big one we started yesterday down first, and then make a start on at least three more. Let's get to it."

The men rose from the patches of ground where they'd thrown themselves and headed into the woods.

Erich had an easy task to start off with – keeping the blade of the two-man felling saw cool with water as the other members of the crew worked the blade through the hard, red wood. The tree was a massive old jarrah, and the day before they'd managed about two-thirds of the cut. Axe men had been chipping away above the incision, knocking away the trunk in the direction that they wanted the tree to fall.

"All ready, Youngster?"

"*Ja* ..." Erich had fetched a bucket from the wagon and filled it from a small tank they carried with them. "Ready when you are."

The two men started, slowly working the blade into the slot they'd created the previous day.

"Watch out! Here it goes!"

With a groan that seemed to tear through the restive afternoon, the great jarrah gave way and with surprising slowness plunged to earth. Erich watched, aware of the unexpected majesty in the tree's death. As men darted from beneath its path, it dropped with a resigned, almost splendid elegance and when it finally crashed into the undergrowth, all present felt the earth shudder beneath them. In the moments that followed the entire bush fell silent, as though mourning the death of that great giant. Then slowly the gentle background rustle would start again, and the men would laugh and joke exuberantly.

"That was a monster, eh Helmut?"

"*Ja.* Even bigger than the one that took Günter's leg!"

Erich had quickly discovered that this was the benchmark against which all tree-fellings were now compared.

"Come on, Pieters, jump to it, Youngster."

"I think he must be tired!"

"Are we keeping you awake?"

The men were grinning.

"*Nein*. I just wanted to let you all feel good about yourselves before I show you up for the old men that you really are." Erich grinned back.

Kaiser replied, "Big words from a little boy."

They all laughed again, and then Erich fell to the task of severing the branches from the main trunk, dropping quickly into his regular rhythm of swinging and chopping, enjoying the solid thump and the bite of the blade into hard wood.

All the time, though, he was aware of the force of the forest. Most of the men seemed unaffected, some even seemed to like it, but working in the dark, muted light between the jarrahs had done nothing to alleviate any of its foreignness as far as Erich was concerned. The feeling that something was watching, observing, was with him whenever he was out there working in the semi-twilight or marching along the rough trails they'd hewn. He felt a presence that followed them out and back and during the days watched the slow destruction they inflicted upon the living timber.

"Hey! Look!"

Kaiser was holding up something. Something small and noisy. The men all stopped and went across to him. Cradled in his hands was a baby bird, a bundle of black down.

"It was in there." He gestured at a hollow junction in the branches of the fallen tree.

The men crowded around. Nests weren't uncommon, but

this was the first time a living chick had been recovered from one. In Kaiser's big hands it trembled and mewed piteously.

"Is it all right?"

"*Ja*. I think so."

"What do we do with it? Can you see its parents?"

"*Nein*. We should take it back to camp."

"What for?"

Kaiser shrugged. "We can't leave it out here like this. Günter can look after it. He's an old woman now!"

The men laughed.

"Youngster, would the doctor or your sweetheart be able to get us a box to put it in?"

Faces turned to Erich expectantly and he felt his colour rise. 'Your sweetheart' had become, despite his protestations, the accepted term used to refer to Alice.

"*Ja*. I can ask."

"Good. In the meantime, it can live in my shirt."

Carefully, Kaiser carried the chick over to where his discarded shirt lay draped across a branch. It was odd to watch his large, scarred hands dealing so delicately with the tiny creature.

"Come on now, you lot, back to it. Now."

When the working party got back to the compound that evening, Kaiser released the bird to Erich and he took it over to the hospital. The tiny creature's heart was beating at a million miles an hour. Erich could feel it beneath his fingertips. The evening was warm, small insects were drifting here and there and the forest beyond the wire was settling into its nightly forage. Erich paused at the door, hesitant, and knocked lightly with his free hand. Footsteps within, and Alice was there.

168

They'd not spoken since the day of his release from detention and now the memory of her anger and his shame came flooding back. She appraised him coolly.

"Erich. Hello."

"Good evening …" Unsure of where to go next, he held out the bird, awkward, embarrassed, uncertain. In his hands it chirruped, the tiny cry the only sound between them. "We found it in the forest."

Alice took the tiny bundle and briefly their fingertips brushed. The contact sent a tiny shiver running through him and he thought the girl stiffened slightly. Doctor Alexander called from behind his desk, "Is that Erich?"

"*Ja*, Doctor."

"Well, come in, son. Don't stand out there all night."

Stepping into the dim light, Erich was suddenly aware of the fact that he'd been working all day and shuffled his feet, feeling embarrassed and dishevelled. The doctor came over and shook his hand.

"It seems like so long since we've seen you. You were going to look in, remember?"

"Yes, Doctor. I am sorry."

"No, no. There's nothing to apologise for. I'm sure you're fairly tired in the evenings."

"That is true."

The girl said nothing but retreated to the shadows by the cold stove and gently stroked the downy bird. That moment of contact with Erich had, what? Scared her? No. It was something different – unsettling. Not fear then. While the doctor and Erich talked, she looked at him, surprised at how different he seemed from the boy who'd stood in almost the same place just a couple of months earlier. The work in the

169

forest had filled out his body, and it suited him, though somehow he still looked ill at ease in it. There was something else about him too, something beyond the physical changes, that she couldn't describe. It intrigued her and Alice felt the vestiges of her anger starting to waver.

"I have something here for you."

The doctor retrieved a package from some shelves.

"They arrived a few weeks ago."

Erich took the heavy bundle, wrapped in brown paper.

"Open it."

Inside were books. Medical texts.

"Are you still interested in doing some more study?" The doctor's eyes were bright. He looked more alive than he had for months, Alice thought.

Erich's brow furrowed with puzzlement. "What would be the purpose? I cannot use it."

"Not now, perhaps, Erich, but you never know. Knowledge is a valuable thing. And I am sure that you would enjoy the distraction."

"*Ja*, thank you." Erich nodded. "I think it will help fill in my spare time."

"Good then."

Alice still hadn't said anything. The bird chirruped again, attracting the doctor's attention.

"And what's this?"

"A cockatoo. A baby. We knocked down its nest today, and Kaiser asked me to find a box and some padding to keep it in."

Alice offered the bird to her grandfather, who took it carefully, scratching its head lightly with his little finger.

"Poor little thing. I don't know enough about animals to

offer much advice, but we'll see what we can do. Alice, would you mind looking under the cupboard there for a small box?" He nodded at the supply cupboard which stood open.

"I can, Doctor." Erich was closer and made a step towards the cupboard, but Alice interrupted.

"No. It's all right. I'll do it." She moved quickly before Erich had a chance. As she bent to search, she could feel his eyes on her.

"Will this do?" She held up a small cardboard box, a little larger than a shoebox.

"We'll put some gauze in to pad it. And give you a syringe to feed it from."

"What should we give it?"

The doctor shook his head. "A little sugar and water, I imagine. To be honest, I'm not sure, Erich. Birds aren't my speciality."

"I will ask the other men. Someone will know something of this."

Outside, the stillness of the bush twilight was broken by the growing wail of the camp siren.

"That is rollcall. I must go, I am afraid."

"That's fine, Erich. It is good to see you again."

"*Ja*, Doctor. And you also." Erich looked at Alice. "Both of you."

The girl looked down, refusing to meet his gaze, remembering the last time the two of them had been alone together.

"You must come back and tell us how your little bird is going, all right?"

"I will, Doctor. But now I must go."

"Goodnight, Erich."

Alice watched him as he left. Clutching the box beneath his arm he cleared the steps of the hospital in an easy bound and loped away towards the mess.

Nineteen

In the morning the bird was dead. Sometime during the night the tiny heart had stopped beating and they found it cold, a black shadow of life huddled in soft white gauze. Kaiser wrapped it gently in an old shirt and carried it back into the forest with them.

The death of the small creature lent a sombre atmosphere to the morning and Erich felt the forest to be somehow more suffocating, more alien, than normal.

Kaiser used his axe to scrape a shallow hole at the severed stump of the jarrah from which the cockatoo had been recovered. Both prisoners and guards stood around as he placed the small bundle in the depression and covered it with rich forest soil.

None spoke. The trees stood watching, impassive sentinels over the strange burial. Kaiser's eyes were wet and Erich wondered at the forces that could move a man like this to tears over the death of a bird. When it was done they stood quiet for a moment, remembering distant places, lovers and

173

times. It wasn't so much a tribute to the bird, Erich realised, as to each of them there.

"Right, then." Kaiser's voice was still unsteady. "Let's get on with it, shall we?" And the men drifted in twos and threes to their assigned tasks.

All day, Erich felt unsettled. It might have been the bird, or something else, but the men laboured the hours in relative silence. During lunch break there were a couple of half-hearted jokes, but nobody had the spirit to carry them on and during the early afternoon a hot, dry wind picked up from the east, blowing hard between the trees and carrying with it dust and discomfort. The wind-howl through the canopy seemed from another world, and when the whistle sounded for afternoon break, all the men stood around, gritty, smoking in quiet conversation as the sweat dried on their arms and backs.

"That's a bad breeze, Youngster."

"*Ja.*" He had not heard Kaiser coming up behind him, but turned to face the former tank commander as he approached.

"Thank you for your help with the bird. It was not too much trouble for you, I hope?"

"*Nein.* It was good to catch up with the doctor again."

"And his granddaughter, I'll bet."

Erich threw a sharp glance at the man, but the easy smile on the pocked face showed that Kaiser was very aware of his own teasing.

"*Ja.* Though I think she is not so pleased to see me now."

"You might be surprised. Women are fickle things."

Kaiser took a final puff on the cigarette he was smoking

and absent-mindedly flicked the butt away into the undergrowth.

"Careful!"

"Damn!"

Rules were strict about smoking in the forest, especially
during the summer. Men were to ensure that their butts were
fully extinguished underfoot.

"We'd better find it, just to be safe." Kaiser plunged into
the spiny shrubs, following the direction of the discarded
butt.

For ten minutes the two combed the bush as best they
could, thwarted by thorns and bracken made dry and sharp
by the desiccating heat, and then the whistle blew again,
signalling the end of the break. Kaiser took a last look
around.

"We'll have to give up. It was out anyway."

"*Ja*," Erich agreed. "There's no smoke."

The two returned to their equipment and their tasks and
the afternoon wore on in hot, uncomfortable silence. Even
the birds, usually so omnipresent this deep in the forest,
seemed to be absent. And, caught in a tiny fork between two
dry branches, Kaiser's cigarette butt, fanned by the hot wind,
glowed, an infinitesimal hidden pinprick of red heat.

"FIRE!"

The shout went up about twenty minutes before the end
of work, accompanied by a frenzied blowing of the whistle.
Men tumbled towards the muster point, but the forest was
already well ablaze, flames hissing angrily and flinging dark
smoke and ash high into the narrow gaps between the

175

tree-crowns. The air, thick with the pungency of burning eucalyptus, seared the lungs.

Erich sprinted through a confusion of shouts in both German and English, the guards as panicked and uncertain as the prisoners. The timber-cart and equipment trailer were already alight, and the angry wall of flame, fed by the hot wind, was visibly spreading, its hold on the tinder-dry forest strengthening with every second.

"Fall back – towards the camp!"

Gradually the cry was taken up and the working party retreated up the trail, away from the blaze. Frantic guards counted and re-counted.

"How many missing?"

"Dunno. At least three or four."

"Bugger me! Who?"

"No idea. They're still comin'."

Between the trees men stumbled through moving, dim yellow light, coughing and blinded by thick smoke. One of the guards, the senior one, was yelling.

"Everyone – further back up the trail. We can't fight it."

Through the stupor of confusion men staggered, some still clutching equipment, some half naked, stripped to the waist as they had been when the call went out. Someone grabbed Erich's arm and yanked it roughly.

"Come on, Youngster! This way."

He followed, feet moving independently from brain, and with each step away from the inferno the temperature dropped perceptibly and he began to shake. The man who had grabbed him ran on ahead, hauling at other, slower men as he did so, and Erich slowed to a walk. For the briefest of seconds in the flames and heat he was back in the burning camp site in the Libyan sands, but then the forest closed in again.

From behind, the roar of the flames was shattered by a crackling explosion and a piece of flaming timber as thick as his forearm whistled past his head, missing him by inches and leaving behind it the searing smell of burning hair.

"*Mein Gott!*" He started running again, but managed only a couple of steps when a ghastly scream tore from the flames behind him. A figure lurched from the bush onto the track, clothes and hair fully aflame, a primal, deathly wail of agony emanating from the maw of his mouth.

Launching himself at the staggering human torch, Erich threw it to the ground and the two rolled over and over in the gravely dirt, locked in a deathly embrace. Some small part of his brain, some reptilian synapse, was vaguely aware of a sensation of heat, and the smell of cooking, but his concentration was on smothering the licking red devils that caressed the man in his arms. Grabbing the man's shirt he ripped and flung it away, then using his bare hands, he hit at the man's blistering legs, again and again, each blow extinguishing tiny tongues of fire.

And all the while the man screamed. And as long as he screamed he was alive and Erich kept on, hitting and hitting until the flames were gone. But even then the man didn't stop screaming and for the first time Erich looked around for assistance.

"Help!" He yelled up the track in the direction of the retreating party, but his cry was drowned by the roar of the flames and carried away by the wind.

"Somebody!" But there was nobody, and gasping with the exertion Erich lurched upright, grabbed the screaming man by the wrist and pulled him up too. It was a big load, but fuelled by adrenalin and fear, the man seemed almost weightless. Erich hauled him up onto his back and dragged him, feet trailing in the dust, away from the devouring flames.

When the others, regrouping in a small clearing upwind, noticed him, Erich felt as though he'd been carrying his burden forever. Then hands were assisting him and men lifted the now-silent body from Erich's back, having to pry his scorched fingers from the other man's wrists. Someone else lifted a canteen to Erich's lips, which were burnt and wouldn't open all the way, and the water was shocking in its coldness as it streamed across his face.

"Bloody hell, mate." It was one of the guards. "That was a piece of work."

"Give him space."

Voices, all talking at once. Indistinguishable from faces and bodies.

"We'd better get him back to the doctor, pronto."

"What about the other one?"

"No hurry there. Not now, anyway."

Then someone took his arm and he was walking. The air was cooler and cleaner, and after a few minutes Erich started to become aware of the pain in his arms and face.

Twenty

February 1944

"Good morning, Erich. Let's have a look at these bandages."

He unwound the gauze gently from Erich's still-tender skin.

"Getting better by the day, I'm pleased to say. We'll be able to let you go back to your own bed again soon."

"Thank you, Doctor."

"Not at all, Erich, not at all. It's healing up nicely. You are very lucky, you know?"

Erich shrugged. "Perhaps. More fortunate than Kaiser, certainly."

The two fell into silence. Erich lay back against the cool pillows. The burns on his face and head weren't as bad as the ones on his hands, which were still smothered in oily cream and swathed in bandages. Outside, Erich could hear the cockatoos calling in the forest.

"Is the fire out?" In the three days since the blaze started, the doctor had been keeping Erich up to date with the progress of the bushfire.

"Almost. This cooler wind from the coast has helped to knock it on its head."

"Good." Erich nodded. "It is a terrible thing."

"Not really."

Erich looked up at the doctor in surprise.

"I've told you before, Erich, sometimes burning is all you can do."

"But surely, Doctor, the destruction …"

"This is true, and the destruction is often appalling. But the fire also brings life. Clears away the dead wood, makes room for new trees and plants. It's a paradox, Erich. A terrible but purifying force."

Erich pondered the doctor's words. It was true, he had been lucky. Several of the men had been burned more severely than him and were under guard in the hospital in Perth. Kaiser hadn't survived his ordeal in the flames, despite Erich's efforts. He wondered what the bush looked like now, in the aftermath of that devilish heat. Despite his dislike of the brooding green expanse, part of him wanted to see.

"Doctor?"

"Yes, Erich?"

"Will I return to the forest?"

"In a few weeks, when your hands are well enough healed. At the moment, though, I doubt you'd be able to even hold a bucket of water, let alone an axe."

"May I have a book?"

"Of course. How about advanced anatomical studies?"

"That would be good."

The doctor retrieved the weighty tome from the shelf, but with his hands swathed Erich found it impossible to both support it and turn the pages. He was struggling to find a way around the problem when the door to the hospital swung open.

"Good morning, Grandfather." She crossed to the old man's desk and planted a light kiss on the top of his head.

"Hello, Alice. How are you this morning?"

"I'm fine, thank you." She turned to the bed. Erich looked at her, and for some seconds there was silence between them, until the girl spoke, hesitantly. "How are you?"

"I am good." Erich dropped his eyes and started struggling again with the pages.

Without a word, she took the textbook from him and settled herself on the bed alongside.

"I'll hold it for you if you'd like."

A rush of blood to his cheeks made Erich's face burn.

"It is all right. I will manage."

"Erich." She touched his arm lightly, towards the top where it was not badly burned. "I'd like to."

Slowly the tingle of sensation managed to penetrate the traumatised flesh of his arm, sending a shiver through him, until he inclined his head in a slight bow.

"If you have nothing else you would rather be doing."

And for the first time in a long time, Alice smiled at him.

"Nothing at all."

While Erich was lost in the pages of the book on her lap she watched him, at first with small sideways glances and then, as she realised that the boy was totally engrossed, with open attention. She watched the thickly bandaged hands resting on the bedclothes, the inclination of his head and the tiny furrows of confusion when he came across a word or passage he didn't understand, the miniscule twitch of a muscle on the back of his shoulder, casting gentle spasms through the cotton of his shirt. And as she watched she became more and more aware of a sensation of warmth, somewhere inside her, and smiled again.

And later, when the doctor had been called out to the Italian compound, the two young people sat in the quiet duskiness of the tiny wooden hospital and talked.

"Alice?" Even now – especially now – Erich liked the way her name felt on his tongue and lips each time he spoke it. "I am sorry."

"Sorry?"

"*Ja.* For the … incident with the scalpel. You know."

And Alice laughed. A light ringing laugh.

"What ever made you bring that up now? It was months ago."

"I know, but …" He searched for the right words, his English uncharacteristically deserting him. "But I am sorry nevertheless."

She smiled again. "That's fine. I'd forgiven you ages ago."

"Really?"

"Really. You just haven't realised it."

"Well, I am never around."

"True. What happened to the bird?"

"The bird?"

"That little one you brought in here."

"Ah. It died in the night."

"Oh, that's so sad."

"It is the way of things. So Günter would say." He hesitated. "They say that the war is coming to an end."

Alice looked slightly perplexed at the sudden change in subject. "Who does?"

182

"The men. The other Germans, the Italians, the guards. Lots of them."

"How would they know?"

"They get letters occasionally, from home. People talk, make guesses."

The girl shrugged slightly. "I'll believe it when it happens. Plenty of people thought that it would all be over by Christmas, and that was more than two months ago now."

"True. But still, it is good to hope."

"I thought you'd be upset at Germany's defeat?"

Now it was Erich's turn to shrug. "Perhaps six months ago, when I first arrived here. Now, though, I am not so sure."

"About what?"

"About a lot of things. My father."

"Your father?"

"*Ja*. Günter thinks that he will be dead before the end of the war."

"Why ever would he think that?"

"Because ..." Erich paused, the silence around them absolute. "He is ... how do I say it? Important. An important man in the German Army, the *Wehrmacht*. Men in my family have always been officers, commanders. This is the reason I joined up, because I thought that I needed to show him that I can carry the honour of the family."

"Not because of Germany?"

"Not because of politics, if that is what you are asking. For my father, Germany and military life has always been more important than that. That is why he is such a respected commander, but it is also why he will remain a prisoner after the war for certain if he is captured."

"Is that why you're always so secretive about him?"

183

"*Ja*. I know that he believes men should not place their personal feelings above their duty to their country."

Alice gathered Erich's bandaged hands into her own, but gently, and stared deep and hard into his blue eyes. "Then, Erich, you must let go of what your father believes, or what you think he believes, and work out what you are going to believe for yourself. It's the only way."

"The only way to what?"

"The only way to be human." She brushed a fingertip lightly across a wrinkled, pale welt on his upper arm. "Most of this scarring will heal up, given time, but in here ..." Her finger traced across his chest and tapped over his heart. "In here scars can last much longer, if they're not treated."

Abruptly the girl stood and crossed to the door.

"I'm going to leave you for a while. To think. We can talk some more tomorrow if you wish."

"*Ja*." Erich managed a thin smile. "That would be most good."

She smiled back.

"I'll see you in the morning."

184

Twenty-one

August 1944

The men marched back to the camp, leaning into the hot wind which dried their sweat, cracked their skin and left them feeling gritty. The scar tissue on Erich's hands and lower arms itched slightly as it always did this late in the day.

Stutt was waiting at the gates, talking to one of the Australian guards, and the two turned to watch the approaching column of men. Silently the guard unlocked the double gate and swung it wide so the men could pass through two abreast. Stutt fell into step beside them and once they were secure again within the compound the senior officer murmured something to the team leader. Erich saw an involuntary glance thrown in his direction. Stutt made his way back along the column to where Erich was.

"Erich, come with me, please."

He angled away towards the hut lines, and Erich followed, puffing slightly from the march, his fitness still not quite recovered after the weeks of soft time spent healing.

Günter sat on the steps of Hut Seventeen, his face impassive.

"Sit down, Youngster." The one-legged soldier slapped the step beside him.

"What have I done?"

"Nothing, Erich. Nothing at all. The commander has something to tell you, and we thought it best I be here also."

When he addressed himself to Erich, Stutt's face was drawn, his eyes tired.

"Erich, today we received word that a month ago there was an unsuccessful attempt on Hitler's life, an attempt to assassinate him with a bomb."

Erich looked at the man, confused. What had this to do with him?

"There were a large number of men involved. All officers. All in the *Wehrmacht*. They and their families were rounded up and executed immediately. Erich ..." Stutt hesitated, wrestling with the words he had to say. "One was your father."

Erich stared, his face blank with incomprehension.

"Excuse me, sir? There is a mistake, surely."

Günter's arm fell lightly around his shoulders. Erich was barely even aware.

"We don't have many details, I'm afraid, but we have a list of names, Erich, and there is no doubt. Your father was implicated and he was executed."

"My family?"

A look passed between the two men.

"We don't know, Erich. Your mother and sister's names weren't on the list so, ..."

A black wave of darkness surged as comprehension dawned on him.

"But ..."

"I know, Youngster." Günter's deep voice was soft.

In a rush, Erich felt his gorge rise and, twisting, he vomited onto the ground.

Everything. Everything he thought he'd believed, his father, his country … it was all a lie. A hopeless, futile, horrible lie. For a moment Erich railed against the hopelessness of it, tried desperately to find something else to have faith in, to hold on to. Then oblivion swept over him like a tide, a black void seemed to yawn in front of him and he dropped into it, embracing the silence, unwilling to feel. The last thing he was aware of was Stutt's voice, coming from a long way off and growing ever more distant: "Look after him, Günter. I'll go and fetch the doctor."

And then, nothing.

Twenty-two

August 1944

The bodies lay in a pit, dragged by the few survivors under the direction of the British soldiers. Blood soaked the surrounding sand, staining it a thick, heavy brown. Staggering, Erich hauled at the legs of the final man, a man he recognised but couldn't remember his name. He was a mechanic from Munich, Erich recalled.

A British soldier bent and removed the steel tags from around the body's neck, then nodded at Erich. Without a word, Erich and another man swung the body as gently as possible into the pit and stepped back. That was the lot.

The British waved their rifles and the survivors clustered together before the unsteady barrels.

"Right then, any of you lot speak English?" The British sergeant was blackened and weary. A cigarette hung lazily from the corner of his mouth. Erich stayed mute.

"That'd be bloody right."

One of the other soldiers slouched across to the sergeant and spoke words too quiet for Erich to make out. The officer spat the cigarette butt into the sand and ground it under his heel.

"Bloody 'ell, Jim, will you look at that pile there. 'Aven't we killed enough of these poor buggers today? Anyways, this lot did well enough just gettin' through that first assault. Somehow wouldn't seem fair to top 'em now, would it?"

The soldier named Jim just shrugged and stared off again into the morning.

Erich studied the enemy soldiers closely. Apart from the different uniforms there wasn't much to distinguish them from his own company, now mostly dead. All were grubby and sand-blown, burnt by exposure and clearly fatigued. Most were in their early twenties.

"You are thinking they are all the same as you, aren't you?"

"What?" Erich spun round.

His father stood a couple of feet away, his uniform pressed and creased perfectly, out of place in the hot desert morning. His decorations gleamed in the early morning sunlight.

"Father?"

"*Ja*. Not so different, are they?"

"What are ..."

"Of course they aren't, my son. Enemies never are. You should remember that."

"What do you mean?"

"Just that, Erich. You must always look hard to find your true enemies, because chances are they will be just like you."

His father turned to leave, walking towards the line of British soldiers, who seemed oblivious to his presence.

"Father!"

The figure stopped and turned. "*Ja?*"

189

For long moments Erich stared at the face of the man who had taught him to hunt, to read. Stared into familiar blue eyes. "Why?"

His father gave a rueful smile. "For Germany."

And with a casual salute he walked between a couple of the British soldiers and faded into the glare off the sand.

"Erich?"

Another voice, this time floating, disembodied, and yet in an odd way more tangible than his father's. More solid. Familiar.

"Erich?"

It seemed to echo around the ragged group of soldiers, but no one else appeared to notice it.

"Erich?"

It came from the air, from above, and Erich let himself be drawn up towards it, and the brightness of the desert faded into nothing...

"Erich?" Alice leaned over the unconscious figure, resting her hand against the boy's forehead. It was hot, clammy and burned beneath the cool skin of her hands. "Will he be all right?"

Doctor Alexander saw the concern in his granddaughter's expression.

"I imagine so, Alice. It must be a terrible shock for him, but he's young and strong. He'll be fine. I'm going over to the mess for a cup of tea."

Her grandfather left, and looking at the sleeping figure Alice wondered if the old man was right. Beneath the sheet Erich seemed small and fragile again. He'd looked the same way the night she'd brought him in from the storm after Günter's operation – as though he might break and dissipate into nothing at any moment. She wiped his hot head with an already soaked hand-towel.

"Erich, wake up ..."

Darkness. Coolness. Nothingness. Drifting up towards the voice, Erich felt peaceful, as he hadn't for months and months. It came from inside him, from the voice which seemed to be washing around him, through him, drawing him to itself with gentle insistence.

Light gleamed in the shadowy air and, like a moth carried by instinct, he let himself waft towards it.

"Erich, wake up ..."

Holding the damp towel to his head, Alice watched trickles of water from the fabric run down his cheeks and neck. Could he hear her? she wondered.

"Erich, it's Alice."

Cold cut like an icy blade across his skin and rolled down his face, and Erich moaned at the exquisite coolness.

"Erich, it's Alice."

Alice? He knew the voice. He knew the name. Somewhere in the empty darkness of his mind memories started to shiver and wake, drawn back into his consciousness by the chill press of cold towelling against his forehead. He felt himself floating further and further from the heat and sand of the Libyan desert, and somehow knew that he'd never be returning there again.

Alice?

Alice ...

"Alice."

He opened his eyes.

Just as the first time she'd seen him, Alice was startled by the blueness – the burning, intense blueness. They bore into her with a strength and energy that almost made her gasp. She was dimly aware that her heart was beating faster than usual.

And he smiled. For the first time that she could remember, his face creased into a proper, full smile, a carefree expression that seemed to lift him from the pillow.

"Alice, you are crying."

Crying? Her hand lifted to her eyes and came away moist. She hadn't even realised.

"Oh, God. No, I'm okay." She looked away in embarrassment. "I'm fine, really."

"Alice ..." He tried to sit up, but fell back.

Wiping her eyes with one of her grandfather's handkerchiefs, Alice wondered if she should go and get him. Tell him. But he'd be here soon enough and she shouldn't leave Erich. Not now, especially not now. She turned again to the smiling young man in the bed and, because it seemed the thing to do, she kissed him.

Even her lips felt cool. Cool, fresh, invigorating.

It was brief. After a couple of seconds she pulled away, startled, embarrassed.

"I'm sorry! I ..."

"Alice ..." He lifted his hand and touched her cheek lightly, his fingertips still wrinkled with scars. "It is all right. It is very fine."

192

His fingers were brushing only lightly against her skin, but heat radiated from them and into her. She knew that her cheeks were starting to flush, was aware of the blaze of warmth rising into them, but it was nothing compared to the fire in that gentle touch from his calloused fingers.

She chuckled at his accented expression and he pulled his hand away, suddenly uncertain, puzzled by her laugh. She caught his hand and held it.

"No, Erich, you're right. It is very fine indeed."

Closing her eyes, Alice leaned her face in towards his again and this time she didn't pull away nearly so quickly.

Twenty-three

May 1945

Sunday. Rest day. A chill wind stirred between the buildings of the camp as Erich trotted towards the hospital. Winter was coming again and the day was cold. Grey clouds hung low overhead, just above the treetops.

At the hospital, as usual, Alice was waiting for him.

"Hi."

"Good morning."

They kissed and for a moment Erich allowed himself to sink into the sensation of her body pressed against his own. Then she pulled away.

"Where is the doctor?"

"He said to tell you that he'll be along in a little while and you should start your revision of last week's work on the respiratory system until he gets here."

With the new textbooks, Erich's medical studies had come along faster than anyone expected. Despite the doctor's appeals, Stutt still insisted that he work in the forest during the weekdays. Surprisingly, Erich didn't mind any more.

Sundays were different, though. Sundays, Thomas usually

accompanied the furlough party into Marinup. Sundays were Erich's days to study in the hospital with the doctor and, of course, Alice.

"I have a better idea than study." He reached for her again, encircling her waist, and she pushed him away half-heartedly.

"Later. He could walk in any moment."

But she let him kiss her again, anyway.

"*Ja.*" Erich smiled at her as he pulled one of the thick, leather-bound texts down from the shelf. "Your grandfather would not be too happy to walk in and find me not doing my homework."

"That's not the only thing he wouldn't be happy with." Alice also fished a book out from her bag. "I brought something to read myself."

The two fell into their respective books with ease and a comfortable silence filled the room. Erich glanced occasionally at the girl settled with her book on the chair by the stove. A beam of pale light reached in through the window behind her. He smiled as he stared and stored the memory of how she looked to carry with him through the week. Outside, a few spots of rain thudded against the tin roof.

Footsteps on the verandah announced the arrival of the doctor. He entered slowly.

"Good morning, Erich. How was your week?"

"The same as the one before. And the one before that. Not much changes in the forest."

"I can imagine. I'm pleased to see you got my message about starting your revision."

"*Ja.* Your grand-daughter is an excellent messenger."

Erich and Alice exchanged a quick smile.

"I'm glad to hear that. I was worried that you might be finding her a little distracting."

"Distracting, Doctor?"

"Just a thought. We might put you through the next of your tests next Sunday. What do you think?"

"I think I will be ready for it by then."

The doctor hummed a popular marching tune as he settled behind his desk.

"Erich?"

"Yes, Doctor?"

"Do you still think about your father?"

"I am sorry?"

The question was unexpected. The old man stared levelly at him.

"I am just wondering, because you haven't really talked about him to anyone, as far as I know. It's been some time now and was clearly a terrible shock to you. I have always believed that it is better to discuss things openly and was wondering if you have dealt properly with his death."

Erich thought for a few seconds.

"When I joined the army, Doctor, I did so because I wanted to impress him – my father, I mean. I thought what he believed in the most was the glory of Germany, as it had been taught to me at school and in the *Hitlerjugend*. And when I was fighting, and in the prison compound, and even when I arrived here, the one thing I never doubted was that I was still fighting my father's war, for him. For what he believed would be a good future for Germany."

"And then they executed him ..."

"*Ja*. When I got the news, all I could think about was that it was all a lie. He didn't believe any of it. He never had, and

196

that left me without anything to believe in. That is why I am not talking too much of these things. I am still trying to find out what it is that I am believing in myself."

"And have you?"

Erich shrugged, but smiled at Alice as he replied, "I am not sure. Perhaps I have."

The girl dropped her eyes, blushing.

The morning wound on quickly, the doctor working through the textbook, with Erich listening and occasionally questioning. He was distracted, though, the doctor's words still in the back of his mind, and later, when the doctor left for lunch in the officers' mess, Alice touched his arm.

"Are you all right? You don't seem quite as focused as usual."

"*Ja*, I am fine. I am thinking about what your grandfather was saying."

"In a way it is good, you know. The way he died. It means you were right about him being a true German."

"Why do you say that?"

"Because" – Alice hesitated, realising that she was on shaky ground – "if he had to die, surely it is better that he died doing something good."

"I think I would rather have him alive. Doesn't his death make it all a lie? Everything they taught me at school? All those men I saw die in Libya, they died for nothing. For a lie too. And me – it means that I am here in this forest because I joined the army for a lie. So many lies."

Erich pulled away from her hand and stood up. Anger welled up inside, sudden and unexpected.

"All I am sure of is that on that night, when Stutt and

197

Günter told me, I felt as though nothing I knew was certain any more. Nothing. Like I had nothing to hold on to."

The girl sat on the bed beside him. "You can hold on to me, if you want."

"*Danke*."

"And I think that your father will be remembered as a hero."

For a while they sat in silence, then from outside came the sound of men yelling, both in German and English.

"What could that be?" Alice looked up, alarmed. Erich was equally perplexed.

"I do not know. It is too early for the men to be coming back from town."

"What are they shouting?"

"I cannot understand it from here. Come." She followed him onto the verandah.

The gates to the camp were open and the Australian guards were standing around and smiling, every one of them. The prisoners were there too – some inside the fence and some outside, milling about, slapping backs and everyone babbling in their own language. The doctor emerged from the crowd and hurried towards them. He too was smiling.

"What is it?"

He strained to hear the words. "I think they are saying that the war is over."

Twenty-four

July 1946

Rain and wind lashed the camp, tearing at the surrounding trees and throwing a storm of leaf and twig litter up against the perimeter fence. Every three or four seconds lightning would rent the grey sky, the crash of thunder following hard upon it. Aside from those brief flashes, the day was dark. Guards huddled in their towers, crouching low to avoid the worst of the weather, paying little attention to anything other than staying dry.

This was ironic, given that Marinup Camp Sixteen had endured more escape attempts in the twelve months since the end of hostilities than in the previous five years of the war. After the initial euphoria of the war's end it quickly became apparent that the men of Camp Sixteen were still prisoners and would remain so for the foreseeable future until arrangements could be made to get them to Europe again. Many of the prisoners, Germans and Italians alike, had received letters from home telling of the aftermath of the war and were less than willing to go back.

Erich paused at the door of the mess. No working party

199

was permitted to venture out into the forest in this kind of a storm. A bolt of lightning crashed into the forest only a few hundred yards away, and even through the noise of the storm Erich heard clearly the sound of splintering timber. He shivered for a moment and then, pulling the collar of his greatcoat high around his ears, sprinted down the slope to the hospital.

"Good morning, Doctor. Alice." The two smiled. "It is a terrible day out there."

"Good morning, Erich. We haven't had a storm like this one since the night of Günter's operation."

"*Ja*. I'd forgotten how wild it can be."

"Have you heard anything from him?"

"Günter? No." Erich shook his head. Günter, as an invalid, had been shipped back to Germany on the first transport, some eight months earlier. "From what the commander says, though, it is not likely that we will, either. Nothing back home is too efficient at the moment."

"I can imagine. It is certainly strange not having him around the camp."

So far, two shipments of German prisoners had been repatriated from Marinup. Already huts were being pulled down, and without the full compliment of men the camp seemed strangely deserted.

"Do you know when you are leaving yet?"

"No, sir. Another shipment is due to depart any day now, but nobody knows how many men or who they will be. It might not even happen for another month."

"Still, you will be looking forward to getting home, I imagine."

"Not really, sir." Erich and Alice made fleeting eye

contact. This was something they'd discussed many times in the last few months.

"No?"

"No. I cannot imagine that there is much left in Germany for me to return to."

"I know, Erich. I am sorry that I couldn't have a little more influence on your behalf, but you know how the military is. All prisoners are to be repatriated, forcibly if necessary."

"Perhaps I should escape?" Erich was only half joking. Looking at Alice a small part of Erich seriously considered trying. She rested her hand lightly on his shoulder. It was a tiny gesture but one that filled Erich with an unsettling combination of fear and affection.

"They caught the three that got away last month, you know?" So often nowadays she seemed to know exactly what he was thinking.

"Did they?"

Eric looked at her expectantly, eager for more information. The three Italians had bolted from a farming assignment and hadn't been seen since. It was widely suspected that they'd had the help of a couple of locals in their escape.

"They caught them trying to get a ride to the eastern states. A lorry driver picked them up near Southern Cross and took them to the police in Kalgoorlie."

Footsteps outside and the door slammed open, another draught of cold wind howling briefly through the warm room.

"Erich, I thought I would find you here." Stutt smiled. "Doctor, Alice." The commander offered a polite bow of acknowledgment to both the Australians, as Erich jumped to his feet.

"Good morning, sir."

"I have some news." Stutt was clearly excited. He spoke in German. "It's tomorrow. They've found extra berths on a transport out of Fremantle three days from now, one travelling to Europe to pick up the last of the Australian troops. They're clearing the rest of us."

"Us?"

"All the remaining Germans and most of the Italians."

"Tomorrow?"

"*Ja*. Wake-up call will be early, 0430, to give us enough time to get up to the city and be processed before leaving." Stutt paused, noticing the sudden droop in the young man's shoulders. His voice softened. "This is going to be difficult, but there is no other choice, you know that, Erich."

"Yes, sir."

"Good then. You will need to pack today. Leave any German military emblems you might have – badges or whatever. They are confiscating them all at the port."

"Yes, sir."

Stutt nodded a goodbye and left, clearly in a hurry to inform the others. Erich slumped into a chair.

"That was it, wasn't it?" Alice started towards him then stopped, fear in her face.

"*Ja*. It was."

"When?"

"Tomorrow." He looked up at her and her lip trembled. "Early in the morning."

The doctor's chair scraped the timber floorboards as he hauled himself slowly to his feet.

"So soon." He hesitated, about to speak further, but then clearly changed his mind. "I will leave you two alone for a

202

while, I think. I have paperwork to do in my hut, in any case."

Reaching into the cupboard behind his desk, he retrieved a small bundle and made his slow way towards the door, stopping only briefly by the chair where Erich still sat slumped.

"Erich."

"Yes, Doctor?"

"You will need to be brave, for both of you."

"*Ja*. Thank you, sir. Will I see you before I go?"

"I wouldn't allow it otherwise. I will be back later this afternoon."

As soon as the door closed behind the old man, Alice crossed silently to the pot-belly stove and stoked it up. It radiated hot warmth into the dimly lit building. Then, crossing to the door, she locked it. It clicked faintly in the silence.

"Alice …"

"Shhh." There was a strange look in the girl's eyes as she took Erich's hand and pulled him from the chair. One he'd never seen before. "Don't speak. Not yet. We'll talk later."

Erich let her lead him to the nearest cot.

In the late afternoon gloom the dim glow from the stove cast tiny, leaping red shadows onto the floor. On the bed the two lay entwined. After the initial hesitant awkwardness, both had fallen to each other with a desperate, frightened hunger. Erich had heard the other men talk about these things, had heard more than his share of bawdy army tales, but the long hours of the afternoon with Alice, with only the rain pounding on the tin roof, had been nothing like that. Nothing like he'd expected.

And afterwards, when they'd lain together, naked, quiet

203

and still, and she'd finished crying, he'd stroked her hair and whispered to her that he would be returning and that it would be all right, until she'd fallen into a gentle sleep. Then Erich had lain there, treasuring the warm softness of her body pressed sleeping against his own and had watched the fireshadow leaping on the timber floorboards, constrained behind the iron bars of the stove. And he'd felt a slight tingle in the fading scar tissue on his face and arms and he trembled at the thought of what might or might not be waiting for him in Germany.

"Are you awake?"

"Hmmm." She stirred against him and her eyes opened. For a moment Erich allowed himself to swim in the two dark pools of them. Then she was sitting up and shaking her head.

"I fell asleep!"

"You did."

"Erich, I'm so sorry."

"No." He kissed her. "No. You are beautiful when you sleep. I am glad I was able to share it."

"But it's your … our last day."

"Only for a little while. A few months."

Without further conversation the two climbed, albeit reluctantly, from the bed, both suddenly aware of their nakedness. They turned from each other and fumbled quickly at their clothes.

"Alice, are you all right?"

She smiled at him again, a kind of sad happiness behind the expression.

"I'm very fine."

"Good. I will need to go and pack."

"I know. I should see to grandfather."

"*Ja*. I will look in again later."

"All right."

At the door, Alice grabbed at his hand before he opened it.

"We might not get another chance." She kissed him then propelled him out side. "Go."

Erich tumbled into the storm-thrashed afternoon and ran for the shelter of the mess hall. There he turned to wave a final goodbye, but Alice had already retreated back into the warmth of the hospital.

PART THREE

1946–1947

5 July 1946, 4.30 am

During a break between rain showers, the night forest falls silent to the rumbling thump of diesel engines and the quiet murmur of men's voices. The foreign sounds echo through the gaps between the trees.

In the tray-backs of the trucks, men hunch, thickly wrapped and huddled together against the bitter cold, grey and anonymous. In the deep darkness of the verandah, Alice trembles and draws the lapels of her coat closer around her. One of the shapes is Erich. This she knows, but her grandfather has forbidden her to come out for the departure, thinking that this will make it easier for both of them. The shadows of the hut are as close to him as she can get undetected, and Erich might as well be gone already, lost among the shapeless forms climbing into the trucks.

The bustle and loading seem to take an eternity and then nothing happens for a while until finally, with a shout and a muffled cheer, the trucks lurch forward, wheels spinning in a brief battle for traction before crunching away across the gravel.

Alice watches the red tail light of the lead vehicle flash briefly as the driver taps the brakes. Are they stopping? Has there been some mistake?

No.

The firefly glimmer vanishes again and the trucks reach the point where the road disappears into the tree-line.

As they slip between the shadowy trunks, the forest seems to swallow them.

25 July 1946

Through the window of her tiny room Alice watches the rain falling. At this time of the year Perth is at its coldest, and though it is nothing like the bitter cold of the Marinup winter, here it seems somehow worse, somehow repressive. The low-hanging clouds sit on the sleepy city, almost embracing the buildings.

She can't sleep. Just like last night, and the night before.

Finally she rises from her bed, retrieves her dressing gown from the floor and slides out into the passageway.

Her parent's home, though bigger than the hut she shared with her grandfather at the camp, seems tiny and cramped. The floorboards in the passage creak slightly beneath the press of her feet but the sound is drowned in the soft grumble of rain on the tin roof.

Her father is asleep in the front room again, slumped in his armchair beside a wireless that hisses only night static into the room. The fire has gone out and he clutches a blanket beneath his chin, shivering in his sleep. For a while Alice stands in the doorway and watches him; the tiny tic and twitch of his closed eyes and the laboured rise of his breathing the only signs of life.

Is he really alive? she wonders.

This sleeping man isn't the same one who left them three years earlier. This man is a stranger who sleeps night after night sitting upright with the light on. This man barely speaks to her or her mother, except when something is wrong. This man has sadness in his eyes and in the way he walks and in the sound of his voice. It seems to pour out of him with every nuance and gesture.

Somewhere in the distance, lightning crashes.

Silently, Alice slips the latch on the front door and steps outside.

Perth is sleeping through another stormy July night. A little along the porch her father's lamp casts a dull yellow rectangle out through the front window and across the verandah into the garden, where her mother's rose plants whip in skeletal anguish. Soon it will be spring and they will bloom, but for the moment they stand naked, stripped by their winter pruning, the thorns and occasional leaves bare to the cold air.

A couple of steps down from the porch and Alice walks out onto the cracked concrete of the front path. The rain is driving now and she is getting wet, but she doesn't care. Her thoughts are somewhere else. Somewhere warm. Out in the endless blue tropical expanses of the Indian Ocean, under a sky peppered with stars, where a troop ship, a converted liner, steams its way through the humid night towards the Suez canal, through the Mediterranean Sea, and then to the ruins of Europe.

Where is he now? she wonders. *Is he thinking of me?*

Her bare feet splash in puddles as dark as blood as Alice walks along the pavement. Her hair is wet and lank now, sticking to her face in long strands. It was like this the night he left, she remembers, and the afternoon before.

When she closes her eyes Alice can remember what he felt like. She can recall without effort the sound of his voice, his accent, his Germanic expression – sometimes so lilting and at other times guttural.

But when she opens her eyes again there is only the rain and the night.

She walks automatically, along empty suburban streets and past silent rows of shops. The greengrocers and butchers are quiet, their painted wooden signs swinging wildly in the wind, their windows dark and empty.

It rains harder and harder, but still she walks, embracing the cold and the wet as she would a lover. Feeling the chill fingers of the storm weave through her hair, slide down her neck and trickle gently along her back.

Somewhere between minutes and hours later she looks up and finds herself standing in front of her parents' house again. Through the window, her father still sleeps in his chair, and the house is as silent as when she left it. The front gate swings wildly – she has forgotten to latch it again on her way out – and Alice steps through, securing it behind her.

The brown and cream tiled bathroom is cold as she steps out of her sodden pyjamas and towels herself dry, her skin blue-veined and goose-fleshed. For a moment she examines her face, her eyes, in the small mirror. Is there something different about them now? At certain angles, when she glimpses herself and looks away quickly, something new seems to hide behind her eyes, something older and more grown up.

The dry flannel of fresh pyjamas feels soft and warm

against her skin and she shivers slightly as her body begins to warm. There is a slight tingle in her breasts and she rubs at them subconsciously. The pyjamas are an old pair of her father's and she has to roll up the sleeves and cuffs to make them fit, but they are warm and comfortable and remind her of her father from before the war.

Silently, Alice makes her way back into the front room. Her father stirs slightly and murmurs something inaudible as she flicks off the wireless. Alice tucks the blanket more tightly around him, kisses him lightly on the top of his head, notices that his hair has begun to grey around the temples, turns off the light and creeps from the room.

Under her mattress is a notebook, leather covered, a gift from one of the sergeants at Marinup. Lately Alice has been writing in it. A diary of sorts. A place to confide to the world at large the things she can't find the strength to tell those closest to her. Alice slides it out and sits at the old writing desk beside her window.

The nib of the pen is old and the ink flows easily from it into the smooth, thick pages of the book. Alice writes. She writes to Erich and tells him about her father, and her mother, and the weather, and her grandfather. And for a few moments it is like he is there again, in the room with her, listening.

Finally, in her own bed again, Alice watches the rain falling until eventually she sleeps.

5 August 1946

Alice and her grandfather sit facing one another on opposite sides of the old wooden table in his kitchen.

Are you certain? she asks him.

213

Yes. He doesn't say anything more. He doesn't need to.

Now that he is back, she spends a lot of time at his house. It is warm and dark and filled with the smell of wood polish and hints of lavender. Her grandmother used to put lavender in all the drawers and in the linen cupboard, and even now, all these years later, pockets of it still linger and waft through the dusty air.

I'm sorry, her grandfather begins, but Alice manages a half smile and a nod.

Don't be.

Alice isn't. Now that her grandfather has confirmed it, she realises she already knew.

When will it show?

The old man shrugs. It could be early, it could be later. Some women manage to hide it all together until the very end. She won't be like that, he knows. *A couple of months at least,* he tells her.

She will have to tell her parents. Does she want her grandfather to do it for her?

No. Alice shakes her head, emphatic. This she will do herself.

Do they know about Erich?

Again, Alice shakes a negative response. Since her return to the city, her parents have been impossible to talk to, outside the pointless conversations of day-to-day life. Her mother is walking on eggshells again. At nights when Alice is lying awake she can hear her sobbing, alone in her room for hours on end. During the days she is quiet, withdrawn and world-weary. Her father has started looking for a job, but there's nothing around for a returned soldier in his forties. There's little around for anyone in Perth at the moment.

On the stove the kettle is bubbling quietly. The fire flickers through the narrow grate and fills the dim kitchen with warmth and the smell of wood smoke.

Another cup of tea?

Yes.

Grandfather makes the tea strong and stewed, like he always does. Alice has to put a lot of milk in hers. The warmth of the mug tingles into the palms of her hands and she inhales the sweet, fragrant aroma. Her grandfather is talking to her.

Just the once, she tells him. *On that last afternoon.*

For a long time the old man says nothing and the silence fills the space between them like a comfortable blanket. *It won't be easy, you know*, he tells her. Alice nods.

Walking home again, Alice cuts through a park. Two small children – a boy and a girl – play on a pair of old wooden swings while their mother watches from a nearby bench. She is young and would be pretty except for a weariness which hangs about her shoulders. The children are having a competition to see who can swing the highest. The mother smiles at Alice as she walks past.

There is a sense of unreality about it all. The sky is grey, but there is no rain, only a heavy curtain of clouds which hangs overhead, muting the sunlight, hiding the blue. As she walks, Alice holds her hands on her belly for a few moments, trying to feel the life in there.

All she feels is her own breathing.

10 August 1946

This bedroom used to be her mother's when she was a girl. Then it was her grandmother's sewing room. Now it is filled with boxes. Alice clutches the eiderdown tightly around herself and allows the faint scent of lavender to fill her.

It is early to be in bed, but tonight, for some reason, Alice feels tired.

When she was a child she would stay here at least once a week with her grandparents while her own parents went out. Her grandmother would tuck her in, just like this, every night. Alice remembers those dry lips kissing her goodnight, just lightly brushing against her hair. She remembers the joy of burrowing deep under the covers, swimming in lavender-scented warmth.

She hopes that one day her child will be able to burrow under quilts like that.

A few yards away, in the main room, her grandfather is reading. It is nice to know that he is out there. It's like being back in the camp again, except this time Erich is much more than just a few minutes walk away. At night in the camp they were separated by barbed wire and searchlights. Here they are held apart by oceans. She still writes in her journal most days. On those pages she pours out the things that would otherwise circle in her mind, building pressure like an oncoming storm. Most often she writes to Erich, but sometimes she writes to herself and sometimes to the world.

She hears familiar voices in the main room. Her parents.

Her first instinct is to dive deeper under the eiderdown, to cover her head and shut out the gentle whispering beyond the door. She knows it won't work, though. No matter how deep she buries herself, she won't be able to shut out the voices from inside her head.

After the warmth beneath the quilt the room seems cold and Alice trembles as she pulls her threadbare old dressing gown around her shoulders. At the door she hesitates. It has been three days since she has seen or spoken to her parents. Three days since telling them about Erich and her, and the baby growing inside her. Three days since her father struck her.

Even now she can feel his slap stinging her cheek. Drawing a deep breath, Alice opens the bedroom door.

They are sitting in the parlour at the front of the house. Her parents and grandfather. The fire is banked and an old spirit lamp burns on the sideboard. As Alice enters they all stop speaking and look up at her. Her parents sit beside one another on the lounge. It is the closest Alice has seen them to each other since she returned to Perth. Her mother has been crying, her father's expression is unreadable. The only thing Alice can see in his face is the usual sadness. No lighter or heavier than it was the last time they spoke.

Did we wake you? There is concern in her grandfather's voice.

No.

Alice ... her mother begins, but stops after that one word. For a long time nobody says anything. Four people in a room with pain holding them apart.

We'd like it if you came home. Her father's voice is flat, neither love nor hate behind the words.

I don't want to.

Alice, says her grandfather, *you should think about it.*

She is startled. She hadn't expected him to be on their side. Then she looks at him and realises that he isn't. The old man is regarding her with nothing but concern as he runs his fingers across his scalp, through his thin white hair.

They love you, Alice.

217

Do you? She turns to them.

How can you even ask that? Her mother starts to cry again. But she knows, she remembers, the things that were said the other afternoon. Before the slap. She knows she used words like *disgrace* and *shame* and talked about convents and *'going east for a while'*. As far as Alice is concerned, these aren't words of love.

The silence fills the room again, thick and engulfing. Alice stands in the doorway. Her parents look at the floor.

Her father stands suddenly and steps towards her. For a moment Alice thinks he is going to grab her, shake her or strike her again. But he doesn't. When he lifts his gaze she looks into his eyes and sees something new there.

Alice ... He hesitates then reaches for her hand. *I'm so sorry.*

Something seems to shift deep in the pit of Alice's stomach.

Excuse me ... I ... She runs from the room, out to the front garden, and vomits into a flowerbed.

17 August 1946

Alice sits in the park and writes. It is a warm afternoon for late winter, but even so she is bundled up against the cold wind which blows up from the south. On her lap the leather-bound journal is filling with her thoughts and longings, and high in the air above, the occasional wispy, white cloud goes scudding past.

Birds sing.

As she writes, a part of Alice's mind detaches itself and simply watches the black ink spidering across the pages. This afternoon she is not writing to Erich but to her baby. She chooses the words she writes carefully.

Voices float down the path and she looks up to see a mother and two children walking towards her. It is the same family that was here two weeks ago on the afternoon she found out. The little boy is running ahead, the girl skipping beside her mother, holding her hand. When they reach the swings, she drops the hand and runs off with her brother.

The mother stands and watches them, then wanders across to the bench and sits beside Alice. There is tiredness in the way she lowers herself onto the hard wooden slats.

Hello, she says, and offers Alice a brief smile.

Hello.

Alice starts to write again, but the sound of laughter is distracting and after a while she gives up and watches the children. The boy is pushing while his sister swings, trying to make her go higher and higher. The little girl is getting scared and tells him to stop, but he doesn't. Finally she screams, her thin voice wailing through the warm afternoon, and the woman beside Alice calls out sharply, *That will do, Harry.*

The boy stops, chastened, and the little girl tries to get off the swing, but she is scared and the swing is moving too quickly and as her feet hit the sand they slip and she pitches forward onto the ground.

Her brother is beside her immediately and Alice can hear him trying to comfort her as she sobs and gets to her feet, stumbling through tears towards her mother, who is rushing over.

You're all right, he tells her again and again, and Alice can hear the desperation behind his words. He wants them to be

219

true. He wants to believe his little sister is fine. It's a selfish sympathy, but Alice feels more sorry for the boy than his sister.

The girl has grazes on her knees and the heels of her hands and a grass stain on her pinafore. She is more upset about this last indignity than about her injuries.

Calm down, Elizabeth, her mother soothes her. *We'll go home and wash it out.*

With the little girl now gathered onto her hip, the mother takes Harry's arm with her free hand and leads him away, back up the path. She throws a last, weary smile – almost apologetic – at Alice as they pass.

19 August 1946

In the evenings the three of them sit together in the front room and listen to the wireless. Her father prefers to listen to music, preferably classical, but tonight a visiting professor is talking about the war.

Usually, whenever the war is mentioned her father reaches out immediately and fiddles with the tuning dial, swinging the needle across the frequencies until he finds something else, anything else, to listen to. Tonight, however, he doesn't.

The professor is British and is visiting Perth on his way to Melbourne to lecture at the university there. His accent is thick and plummy and he is talking about the Germans and the rumours that have been circulating. He talks about death camps and propaganda and makes it sound as though all Germans are little better than animals. Alice wants to scream at him, to shout into the radio set and tell him about people like Erich and Günter and Commander Stutt, tell him about

220

their families and how they are just men like him. She doesn't though.

The voice is scratchy and distant, but each time the professor makes a point, Alice's father nods his head and makes noises of agreement.

The German people as a whole find it difficult to stand up against the group instinct, says the radio. *Hitler was able to use this aspect of his people's mindset to manipulate them for his own depraved ends …*

Alice's father mutters, *Exactly*!

Unconsciously, Alice's hands creep to her belly and rest there, protectively. Does her child have the 'German mindset'? She knows it doesn't. She knows the professor is wrong.

She says nothing.

Finally, the interviewer thanks the professor and their voices are replaced by music. A brass band plays a popular dance tune from the days of the war.

That was interesting, says her father.

It was wrong. Alice walks from the room.

Later, she lies in her bed in the dark staring out the window. Her bedroom door creaks. She feigns sleep, doesn't turn her head to see whose footsteps are padding across the room. Her mattress sinks slightly and her mother is perched on the edge of her bed. She doesn't say anything. She knows Alice is awake. She runs her hand over Alice's hair, stroking it gently, and her fingers are warm. Then she rests her hand lightly on her daughter's belly and Alice can feel the distant pulse of her mother's heart beating through her fingers.

For a long time mother and daughter sit like that, and the soft warmth of her mother's touch seems to creep through

Alice's skin, into her womb, calming and soothing, and Alice slips off to sleep. Finally her mother leans down and brushes her lips against her daughter's forehead. Then she leaves quietly.

Alice wakes in the night and can hear her mother crying through the wall.

2 September 1946

Her grandfather is asleep in his chair in front of the fire when she arrives. On his lap is the framed photo of his son, Paul, in his uniform. She doesn't want to wake him, so Alice tiptoes into the kitchen, stokes the fire in the stove and puts the kettle on.

Is that you, dear?

Yes, grandad. I'm making tea.

Lovely.

He walks in and sits at the kitchen table and Alice watches him. He is looking older, she thinks. Each step seems more of an effort, and even sitting takes time.

How has your day been? He always asks her this. *Fine*, she always answers. She considers telling him the news – the neighbourhood women have somehow found out about her 'condition' – but she decides against it.

Sipping his tea, he makes appreciative noises and, when their cups are empty, gets up as slowly as he sat. *All right, let's take a look at you.*

His battered old medical bag is in his bedroom. He takes her pulse, timing it with a small stopwatch, then her temperature, then he feels her belly. His touch is soft, his hands cool.

You will need to see someone else from now on, he tells her. *A specialist.*

She protests, but the old man shakes his head. *I'm too old. I haven't done a pregnancy in years.* He gives her a name, writing it in his precise copperplate hand on a piece of card and she promises to make an appointment tomorrow.

They sit again at the kitchen table, opposite one another.

Do you still think about him? he asks.

All the time, she answers.

And she does. But recently it's been different. She doesn't tell the old man this, though. Lately Alice has found herself wondering about Erich, not with the longing, not with the desperate hunger that she felt when he first left, but with a strange sort of detachment, treating his absence and her feelings for him like a puzzle. Most nights now she writes about this in her journal, trying to sort out what she feels.

Of course, there has been no word. Not yet. She knows it could be months. And so she waits.

On the way home she stops in the park. Usually, at this time of the day, the mother and her children (what were their names again?) are having their afternoon play. Not today, however, and after a few minutes Alice continues on home. Turning the corner at the end of her street, she sees Mrs McKaigh in her front yard, weeding.

Good afternoon. Alice smiles. The woman doesn't reply. She offers nothing more than a reluctant grunt, before pointedly returning to her roses.

It's been like that for a week now. And Alice knows she is the main topic of discussion down at the markets each morning. She knows the question they are all asking each other. *Who's the father?* Nobody has been brave enough to ask her, though. Not yet.

Even when they do, she won't tell them.

Let them wonder.

3 September 1946

It's a perfect day. Sunlight trickles between the branches of the weeping willow beside the playground. A magpie perches on a telegraph pole at the edge of the park and warbles at the sun. The air is warm, filled with the beginning of spring. Harry and Elizabeth and two other children chase each other around the playground while their mothers stand and gossip nearby.

Alice sits on the bench.

In her journal on her lap she is making a list.

Things she doesn't know about Erich.

His mother's name. His sister's date of birth. His shoe size. The names of his grandparents.

The children are playing some kind of tag game. Elizabeth is 'it' but the other three children are too big and fast for her and she can't catch any of them. She is starting to get frustrated when her older brother, Harry, pretends to trip and fall and his sister is on him in seconds, the two of them giggling.

The size of his home. The names of his friends from school. His favourite subjects. His favourite book.

Harry and Elizabeth. Harry and Lizzie. In a few minutes, as usual, their mother will gather them up, wrap their coats around them again, and walk them home. What is their house like? Alice wonders. Is it a lovely little semi-detached cottage, where their father will be home from work and waiting for them? Their father …

What he looks like out of uniform. What sort of music he listens to. Whether or not he has had any other sweethearts.

Their father. These two lovely children would have a father, of course. He'd be young and handsome, and would probably read to them or play with them every night. And whenever they needed him, for a hug or a story, he'd be right there for them. Right there always.

Tears escape as she watches the children playing. Her list, abandoned now, sits on her lap.

Are you all right?

The children's mother is standing beside her, concern written across her face.

Oh. Yes … I'm sorry, I…

Alice fishes in a pocket for a hanky, can't find one, rubs ineffectually at her eyes.

Here, use mine. A fresh, crisp square of linen is pressed into her hand. The young mother sits beside her.

Thank you. I'm okay, really. I don't usually … Alice stops. Breathes. Tries to get herself back under control. *You have a lovely family.*

Thank you. The woman offers a brief smile and glances quickly at her two children, who are tickling one another on the grass. *They keep my hands full.*

I can imagine.

The magpie sings into the silence.

I'm Anne.

Alice. Alice Andrews.

The two women shake hands.

Are you sure you're all right?

225

Yes. I am now. It is good to talk to someone. Someone new. Someone outside her family. *It's just that …* Alice stops.

That's fine. You don't have to talk about it.

Alice says nothing for a few moments. Then, *I'm pregnant. And I was making a list …*

She stops again and the other woman says nothing. After a moment or two, though, she places a hand on the girl's arm. It feels warm and slightly rough, but the moment of human contact, of reassurance, is enough.

The father?

In Europe somewhere. I don't know. I miss him.

I know. I miss my husband, too.

He's gone?

Killed. In Africa.

Oh.

The little girl disengages herself from her brother and runs, still giggling, across to the bench. *Mummy, can we stay longer? Please?*

Just a little while. Elizabeth, this is Miss Andrews.

Hello.

Hello, Elizabeth.

For a long time the two women sit, arm in arm, watching the children.

25 September 1946

In her parent's bedroom there is a full-length mirror, the only one in the house. Alice stands before it, naked.

It is afternoon. Her father is job-hunting and her mother at the shops. The house is silent. Alice turns this way and that, studying her reflection closely, looking at her body.

It is changing.

226

Her breasts seem a little fuller already. They feel oddly heavy and pendulous even though they look much the same as always. She stands side-on and runs her hands over her stomach. It might be her imagination, but she thinks there might be a lump, or at least the beginnings of one.

She still throws up in the mornings, but not so much any more.

Alice slips back into her clothes and studies her face closely. It seems more lined than it used to. There are dark bags beneath her eyes – she hasn't been sleeping well. She looks older, she thinks.

In the front room she sits and opens her journal. She hasn't written in it since that day in the park. The last entry is her list. She reads it again and is half embarrassed by it.

She thinks about Anne.

Most afternoons now they meet at the park and talk while her children are playing. Alice sometimes feels that she knows more about Anne's husband than she does about Erich. She knows his name was Jim. She knows they were married only three years before he went off to war. She knows he never laid eyes on his daughter, and that his son was too young to remember him properly. She has seen his photograph. She knows he had light hair and a strong chin. In his army uniform he reminded her a little of Erich. She knows he liked roast potatoes.

All she has told Anne about Erich is his name. Nothing else, and Anne hasn't asked for any more. Alice is scared that she will.

She is scared she'll have to lie to her friend.

29 September 1946

Alice? The voice behind her is unfamiliar. Alice stops and turns.

I thought it was you. It's me … Victoria.

Victoria. Vicki. Alice remembers her from primary school. They sat beside each other for a year. The boys used to dip her blonde pigtails in the ink wells. *Victoria …* Alice's voice sounds strange, even to her. *How are you?*

I haven't seen you in years. Victoria is one of those people who don't seem to hear anything anyone else says. *How have you been? What are you doing now?*

Nothing really.

I'm working in the city, in a dress shop. It's wonderful work. Mr Williams, who owns the shop, says that I have a real eye for it. And of course it's nice to have a little bit of spending money for dances and things like that …

Alice just nods.

Victoria is engaged. She shows Alice the ring proudly. It has a tiny diamond, little more than a chip of glimmering rock, set between two small rubies.

Of course it's not very big, but it was all that Allen could afford on his Army pension and everything. He's got a job now, though, driving timber trucks, so we're planning a lovely wedding. But I'm talking all about myself. What about you? Is there a young man in your life?

Unconsciously, Alice's hand brushes lightly across her belly, as though trying to shield it from her words.

No. Nobody.

That's sad. Victoria touches her arm. *I know, there's a dance this Friday night, in at the Empire. Allen and I are going – why don't you come with us? It would be great fun, and I could intro-*

duce you to some of Allen's soldier friends. They're lovely blokes. What do you think?

Thank you, but no. Alice shakes her head. *Not this week.*

Oh. The other woman seems taken aback by her refusal. *Well, perhaps another time, then?*

Perhaps. They both know Alice is lying.

Anyway, I must go. Have to get home. It's been good catching up with you, Alice. We must do this properly some time. Perhaps over a cup of tea?

That would be nice.

Alice watches Victoria walk away up the pavement towards the tram stop. Should that have been me? she wonders. Young, pretty, engaged, working in a dress shop and going to dances on the weekends? Perhaps if she'd never gone out to Marinup ...

Shaking her head, Alice continues on towards the park.

Anne and the kids are already there by the time she arrives.

Hi. Alice plonks herself down on the bench. She feels bloated and heavy.

Hi. How are you feeling?

Not too good. She pauses for a moment and then tells Anne about the meeting and conversation with Victoria. When she finishes, the other woman looks at her.

Why didn't you at least tell her about Erich?

In the silence that follows, the sounds of the afternoon, the children playing, the birds calling, all seem to become muted and distant. Alice knows she needs to tell her. Wants to tell her.

I haven't even told you about Erich. Not properly.

I know. Anne nods. She isn't looking at Alice now, but is

staring straight ahead, out to the park, watching her children. *I supposed that you would when you were ready.*

Alice sneaks a quick glance at the woman sitting beside her. The lines on Anne's face seem to echo the ones etching themselves into her own skin.

He wasn't Australian. He was … German. Now Alice turns, and watches the other woman's reaction closely. *He was a prisoner here. In the camp down in Marinup. I lived there with my grandfather during the war.*

Where was he captured? Anne's face is blank. Unreadable. There have been stories in the newspaper about German immigrants being beaten by gangs of returned soldiers. Germans aren't popular in Perth at the moment.

Africa. Alice pauses. *Annie … I wanted to tell you all about him. I really did. I just … didn't know how.*

Anne sits perfectly still, says nothing, watches her children. Finally, she speaks.

So then, she says, *tell me about him.*

And Alice does. She talks about how they met. About life in the camp. About the hospital. She tells Anne the little she knows about Erich's family, how his father died, how Erich reacted. Then she talks about the other prisoners, about Günter and Stutt, and about the last afternoon she and Erich spent together. She describes how she felt that night, hiding in the shadows of the verandah in the rain, watching the trucks vanish into the darkness. She tells Anne how every day she rushes out to check the mail, even though she knows it is far too soon for him to have written. She tells Anne everything and for a long time Anne says nothing, her gaze still locked on her children.

Annie? There is uncertainty in Alice's voice. *Is everything all right? Are we all right?*

You know something, Alice? Anne turns and looks at the girl properly and there is something in her eyes, not anger, not tears, something indescribable. *One day our kids are going to play together on those swings over there, and if I've got anything to do with it, then none of them, not yours or mine, or anyone else's for that matter, is going to give a bugger about where their fathers came from.* And she links her arm through that of the younger woman and leans her weight into Alice's shoulder. *Thanks for telling me.*

28 October 1946

The doctor's hands are cool from the soaping he gave them just before the examination. For a few moments he presses on her belly.

And who is the father? he asks.

Alice tells him. He doesn't react.

Everything here seems fine. Are you drinking plenty of water?

He concludes their appointment by asking Alice to pass on his regards to her grandfather and telling her to come back in four weeks' time for another check.

Walking to the train station, Alice feels large and unwieldy among the lunchtime crowds. The city is so busy and as she makes her way across Hay Street a tram rattles past, almost knocking her off balance. She wanders through Aherns, stopping a couple of times to look at things she can't afford. In Murray Street a group of schoolgirls walk past in twos, led by a nun. Their uniforms are crisp and starched and they giggle to one another. Alice feels as though they are giggling at her.

231

Since her belly started to show, even though it is still just a tiny bump, she feels self-conscious and ungainly and, apart from her afternoon walks down to the park to see Anne and the kids, she has stopped going out unless she absolutely has to. At the shops the other neighbourhood women raise eyebrows at one another whenever she enters and she can feel their speculation on her back as she does her shopping.

Now she has to come into town to see the specialist, and while part of her savours the anonymity of the crowds she still feels too big and obvious to be properly comfortable. In Forrest Street she rests for a moment on a bench in front of the GPO. She knows that her father is inside somewhere, sorting mail. His new job.

The early afternoon sun makes her hot, sweaty and uncomfortable. Her dresses are all becoming too tight and her mother is already making her a new, bigger, looser wardrobe.

Alice?

It's Victoria. She's wearing a pretty floral skirt and a crisp white blouse. She looks fresh and clean. There are two other women with her, both about the same age, both similarly dressed.

Victoria, hello.

Imagine meeting again so soon. I was telling Allen about you just the other week. Her eyes drop to the small lump in Alice's lap. *Oh. You're pregnant. I thought* ... Victoria turns red. *Anyway, we're on our break and we must keep moving, mustn't we, girls* ...

There are mumbled goodbyes and Alice watches the three women cross the road and disappear into the front doors of Boans. She feels so much older than all of them.

232

30 October 1946

Erich is back. He stands in the doorway of her home, in his uniform, clutching his hat. Alice tries to rise to greet him, but the weight of her belly is too much for her, and she can't rise from the chair. *Alice.* His voice is exactly the same as she remembers it. Accented. Formal. Like he is forcing his words through some kind of barrier. *I cannot stay, I am afraid. I need to get back home. Back to my wife. My ship is leaving soon and I must go now. Goodbye.*

Wait! she calls, but the doorway is empty. She struggles to get up but the weight holding her down seems to grow heavier and heavier, pushing her into the chair until the hard wood of the backrest is digging into her shoulders and the edge of the seat into the back of her knees. *Erich!* she calls, but the shout is futile and echoes through the empty house.

Alice? Anne is there beside her. *Alice, get up. Go after him.* But she can't. The baby in her belly is too heavy, and Alice kicks futilely against the floorboards. *Alice, he's going …*

She wakes to find late afternoon sunlight warming her face. Her mother is in the kitchen, the sounds and smells of her cooking wafting through the house. Alice rises and walks towards the noise.

Are you all right, darling? Her mother looks up from her kneading, noting the sheen of sweat beading her daughter's forehead.

Yes. Just had a bad dream.

At the tank in the back yard, Alice sluices water onto her face. It tastes of tin and cold. Birds are playing in the leaves of the whitegums that shade the yard and Alice lowers herself onto the back step, watching them. After a few moments her mother comes out and sits beside her. The flyscreen door bangs behind them. *Anne and the kids came by earlier,* she says. *They didn't want to wake you, though. I like her, Alice.*

Me too, Mum.

Lately her mother has been a lot better. Since her father found work at the post office, since he stopped being around so much of the day, she has seemed less nervous, less tired all the time. He's changing too, Alice thinks. He still sleeps in the chair in the front room, but more often than not he turns out the light and the radio before he nods off.

I think it will all be fine, darling. Her mother wipes floury hands on her apron. *The more I think about it, the more convinced I am. Your grandfather is too.*

I know.

In the house behind them the front door slams and her father's voice echoes up the hallway.

Out here, dear. On the back steps. How was your day?

Her father's day was fine. So was her mother's.

Her mother goes back inside and Alice watches the evening sunlight playing upon the white trunks of the eucalypts. The trees seem to glow an iridescent pink against the darkening, purple sky. A few pink and grey galahs flit past, crying to the sunset and reminding her a little of the way the black cockatoos used to haunt the camp in Marinup.

She feels lost. She has a sense of marking time somehow and going nowhere. When she writes in her journal at nights, she is finding that she has less and less to say. As though her body and mind have somehow slipped away from her, out of her control. The days and nights crawl past, and Alice feels more and more detached from reality.

She knows she is having a baby, that there is a new life

234

growing inside her, but somehow it doesn't seem quite real. She keeps expecting to wake up and find that her life is as it was before.

12 November 1946

The daily walk out to the letterbox has ceased to hold any anticipation. It has been so long with no word from Europe that it is easier to avoid the disappointment of silence by not expecting anything else. Now Alice goes out as she does every day, more from habit than for any other reason.

The card is in a white envelope, slightly yellowed and stained at the edges. The handwriting is unfamiliar, but the name and address on the front are hers. For a few long moments she doesn't register that this is what she has been waiting for, then she tears the envelope open, then and there, not even waiting to get back inside.

I am fine. I love you.

The first six words make Alice's mouth dry and her bladder loosen so that she has to dash inside to the lavatory. *The joys of pregnancy*, she thinks wryly, but she is smiling all the same.

His family home is gone. Bombed. His mother and sister also missing. No sign or word from either. He has found lodging with an old school friend and will write properly soon.

He is fine. He still loves her.

She has an address.

Still smiling, Alice hurries to her writing table and starts a letter.

25 November 1946

The days are getting hot now and in the afternoons Alice usually rests in an easy chair on the back porch, which picks up the sea breeze. She is asleep when her grandfather arrives and he wakes her with a light kiss on her head. His lips are dry, like old leaves.

How are you feeling? Automatically he rests a cool hand on her forehead, feeling her temperature.

Fine. Fat.

You're only going to get bigger, for the next little while, at least.

I know.

It's a scary thought. Already her back aches if she stands too long, and it's difficult to get comfortable at night.

You have some visitors. Her grandfather is smiling, and for the first time Alice notices that something is different about him this afternoon. More animated. There are voices inside the house.

Visitors?

Come along. The old man helps her up, takes her arm and leads her through the flyscreen door, up the passage and into the front room.

The first person she sees is a young woman with dark, olive skin and long straight black hair. She is cradling a little baby, a girl, in her arms. Alice doesn't recognise her, but she knows the man standing by her side.

Günter!

Alice flings herself at the grinning man and throws her arms around him, nearly knocking him off balance.

Oops! He laughs. *Must being careful … my leg is … wood.* His English is worse than ever, rusty from lack of practice. Still, he stumbles through the introductions: *My wife, Francesca. Italian. Daughter ... Claire.*

Alice laughs. *Claire isn't a German name!* Günter smiles back. *She will not being German child. Being Australian!* There is pride behind his words.

Questions flood out. How did they get here? When did they arrive? When was the baby born? What is it like in Germany now? Did they see Erich at all? And Günter struggles through the barrier of language. Occasionally he has to stop and speak to Francesca in German or Italian, but slowly, with a lot of pausing and hand signals, he manages to provide answers.

On the steps of the back porch, with the cool breeze curling around them, he relates how he and Francesca left Europe again almost as soon as he arrived there. He tries to describe the destruction, the suffering, but words desert him, and all he can do is shake his head and make tiny, hopeless gestures.

They haven't seen Erich. They probably passed in mid-ocean.

And, Alice ... Günter stops, searches for the right word, then gives up and simply reaches across and pats her lightly on the belly, the question in his eyes.

Yes, Erich, she tells him and he laughs, the big, full, loud laugh she remembers so well. *But he doesn't know yet.*

It will be a surprise! The idea seems to delight him and he translates the news to his wife, who also laughs.

The afternoon winds on and cools into evening, and they drink tea and talk. Her grandfather sits in the easy chair and eventually nods off. Her mother arrives home from shopping and is introduced. Günter startles her with a massive bear hug, and when she extricates herself she disappears inside to find food for everyone.

Where will you stay? Alice asks. Günter gestures at the sleeping doctor. *Your grandfather is ... agreeing ... to ... (what is the word?) ... sponsor? We stay with him for now, until find house. Become Australians.*

Alice looks at the old man. Did he know about this before today and not tell her? He is smiling in his sleep.

The front door bangs and her father's voice echoes through the house. Alice listens as her mother rushes down the passage. There is a whispered conversation. An explanation. Preparation.

When her father comes out onto the back porch, he is standing stiff and erect. It is a military stance. After so long watching him stooped and sad it is strange to see him this way.

There is a long moment of silence. Günter rises ponderously to his feet, scraping his false leg under him. Even with his missing leg, he seems to tower over her dad.

Dad, this is Günter and his wife Francesca, and their baby, Claire.

They look into one another's eyes. Ex-soldiers. Ex-enemies.

How do you do? Günter offers a large hand and for a moment it hangs there and Alice thinks her father is going to refuse it, but then he returns the handshake.

Well. And yourself?

Good.

The two men regard each other a moment longer. Then her father asks, *Where did you fight?*

Italy. Then to Africa. Then to Australia for camping trip!

238

Alice's father laughs at that and the tension seems to slip out of the evening. They talk for a few more moments before he excuses himself to change out of his work clothes.

Sitting on the stairs again, Günter says something in German to his wife and the two of them smile.

What did you tell her?

It will be all right. Here. Australia.

Did you think it might not be?

Günter shrugs.

Soon, the baby is tired and needs feeding and sleep, and her grandfather and the new arrivals have to leave. Alice and her parents walk out to the front porch with them.

Thank you, Günter says at the gate.

For what?

For your welcome. He is looking at her father, who nods.

26 November 1946

There was a story in the paper this morning. An Italian market gardener was badly beaten in a pub the night before. He and his family have lived in Australia for thirty years. Alice shows it to Anne.

Günter will be all right, though, Alice says. *He's … different.*

I hope so.

They decide to give Francesca English lessons.

Anne asks if there has been any more news from Erich. Alice goes quiet for a moment before she fishes out the letter. It arrived in that morning's post and was the first since the card. This is a proper letter, though. Three pages of bad news.

Five thousand people executed at the same time as his father: families, children, friends of the conspirators. Five thousand. Too many people to imagine at once. The two women sit silently.

He is certain that his mother and sister are dead.

So will he be back soon?

I don't know. He needs to search first. He has to be certain.

But what about you?

He knows I'm alive.

Harry runs across. He wants an ice-cream on the way home. *We'll see*, his mother tells him. *Where will he look?*

I don't know. He wrote something about a camp, but I couldn't understand it.

Has she told him about the baby yet?

Yes. I wrote straightaway. It'll be months before I get a reply, though.

Suddenly the distance between them seems too great and Alice finds herself starting to get teary. This hasn't happened for a while, and she wipes at her eyes, embarrassed in front of her friend. *I'm sorry ...* she begins.

Don't be, says Anne. *It's how we met, remember?*

They both laugh at that.

Her grandfather is waiting at her place when she gets home. *Is it moving yet?* He nods at her lump.

I don't think so, not yet.

The two of them talk about Günter and Frannie. The old man is worried. He too read the story in the paper this morning and is afraid for them. To distract him, Alice tells him the news from Erich, and this time it isn't so hard to talk about.

That night, for the first time in weeks, Alice digs her journal out from under the bed and begins to write. She writes about Günter and Francesca and then Erich. She writes her loneliness and frustration, her fear and anger, her love, her hope. She spills it all out onto the page in black ink and when she is done it reads like a prayer.

13 December 1946

She is beginning to dread the letterbox. She recognises his handwriting now, and it seems that each little white envelope brings nothing but bad news.

His sister is alive.

Alice knows she should be happy. But she isn't.

His sister has tuberculosis. She might be curable. But it will be months, perhaps even years, until she can travel.

She is all he has left of his old life. Of his family.

And Alice knows she can't ask Erich to leave Europe. Not now.

In the afternoon Anne brings the kids around and they play in the back yard while Alice has another cry on her friend's shoulder. She is feeling pathetic at the moment. But it is so hot and she feels so bloated, and Erich is so far away.

You can't be jealous of her, sweetie. You just can't afford to let yourself. Anne is right, of course, Alice knows.

She drinks her tea, calms down a little and by the time her mother arrives home she has got herself together enough to relate the day's news. Her mother goes very quiet.

That night the baby moves, properly, for the first time. Not just a little kick or a poke, but it seems to almost turn a somersault inside her. It leaves Alice gasping with a strange combination of joy and nausea, and she lies on her side on her bed, hands resting on her belly, and she talks to her child.

In the cool, late evening she tells the creature growing inside her all about its father, and grandfather, and great-grandfather. She talks about Marinup. About the war. About the Germany that Erich has described for her in his letters.

She tells her stories to her child in the darkness.

20 December 1946

The car is a Ford, an old Model T, and Frannie is driving. It bumps and jolts across the Subiaco tram lines and Alice has to cling to the leather handle attached to the door to steady herself. The rear seat is heavily sprung and cushioned, so it isn't too uncomfortable. She laughs.

Günter refuses to tell her where he borrowed the car from. Whenever she asks, he just winks and taps the side of his nose.

People are watching them from the sidewalks.

How does she know how to drive?

Günter explains that Francesca drove a munitions truck during the war. *So this is … how do you say it? Easy driving for her. No chance of you exploding.* He grins at her over the back of his seat and Alice can't help but laugh.

Not for a few months yet, anyway.

Cottesloe beach shimmers in the heat, the sun gleaming off white sand. The sea breeze is not yet in so the water is calm and the beach busy with children enjoying their summer holiday, looking forward to Christmas and playing in the shallows under the watchful eyes of mothers. Beach umbrellas dot the shoreline, their bright colours splashing vibrantly against the sand.

Her bathing suit is far too tight. She gathers the clasp together behind her neck and has to breathe in to make it

242

fasten. She feels like one of those barrage balloons they used to show on the war documentaries, or perhaps a whale.

With a towel gathered around her waist, she and Frannie step out from the change room and meet Günter at the bottom of the steps. The sand burns underfoot and the three of them hop across laughing until they are close enough to throw their towels down and stand on them. Günter has to plonk himself down and unstrap the leather bindings which hold his leg in place. *Now we swim, yes?* Without waiting for an answer, he leaps down the sand in giant hops and plunges into the water.

Frannie is more hesitant. With Claire clutched protectively to her chest, she follows her husband down into the shallows and stops when she is only ankle deep.

Come on! He splashes her and teases in German, and she giggles and steps in a little deeper.

Alice is aware of people's eyes on her as she drops her own towel and walks to the water's edge. She can feel the judgment in their gazes. She can feel the other mothers sitting under their umbrellas and radiating disapproval at her. She knows she doesn't look respectable, swimming at a family beach in her condition. Especially with Germans.

Once she is in the water, she stops caring.

The Indian Ocean is cold, icy after the baking, radiated heat of the beach. It wraps itself around her body and lifts the weight from her belly and the ache from her back. She slowly flops forward, gasping as the cold water rushes over her breasts and head. She passes through the mirror-surface of the ocean and into the world underneath.

Underwater, the sounds of the day vanish and Alice allows herself to float there, suspended, enjoying the coldness and the muted half-light and the lack of gravity pulling on her. She holds her breath until it bursts out of her and she has to push herself up from the sandy bottom into the daylight.

Slowly, luxuriantly, Alice breast-strokes out towards the shark net pylon a little way off shore. Behind her, Günter has splashed Francesca again, and she is squealing at him. Neither of them are strong swimmers, but Günter is determined that Claire will grow up used to the water. *A real Australian water-baby*, he says.

Halfway to the pylon, Alice stops, rolls onto her back and floats there, looking up into the blue vault of the sky. Like the beach, it seems to shimmer and sparkle in the summer heat. The moment stretches on and on and she lets herself imagine Erich here with her, instead of Günter and Frannie. They would swim out together and touch the concrete shark net pylon.

She treads water again and looks in towards the beach. Günter has finally persuaded Francesca to come deeper and the two of them are standing together, water up to their chests now, holding their little girl between them and playing with her. Alice can hear Claire's baby giggles as the water splashes around her.

Then Günter hands the baby back to Frannie and swims out towards her. His dog paddle is laboured, awkward and inefficient, but he presses on until Alice, fearing he won't make the distance and that she'll have to rescue him, strokes back and meets him halfway.

Water is good, yes?

Lovely, Günter. Thank you so much for organising this.

Is no problem. He offers a wink. *Good for me, too. One leg not important in the ocean.* At that, he tries to tread water and discovers that having one leg can make a difference. He slips under and then splutters frantically to the surface. *Perhaps ...*

Yes. Let's go in.

Soon there is sand underfoot and they wade up into the shallows. Alice allows herself to stop for a last moment in the deep channel that runs along the beach, savouring the delicious lack of weight before climbing out, back into the hot, public glare of the beach.

24 December 1946

In the afternoon a massive bushfire in the hills blankets Perth with smoke. Sitting with Anne in the park, Alice can smell the familiar scent of distant, burning eucalypt. She remembers the smell from two years earlier and if she closes her eyes it takes her back to the camp, the day Kaiser died, the afternoon they led Erich into the hospital, blackened and burned. Now she remembers his scars, the new, wrinkled pinkness that grew onto his hands and arms. Strangely, though, even when concentrating hard she can't picture the rest of him. Only the scars.

Are you all right? Anne is concerned. Her friend is too quiet.

I'm fine. Just remembering.

The other woman nods and they watch the children in silence for a while.

What are your family doing tomorrow?

Mum is having everyone around for a traditional Christmas dinner.

Does she know it's going to be a hundred degrees in the shade?

Alice answers with a smile and a shrug. *You know my mother*, the gesture says.

25 December 1946

Günter and Francesca arrive in the afternoon, bringing with them a basket of delicate, sweet, iced Italian biscuits. Francesca spent most of yesterday making them, Günter announces proudly.

You shouldn't have. Her mother's concern is genuine. Günter hasn't found work yet, and the little money they made from the sale of Günter's farm in Germany is nearly gone.

Happy Christmas, Günter answers, and everyone takes a biscuit.

Alice nibbles at hers. It is too sweet and she already feels sluggish and bloated from the Christmas lunch their mother made them all eat. Turkey and ham and even pudding and custard. Her feet have swollen and the marzipan sweetness of the biscuit stirs nausea inside her.

Outside, in the back yard, it is little better. The air is hot and listless and seems to sit in the yard. On days like this the sea breeze is usually late and weak and Alice collapses into her easy chair. She wonders what it is like where Erich is at the moment. On the radio news the other night they said that parts of Europe are experiencing record snowfalls, and that with all the post-war homelessness people were dying every day. She tries to imagine what it must be like, the cold whiteness of it, but in the heat of an Australian summer afternoon it seems an impossible dream.

The back door opens and Anne comes out, Elizabeth and Harry in tow.

Happy Christmas.

Thanks. You too.

She has brought a present. A little wooden cot, freshly painted.

It was originally Harry's, and Lizzie is too big for it now. Alice doesn't know what to say. She hasn't got anything in return.

Don't worry about it. Anne smiles and gives her arm a squeeze. *How're the puffy feet?*

Terrible. Alice manages a grimace.

Anne has to leave. She is taking the kids to her parent's place for Christmas tea. They decide that if tomorrow is as hot they'll catch a tram into the city and go for a swim in the river, out at the Nedlands baths.

Günter and her father come out into the yard to share a cigarette. Her mother won't allow them to smoke in the house. In the hot still evening the scent of the tobacco drifts languidly as the two men watch the sunset, standing side by side in silent companionship. They have been doing this a lot lately, Günter and her father. Building a strange sort of friendship. Alice suspects that part of the attraction is the fact that Günter doesn't speak much English. Her father likes silence.

Night brings little relief from the oppressive heat. The air is still warm, scented with the smells of summer – dust and smoke and sweat. Insects hum around the porch light, and Alice's dress clings to her.

At half past nine she goes inside, bids everyone good-night, writes a Christmas message to Erich in her journal and goes to bed.

With the light out, there is at least the impression of cool-ness.

In her sleep, Alice dreams that the camp is burning. Around the perimeter fence the trees are exploding in eucalyptus-fuelled frenzy and ash thickens the air. She is in the hospital and the door is locked. Heat radiates onto her from the walls and roof. Erich is outside. She knows it, she can feel him there, but the door handle is too hot to touch and she can't open it. He calls to her, *Alice*, and his voice seems much more distant than it should be. Outside the fire is roaring now, and finally, ignoring the searing pain in her hand, Alice grabs the handle and flings the door open.

Filling the doorway are roaring flames. A curtain of fire. Alice gasps and steps back. Erich is out there, but the heat rips into her. Through her.

Alice … The curtain flickers briefly and she can see him there. Standing, calling to her. Hands outstretched. Burning.

Again she tries to escape, running at the door, but as soon as she draws close the flames rise up again and he vanishes behind them.

Finally she closes her eyes, breathes in and throws herself into the red-orange maw of the door. The flames lick across her skin and the burning starts inside her womb …

Alice wakes up crying, gasping. Inside her the baby is kicking, hard.

1 January 1947

This time last year the two of them had sat together on the steps out in front of the hospital and talked about the future. Erich had spoken of his plans to return to Australia. To her. Now Alice sits alone on the back steps of her home in Perth trying to read. Her grandfather has given her *Wuthering Heights* for Christmas, but the story of Heathcliffe and Katherine somehow doesn't ring true for her at the moment.

There hasn't been a letter for weeks now. *No news is good*

news, she tells herself. The old cliché. Somehow it gives little comfort.

In just over three months her baby will be born. A little version of herself and Erich. She wonders if that will make her feel closer to him.

Last night, at midnight, she sat out the front on her own. Her parents had gone to bed hours earlier. It was another hot night, still seventy or eighty degrees even that late in the evening, and somewhere nearby a group of people were singing.

Auld Lang Syne.

Should old acquaintance be forgot? Alice asks herself.

It's hard to remember what he looks like now, even when she closes her eyes and struggles to recall his face. Occasionally she'll get a glimpse of him, veiled by the passage of time and memory, but usually nothing. She is left with odd impressions, the memory of a touch, or a smell. She can remember the sound of his breathing on that last afternoon and the gentleness in his voice when she woke up.

But not his face.

She remembers that he had blonde hair. Blue eyes. A square, clefted chin. But not his smile. She has the pieces there, but as the summer draws on and the days elongate, it is harder and harder to put them all together.

In a little over three months her baby will be born and she can't remember what its father looked like.

14 January 1947

They walk to the shops early in the day, before the heat really sets in. Francesca pushes Claire in an old stroller that Günter found somewhere, and the two of them walk slowly. As they stroll, Alice points out things to the other woman, teaching her the words in English.

Gate. Gumtree. Dog.

Frannie repeats them back, struggling to get her tongue around the unfamiliar phonetics.

Fence. Garden. Wheelbarrow.

Already the butcher's is crowded and the conversation lulls momentarily when they enter, as it does every time. The pregnant girl and the German woman. While they wait to be served, though, the other women return to their gossiping, pointedly ignoring them.

Mr Johnstone, the butcher, winks at them. *What'll it be, girls?* Francesca points at the clustered sausages hanging from a hook behind the counter. *How many pounds, love?* Puzzled, she looks desperately to Alice. *Ein ... this is ...*

Just one, thanks, Mr Johnstone.

No worries.

In the grocer's, there is a new boy behind the till. A teenager. Pimples dot his cheeks and his fingernails have dirt clinging to them.

Yes?

I would like please ... are you having ... Again Francesca loses the words, and this time lapses into German or Italian, just a few words, too quick for Alice to make out. She tries to mime what she is looking for, a round fruit of some kind, either an apple or an orange, Alice thinks, but before she can ask, the boy snorts, *Bloody hell! A kraut. Who let you into the country, eh?*

Frannie looks confused. She doesn't understand the words. The meaning is clear though. She tries again in English. *I am sorry, I would like to buy ...*

250

But the boy interrupts again. *Whatever it is you want I haven't got time to stand here listening to you babble on all day.*

Now it is Alice's turn to jump in. *Then why don't you just be quiet for a moment and let her explain?*

'Cause she's got no right bein' in this country in the first place. She's the reason me old man got shot in the leg. Now piss off, both of you.

Francesca is getting upset now and says something in Italian, louder than before. A woman in the line behind them taps Alice on the shoulder, not gently. *Would you mind getting this woman out of our way? Some of us have things to do, you know.*

When we've done our shopping, Alice replies.

Really! If she can't be bothered learning English …

Mr Chesterfield comes over. He's owned the shop for years. *Is there a problem, Michael?*

This kraut here won't speak English, sir. Haven't got a bloody clue what she's after.

Nobody speaks while the older man looks the boy straight in the eye. *Michael*, he says finally, *I'd hate to have to give you your notice on your first day.* Michael is sent to sweep the floors while Mr Chesterfield serves Alice and Francesca himself. *I'm sorry about that, Alice.*

It's fine.

But it isn't fine and on the walk home both women are quiet. There are no more English lessons that morning.

20 January 1947

Günter gets a job at a saw mill unloading timber from the logging trucks. After his first day he arrives home with a black eye. *How did this happen?* everyone wants to know, but

251

he refuses to say, just offers a pained wink with his good eye and shrugs.

I must not be so clumsy, no?

That night her grandfather comes over and sits out the back with Alice. *I'm worried for them*, he tells her. *It's so hard for both of them.*

What can we do?

Just be their friends. That's all.

Francesca is withdrawing further and further into herself. She hasn't come around for an English lesson for almost a week now, ever since the incident in the grocery shop. *There must be something else*, Alice thinks.

For a while Frannie would bring Claire down to the park in the afternoon, to sit with Anne and the kids, but she's even stopped doing that. *She needs to keep learning her English*, Alice tells her grandfather. *That's more important than anything.*

Doctor Alexander sighs. *There's no way we can force them, Alice. She's not a child. Neither of them are.*

Then talk to Günter about it.

I've tried, but … The old man hesitates. *They're fighting a lot. I don't think she's listening to him. Anyway, he'll be away for a few days next week, so perhaps we can talk to her then and have some more success. She'll need the companionship.*

Where's Günter going?

Down to Marinup.

Alice gives her grandfather a sharp look. *Why?*

I think he just wants to see what's become of the place. Sort of a letting go of the past, I imagine. He can get a ride down on one of the timber lorries.

Alice goes quiet. It is strange to think of Günter and Francesca fighting. They always seem so sweet and close when they are together. She wonders for a moment about herself and Erich, and if perhaps it is a good thing that he had to go, but she dismisses the thought, suddenly angry.

I must go. Doctor Alexander takes a while to climb to his feet.

Are you all right, Grandad?

Yes, dear. He reaches down and rests his hand lightly on the top of her head. Alice can feel his fingers pressing down through her hair. There is little weight behind them now. *I'm fine. Just feeling my age, that's all.*

I'll walk home with you.

Goodness no, not at this time of day. Besides – he chuckles lightly – *don't be offended but I think even I can probably get there faster than you, nowadays.*

Alice laughs too, hauls herself off the step and follows him inside.

After he has left she goes into her room and gets out her journal. It is starting to look a little tattered and worn and Alice carries it back outside. Sitting under the porch light, she reads through the entries, right back to the day she started writing, in the late afternoon of July fifth, sitting among the flower gardens in the prison camp. She looks back at those early pages, at the words written before she knew she was pregnant. She reads the longing, the pain that she poured out.

By the time she finishes reading it is getting late, but Alice picks up her pen and starts to make a list.

Boy. Johnathon, Paul, Erich.

Girl. Emmaline, Elsie, Matilda.

In the hot night she stares at the six names. She thinks about the baby, its family – both those here and those gone.

After a long time she circles two names. If it's a boy – Paul. If it's a girl – Matilda.

And looking at the name, she wonders how Erich's sister is going. She wonders when the next letter will come and what news it will bring. She no longer writes to him every couple of days; now it is usually about once a week.

The moon is rising out of the eastern sky. It slips into the air above the hills, painted bloody by the smoke of distant bushfires, and it seems too big, too close to be real. It is hard to imagine that this same moon was looking down on Germany just a few hours ago. Alice wonders if Erich, wherever he is, sat like this and watched the moon last night.

In the camp during the war she used to listen to Erich and Stutt and Günter talk to one another about the places and people they knew back in Germany. It was like listening to the guards discussing their lives back in Perth. They talked about the same things, in the same way. They told the same ribald jokes and made the same digs at one another. And the news; when Broome and Darwin were bombed, people in sleepy little Perth were digging bomb shelters in their backyards and filling them with supplies. It seemed as though Germany and the war were only just around the corner.

But then the war ended and Erich left, and the world seemed to grow again. Germany once again became something, somewhere distant. Somewhere lost to her.

Tonight, even the moon seems closer.

23 January 1947

The letters arrive in the morning post. Alice immediately recognises the familiar creamy white envelopes and spidery

254

handwriting and tears the first one open then and there, standing by the letterbox.

He has her letter. He knows about the baby. He is happy.

The news comes rushing over her like a tide and she needs to sit down.

In the kitchen she pours herself a cup of tea, sits at the table and then reads the first letter again. Slowly this time.

He is delighted at the prospect of being a father, but he is also terribly sorry for having put her in that position. Of course he will come back to Australia and marry her as soon as his sister is fit to travel. The two of them will come together, so that the baby will have a father and an aunt.

The warmth of the tea sits inside her like a solid, comforting lump.

There is more, much more. News about Germany and Mathilde and the progress of her TB. He has hopes of getting her into a specialised hospital. He has managed to track down a little of his family's money, which is lucky. He is looking for work.

The second letter lies beside her. The same type of envelope, the same handwriting, the same address. Without examining it, Alice pulls it towards her and opens it. The first words leap from the page.

Dear Doctor Alexander,

I hope that this letter finds you in good health, and that you are not displeased to hear from me …

Stopping, Alice looks at the envelope again. It is addressed to her grandfather, care of her. For a moment she hesitates. She should simply slip the letter back inside and deliver it to him. But she cannot help herself. She reads the next lines: *I would like you to know that I received Alice's communication yesterday, and am ashamed that I can not be there to do the honourable thing. I do hope that this has not altered your judgment of me and would like to reassure you that I will be returning to Australia and to your grand-daughter as soon as it is reasonably possible for me to do so. My sister, however …*

Alice stops herself. She slides the letter back into the envelope and re-seals it as best she can.

The walk across to her grandfather's takes an age now, as she has to stop and rest a number of times. When she arrives Günter meets her at the door. He is on his way to work.

What are you doing here? I thought you were going to Marinup this week?

On the weekend, he replies. *Friday afternoon go down, Sunday come back. That way not miss any work.*

Her grandfather is sitting at the table in the kitchen, doing a crossword. Francesca is trying to help, but crossword puzzles are still a little beyond her.

Alice! This is a surprise. What brings you over?

This. She hands him the envelope. *I'm sorry, I opened it accidentally. It arrived at the same time as another one and I thought they were both for me. I haven't read too much.*

That's fine, he tells her.

She watches his face intently as pulls the pages out and reads them. Behind his moustache he gives little away. *Can I ask you a favour?* he says finally.

Of course.

I should like to write a reply to him. There are things I need to tell him. Would you be able to give me his address?

Alice writes it on the back of the envelope and her grandfather smiles and pats her hand.

256

Thank you, dear. You have nothing to worry about, you know that, don't you? He'll be coming back as soon as he can.

I know, she tells him. But looking into his eyes, she senses that there is something more.

Alice … he begins, but stops. She waits. *You understand that his sister's tuberculosis will require quite some time to recover from?* Alice nods. *Good. Provided you know. Your baby might even be one-or two-years-old by the time Erich and Mathilde can get back here, but it would be unfair to ask him to come any sooner.*

Grandad, I know. Alice stands and kisses the old man on the top of his head.

I'm sorry, dear. I should understand you better by now.

The park is empty on her way home and Alice stops by the playground, remembering the first time she met Anne. It was only a few months ago, but it feels like an age. Her pregnancy seems to be stretching forever through the dusty months of the Perth summer, and she can't even recall the last time she felt light on her feet, or clean or cool.

Her grandfather's words ring in her ears. *Your baby might be one-or two-years-old by the time Erich can get back here.* She told him she understands. And she does. But still …

There is a part of her that doesn't want her baby to miss its first two years of having a father. There is a part of her that doesn't want to be an unmarried mother for that long either. She is also scared. Already, after only six months, she can't properly remember him. What about him? Can he remember her? And how will it be after two years?

Re-reading her journal the other night, looking over those early pages, Alice was shocked to discover how she felt when she read back what she had written. She was embarrassed.

Embarrassed by the rawness of the emotion. By the desperation. By the longing. Embarrassed that she should have felt that dependent on him, on anyone.

She doesn't feel like that any more. How will she feel in two years?

A couple of pelicans are soaring languidly overhead, riding a warm column of air high up into the sky. Alice watches them, faintly envious of their freedom, their detachment from the earth. Nothing holding them in place. They are so high it looks as though they could angle off now in any direction, to any place they choose.

Alice makes a decision.

She will not wait for him.

Not for two years.

No. As soon as the baby is born, as soon as it is old enough, the two of them will get on a ship.

They will go to him.

That night Alice sleeps better than she has in months.

1 February 1947

Günter is back from Marinup. When Alice asks him about the trip he doesn't want to talk about it.

Things seem even more strained between him and Frannie. They no longer smile and laugh at each other, even in company, and she has become pale and withdrawn. The hot nights are uncomfortable for everyone, but especially for a baby, and Claire cries a lot, so neither of them is getting very much sleep. When they arrive with the car to pick Alice up for her weekly swim, though, Günter is in good humour.

I tell you a funny story, he begins.

Yesterday, after work, he had gone to the pub with the

other men from the mill. It seems that most of them have managed to overcome their differences with him and they are now getting along well. In the pub, while he was drinking his beer, someone grabbed him on the shoulder. A policeman.

And so I turn around and look and who do you think it is that I am seeing?

Günter is laughing in anticipation. He doesn't wait for Alice to guess.

Guard Thomas! Erich's good friend! Except now he is in a police uniform and he is trying to arrest me for being 'illegal alien'!

He seems delighted at the term. *Illegal alien*, he repeats, still laughing. Even Francesca, behind the wheel, giggles a little. She's obviously heard this story before.

And so now I am telling him that, no, I am sponsored Australian, with passport and everything, but he is not believing me and is trying to take me to police station when Jim from the mill taps him on the shoulder. "Excuse me, officer, but I don't think you should you be drinking in a pub while on duty!" he says and all the men laugh and say for him to "piss off!" and he turns very red and goes then.

Now Alice can't help laughing herself. *I wish I'd been there to see it*, she tells him.

Ja. It was very funny, he replies. *Still …*

Günter becomes serious. They have to make a stop on the way to the beach, he tells her, at the police station, to show their passports and immigration papers to the sergeant to prove that they are legally allowed to be back in Australia.

But why?

Ach … He makes a tiny hand gesture. *Still there are some prisoners, Germans who escaped, in 1946, you remember?*

259

Alice remembers. *I thought most of them were recaptured.*

Most, he agrees, *but still, one or two …* He says nothing more, but there is a sly expression on his face.

Günter, Alice asks slowly, *do you know something about this?*

He doesn't answer, just throws her another grin and a wink and it might be her imagination but his right hand seems to be making a small tapping gesture on the seat between them.

At the beach, Alice gets out of the water early and makes her way up the sand to where Frannie sits on her towel. Günter is splashing in the waves with Claire, but the ocean still frightens Francesca, so she usually paddles for only a few minutes or stays out all together. A couple of young women make disapproving clicking sounds with their tongues as she passes, but Alice has given up caring. She fixes the two with her biggest smile. *Good morning!* And she pokes her swollen belly out in front of her as far as she can.

Not swimming? Frannie shakes her head and Alice sits on her towel beside her. The sun is hot and she can feel it burning her pale skin. *Shall we sit in the shade?*

There is grass below a couple of Norfolk Island pines a little up the beach, and they drop their gear there before settling in the speckled shade. *Alice …* Francesca's voice sounds small, lost. *How you are being so strong?*

Strong?

Ja. All these people are looking at you always and doing … uhm – she makes a fierce frowning expression – *doing this, and you still being brave and nice. How are you doing this?*

Alice puts her arm around the Italian girl's shoulders. *Sometimes that's all you can do, Frannie. Sometimes you just have to.*

They sit silently for a while, watching Günter and his baby daughter splashing so much that a lifeguard paddles out to check on them.

You are missing him, yes?

Yes. But we're going to go to Germany. Me and the baby, when it's born. Don't tell Günter or Grandfather.

No. She looks at Alice and there is a little envy in her expression. *You are lucky. Germany is beautiful. Not hot. Green.*

You don't like Australia, do you, Frannie?

Australia is … very wild. Some people are nice. Günter is happy here. It is a good place for Claire, he says.

Günter hops into the shallows and waves at them. With a sigh, Francesca slips on her shoes and trots across the sand to retrieve Claire from him, so that he can manage to get himself out.

28 February 1947

Something is wrong. She knows it as soon as she wakes. The morning sun is slanting in through the eastern windows like always, the air is cool, and she can hear the magpies calling to the dawn. Everything seems normal, but even through her sleep-addled mind Alice knows that something is wrong.

She sits up a little in her bed and then it hits her.

Pain.

Not a stabbing pain or anything like that, but a dull, deep ache, heavy and insistent, deep inside. In her womb.

Mum! She calls before she lets herself think too much.

Her belly feels harder than it usually does, muscles tense beneath the skin. Her father rushes to get her grandfather. The baby is not due for at least another month.

Something is wrong. Lying, waiting, Alice is surprised to

261

discover that after all these months she can suddenly remember Erich again. If she closes her eyes, he is standing there beside her in perfect clarity. *I'm sorry*, she whispers to the empty room.

What if he never sees his child?

Then Grandfather is there by the bed and he gets her to describe the pain and takes her temperature and sends her father down to the telephone to call for the specialist and tells her to be calm. *This sort of thing isn't unusual.*

For a long time nothing happens. The morning stretches on and the day warms up and the pain doesn't go away, but it doesn't get worse either. Alice drinks a cup of weak tea that her mother brings her and tries to relax, like she has been told.

But whenever she closes her eyes, he is right there, as clear in her mind as the day after he left.

She dozes and in her dreams they are back together in the hospital. It is winter and the fire is burning in the pot-bellied stove and they are holding each other. She wakes up to feel the cool hands of her doctor examining her.

How does it feel now? She tries to describe the pain. It might be her imagination, but while she has slept it seems to have changed, become more muted. The doctor puts a stethoscope to her belly and the round circle feels icy against her skin. *Can you breathe in deeply for me? That's good. Hold it, and now out. There. Thank you.* His voice is calm, unworried. She draws some strength from that.

Has it been moving a lot lately?

She nods.

Good.

He mixes a white powdery substance in some water and

gives it to her. *Drink this. It's just a relaxant and digestive. I think it will help.* The fluid tastes chalky and slightly bitter.

He speaks to her grandfather, who has been waiting by the other side of the bed. *I don't think it's anything too serious,* he says. *A little stress and perhaps a touch of indigestion. The heartbeat is still strong and regular and there's no false contractions so I'm not too worried. I'd say she just needs to rest.* He is talking about Alice as though she isn't in the room. As though the baby belongs to someone else.

The two men shake hands, and the specialist gathers his equipment together, placing it back into his bag. Finally he talks directly to Alice. *I want you to rest for the next couple of days. Drink plenty of fluids, especially in this heat, and then come into my rooms later in the week so that I can check everything again. I don't think that at this point you have anything to worry about, but I'd like to keep a close eye on things.*

With a nod to her mother and a handshake for her father, the doctor leaves, and a few minutes later the pain seems to subside a little further.

That afternoon Anne visits. She has left the kids at her mother's. *Are you all right?* she asks. She is the first person today to want to know.

Alice describes the morning, and the pain, and the fear, and Anne nods sympathetically. She had a similar experience with Harry.

It's so scary, I know, she says, and strokes Alice's forehead with cool hands. *But it'll be okay. You're strong.* She thinks for a moment. *Are you worried about the birth?*

Alice nods. So far only her doctor has talked to her about it, and he described the process in cold, clinical terms. *I'm scared,* she tells Anne.

I was too. But you get through it. And once it's over and you're holding your baby, trust me, it's all worth the pain.

And they talk about it, and Anne tells her all about her two experiences. By the time her friend leaves, Alice feels much better.

In the late afternoon she can't bear the thought of staying in bed any longer, so she gets up and pulls on a dress. It is the one her mother made her for Christmas. On a hanger it looks like a cross between a tent and a flour sack. When she shrugs it over her head, though, it fits her perfectly.

She splashes cold water over her face and straightens her hair. Her skin is terrible at the moment, but she knows it could clear up again almost overnight. It doesn't worry her.

What are you doing up? There is concern all over her mother's face when she enters the kitchen. *Is everything all right?*

I'm fine, Mum. She sits at the table and watches her mother prepare the dinner. Watching her chopping carrots, she realises for the first time what fine fingers her mother has. *You've got lovely hands, Mum.*

Her mother stops for a moment, puzzled, flexing her fingers and looking at them closely. *They're like my mother's. If the baby has them perhaps we should give her piano lessons. I always wanted to play the piano.* There is a slight wistfulness in her mother's voice and eyes, and Alice watches as she visibly shakes it off. *Do you feel up to hanging out some washing for me?*

Of course, Alice replies.

That night, she begins a new list in her journal.

To learn to play the piano. To camp in the bush. To swim at Cottesloe with his or her father.

The experiences her baby will not miss out on.

7 March 1947

Frannie has borrowed the car to drive Alice in to town for her check-up. *It is too hot for you to be catching trams*, she says.

In Perth they find a parking spot not too far from the doctor's rooms. Frannie says that she will take Claire and go shopping, and they will come back in half an hour. Alice watches her go, carrying her baby. Soon they will be able to take their children for walks together.

She is sweating heavily by the time she has travelled the few hundred yards to the surgery. A nurse offers her a glass of water which she gratefully accepts. Another woman is waiting for an appointment ahead of her. She is also pregnant, probably five or six months, Alice guesses.

The other woman smiles across the room. *Not long now for you, by the looks of things.*

No. Alice smiles back, though she doesn't feel very happy. *Just another three or four weeks.*

You lucky thing. You must be excited.

No, not really. Alice thinks for a moment. *It doesn't seem quite real.*

Oh. The other woman returns to her magazine and after a few moments the nurse comes and takes her through to the doctor. *Won't be long*, she tells Alice over her shoulder.

Alice picks up a magazine but nothing in it grabs her interest and after flicking idly through the pages she drops it back onto the low table and just stares out the window.

The sunshine today seems different from normal. It seems to have lost some of its bright brilliance and there is a hazy, subdued feel about it. It is humid, too, and Alice can feel her dress clinging to her, and her hair frizzing.

Finally the other woman comes out and it is Alice's turn to go into the tiny office.

Good morning, Alice. The doctor greets her. *Would you mind climbing up onto the bed here for me?*

The examination takes only a few minutes. The usual routine of temperature, stethoscope and gentle probing of her abdomen.

No more problems with pain? he asks her.

No.

Excellent. He washes his hands at a small sink while she slides off the bed and back to her feet. *Well, both you and the baby seem to be in perfect health as far as I can tell. Only three weeks to go now, right?*

That's right.

Good. Well, make sure you get plenty of rest to build your energy up, but do a little bit of exercise each day if you can. Just gentle walking, that sort of thing. If you find your back getting too sore, a hot bath might help.

With the weather the way it is, Alice can't imagine anything worse than a hot bath.

Then there's not a lot else you need to do now. Apart from knitting some baby clothes, of course. He smiles a little. This is his idea of a joke and Alice fakes amusement.

Have your father call me if you need anything. Other than that, I'll see you again in a week.

Francesca is waiting in the car by the time she gets back. *Everything is good?* she asks.

Fine, Frannie.

Alice holds Claire as they drive home. The little girl gurgles and tries to grab a handful of Alice's hair, but still doesn't have the coordination.

Where do you get this car from, Frannie?

Her friend gives her a sly look. *You are not telling Günter I told you this … she begins.*

I promise. Our secret.

He is borrowing it from some Australians, some people who were living near Marinup but now are being in Perth. They have boarder, a German man, friend of Günter's, also from prison camp. He is … how do you say? Escaping? Not going back to Germany.

Alice laughs. *That's why he won't tell me.*

Si. Very big secret. His friend have new name now, and also sweetheart here.

As they round the corner at the end of her street, Alice smiles and plays with Claire.

28 March 1947

The last few weeks are the worst. They seem to drag out for almost as long as the previous eight months. Each day brings with it routines and habits, and Alice moves through them feeling disconnected. Like acting a part in someone else's play.

More letters arrive from Germany. Mathilde has been moved into a good hospital, on the outskirts of a small village near the Black Forest which hasn't been too badly damaged in the war. It is costing most of the family money that Erich has managed to recover, but it is her best chance of a quick recovery.

He is well too, working as a labourer, clearing rubble and debris from bombed-out sites, and visiting his sister whenever he can find the time. He is missing Alice, is worried about their baby, wishing he could be there for the birth.

267

She writes back. Stories about her and her grandfather, and Günter and Frannie, and Annie and her kids. *Don't feel like you need to return before you are both ready. I understand*, she tells him, even though inside she really wants to beg him to come back: She'll be all right in the hospital now. Let someone else look after her …

But instead she writes *I love you*, signs her name, and slips her understanding into an envelope. She addresses it carefully, stamps it and consigns it to the red mailbox in front of the greengrocer's, knowing that by the time it reaches its destination its recipient will be a father.

Walking to the park is too much effort now, so most afternoons Anne brings the kids around and they play in the back yard, climbing the old Moreton Bay Fig at the bottom of the garden, while their mother and Alice sit on the back porch and drink tea and chat. Frannie often joins them too, things seem to be a little better between her and Günter now.

It'll all be over soon, love, Anne tells her. *Nothing to worry about.*

But she does worry, and she lies in her room at night and listens to the house ticking and cooling around her, and feels her child kicking inside, and knows that tomorrow morning will bring the same routines, the same sensations and aches and pains, and she just wants it all to be over, now. Alice has had enough of being pregnant.

5 April 1947

All day the humidity has been building, and in the early afternoon a low cast of thick grey cloud rolls over the city. It traps the heat close to the ground and the temperature climbs into the eighties, then the low nineties. Alice dozes in her chair on the back verandah, a fitful, disturbed sleep.

When Anne arrives and wakes her, the air feels charged, electric.

I think we're in for a bit of a storm, you know that? Anne has told the kids they're not to climb the tree this afternoon.

Frannie isn't coming by today. She and Günter are looking for a house to buy. They have some money saved and want a place of their own. Günter wants to find somewhere near bushland, on the outskirts of the city, where there are birds.

Are you feeling okay? Anne notices that her friend is very quiet.

Yes. Just a little strange. I think it's the weather.

Evening approaches and her mother comes outside to sit with them. The dropping sun slants up from below the cloud layer, illuminating everything with a dirty yellow light. Alice watches dust particles float, suspended in the air.

We'd better get moving. Kids! Lizzie and Harry come tumbling in off the lawn. *It's time to go. Give your Aunt Alice a kiss.* Harry dutifully pecks her cheek, his face serious and round, hands in the pockets of his shorts. Lizzie tries to throw her arms around Alice's middle, giggling. *Can I feel the baby?* she asks. *Of course.* The little girl's hand is warm and sticky against her belly, and, almost as if in response, the little creature inside her kicks out, making Lizzie squeal and pull her hand back quickly. Everyone laughs.

He's restless tonight, Alice says. Anne and her mother exchange a look.

A few minutes later, with the light fading, the first fat drops of rain fall. They make miniature craters in the dusty patch at the bottom of the stairs and plonk a sporadic chorus onto the tin roof. They are accompanied by a peal of distant thunder.

Anne leaves and her mother goes back inside to prepare dinner. Alice sits alone again, watching the rain. It isn't a constant fall, just random drops which have forced themselves to earth. The rain does nothing to release the tension in the air, just the opposite in fact. As the evening grows darker, the air seems to get thicker, dryer, more charged, more claustrophobic.

After dinner, Alice goes to bed early but can't sleep. The baby is kicking, hard. Sharp little stabs of tiny feet against the inside of her uterus. She runs her hands lightly over the curve. *Shhh. Sleep*, she tells it.

But it doesn't and both of them are still wide awake at half past ten when the storm finally breaks over Perth with a roar of water. The downpour is almost tropical in its strength, and finally Alice rises from her bed and makes her way through the darkened house out to the front verandah. She remembers making this same trip all those months ago, kissing her father, turning off the light and the radio, walking in the winter rain. Tonight the front room is empty and silent. Her father hasn't slept there in several months. Tonight, as every night now, her parents share a bed.

She stands under the shelter of the verandah, watching the energy pour itself from the sky. The rain seems to pound into the pavement with an almost living strength. The street is flooded, the drains not able to cope with the flow.

Alice steps into the deluge. Unlike last time it is warm, blood-like. She is instantly soaked, her nightdress clinging to her and the water cascading around the bulge of her belly, down her legs, pouring into the ground. Alice laughs and spreads her arms wide to the sky, savouring the sensation, the incredible release of it. The baby kicks again.

Then the first contraction shudders through her and she gasps and has to sit down, right there, in the street, in the rain which continues to pour down onto her.

Through tears that mix with the rain, she laughs again.

6 April 1947

By morning, the contractions are close. The midwife has been there, since being summoned in the middle of the night.

We need to get her to the hospital. Soon. I can't understand why her waters haven't broken.

Günter and Frannie have gone to fetch the car. They should be here any moment.

Alice's hair is sticking to her scalp and with each new set of contractions she whimpers and shudders. Her mother holds her hand. She hasn't let it go since the previous night when her daughter, soaked and trembling, had stumbled into their bedroom and announced that it had started.

Her grandfather is standing on the other side of the bedroom feeling helpless.

Can I have some water? The old man leaves the room to fetch a glass for her.

The car arrives and they carry her out to it. She tries to walk, but her legs keep collapsing beneath her as waves of pain spasm through her body. Her father supports her on one side, the midwife on the other.

Alice lies across the back seat, and Frannie and her parents

271

are in the front. The midwife squeezes herself in beside Alice. *Now go!* There is urgency in her voice.

The hospital is in Subiaco. The doctor is already there.

How long between contractions? he asks.

Three minutes, now, the midwife replies. *Still no waters, though she's almost fully dilated. I don't understand it.*

Another cramp squeezes her and this time the pain is different, sharper. Harder. Like it has an edge. She screams.

Get her into the theatre, I want to have a look.

In the operating theatre, Alice is laid on a table, her legs stirruped up into the air like some absurd puppet. The doctor and two nurses are wearing robes and masks which make them look distant. Impersonal. *What's wrong?* she asks.

It's fine, Alice. Just try to relax, the doctor tells her. One of the nurses wipes her head with a damp cloth. Another contraction, and the doctor is probing into her with some kind of tool now. She can feel the coldness of it inside her. She feels like she is burning up.

I think it's the placenta, he tells one of the nurses. *It's fixed over the birth canal instead of at the top. Prep her for a caesarean, please.*

He leaves the room.

Then her mother is there again, holding her hand once more. She's also wearing a robe. *Everything will be fine, honey. Just stay calm.*

But it's too hard to stay calm. Alice cries out in pain as another set of contractions takes hold, and inside herself she feels something tearing. *I just want it to stop. Please!* she begs her mother. But it doesn't stop. There are more cramps and more tearing, and she feels something warm and sticky running out of her and pooling on the table beneath.

She's bleeding, doctor!

The doctor swears and her mother is bundled from the room. Alice wishes she still had her hand to hold on to. The pain is constant now, a deep sharp burning inside her, even between the contractions. The room blurs and spins through her tears, and then there's an injection and a kind of floating sensation, and then, for a long time, nothing.

There are voices in the room when she wakes. The doctor. Her parents. Her grandfather.

The baby is fine, but it took so long to get her here that there has been a lot of haemorrhaging and internal bleeding. She's not in a good way …

Who? Alice tries to speak. No words come out, only a croak.

She feels so cold, so tired.

Someone strokes her forehead. Her mother. Her long fingers feel like fire.

I'm cold.

Shhh, honey. her mother soothes her. The voice washes around her.

Something is pressed into her arms. Something tiny, hot and wriggly. Alice tries to lift the little bundle to her lips, but can't. Her arms don't seem to be working properly.

It's a little girl. A perfect little girl, Alice. Her father is standing at the foot of the bed. He seems to be a long way away. *We're so proud of you, honey.* She doesn't understand why her father is crying. He never cries. *So proud …*

With an effort that makes her gasp, and ignoring the pain that sears through her belly when she does so, Alice finally manages to raise her child to her lips. She breathes in the baby smell. The little creature coughs and hiccups and

273

squawks. *Matilda.* Her voice is only a whisper, but it's all she can manage. It's enough. She whispers it again into the tiny, perfect ear. *Matilda.*

She is so cold, even with all these blankets on. And the room is dark. Why doesn't someone turn on a light?

For a moment Alice closes her eyes. Just for a moment.

When she opens them again, there are new people in the room. Strangers.

Alice.

An old woman is there with a young man. She is vaguely familiar. She smells of lavender.

Get up, now. It's time to go.

Go?

Come. This is your Uncle Paul. There's other people who want to meet you too.

The old woman's eyes crinkle when she smiles. It's warmer and brighter all of a sudden, and there are other people there. More strangers. A handsome man with blonde hair and a woman with him. She has never met them, but she knows them. He has piercing blue eyes. She has seen those eyes before. *Hello, Alice.* The woman reaches out and takes her hand. Her voice is soft and accented. Alice stands.

But my baby ...

Don't worry, her grandmother says. *You'll be able to watch her, see?*

Alice looks behind her, in the direction that the old lady is pointing. It's much darker over there. Her parents are there, and her grandfather. They are all crying.

She'll be fine. We promise. The blue-eyed man steps over and wraps an arm around her shoulders, protectively, welcomingly. *We'll all watch over her. Now come ...*

It is much warmer here. With a last, lingering look behind, Alice follows …

7 April 1947

The old doctor's hands tremble as he pulls the paper towards himself. On the desk a lamp casts a dull light across the empty page. In the bin by his side rest seven similar sheets, all half-written, all discarded unfinished.

He can hear his daughter and son-in-law talking in the kitchen next door. They speak quietly, but he can still hear the shock, the despair in their voices.

Doctor Johnathon Alexander feels empty, drained, old. Almost too bereft to mourn. But he has to write this letter. He has promised his daughter and son-in-law and, even if he had not, the duty should still be his anyway.

Finally, he puts down his pen and stands slowly, crossing to the window and looking out to the east. The first stars of night are starting to wink into life, pinpricks of heat, billions of miles distant. *Is she out there somewhere?* he murmurs to the empty room. He is not a religious man, the doctor. But tonight he wonders.

The storm has passed completely, scrubbing the air and the land, settling the summer dust and washing it away, and the evening is crisp and clear. The doctor breathes in deeply, feeling the coolness of the air flowing into his old, tired lungs. He tries to imagine himself drawing energy from it.

On the other side of the room, the cot that Anne gave Alice for Christmas sits empty. In a few days it will be occupied with life, and then, hopefully, the healing will begin. Anne had appeared at the hospital that afternoon, expecting to find mother and baby alive and well. One of the nurses told her before anyone else got a chance.

Some kind of night-bird calls and the old man closes his eyes for a few moments, breathing in the night and remembering the sounds of the night forest in Marinup, remembering his grand-daughter and the boy who was his orderly, gathering his thoughts, and his strength.

Turning back to his desk, he begins to write.

Perth, 7 April 1947

My Dear Erich,

I know that I told you I would not write again, but only I can send you this news, I am afraid. I am really not sure how to express this – all my years of medicine and working with people leave me totally unprepared for the news which I must impart.

Firstly, congratulations – you are the father of a baby girl, Matilda Alice Andrews, born weighing nine and a half pounds yesterday, April 6th. You will no doubt be pleased to know that she is in perfect condition. Unfortunately, Erich, I have some terrible news which must come hand in hand with this joyful announcement. There were complications during the birth, and Alice suffered a great deal of internal haemorrhaging. By the time we managed to get her to hospital, there was little that the medical staff could do. The baby was delivered by Caesarean distressed but healthy, but Alice died in hospital late last night, at about 11.30.

Erich, it pains me so much to have to convey this news to you in a letter, but there is no other feasible way. I debated the wisdom of trying to telegraph you with it, but by their nature telegraphs are brief and impersonal, and there is little or nothing that you can do about the situation now, so I decided upon a letter, which will at least lend me greater clarity of expression.

As you can imagine, everyone here is distraught. Alice's

mother, my daughter, is in shock and her father is only just in control. This is why I take it upon myself to be the bearer of this news. It is a terrible thing for a parent, any parent, to have to bury their child, and while their grief will, in time, no doubt be tempered by the beautiful little girl their daughter brought into this world, it will still be a long time before they will be able to fully come to terms with their loss. Of this, I have some experience.

We will be holding Alice's funeral tomorrow, and I have taken the liberty of having Günter organise flowers in your name. My son-in-law has also asked me to convey in this letter that he and my daughter will look after Matilda here for you until such time as you and your sister are able to make the journey back to Australia. This is what Alice would no doubt have wanted. They understand that it could be years until Mathilde is well enough to travel, but they will welcome both of you upon your return.

I would also reiterate my own hope for your return. The gift I spoke of in my last letter to you will remain in place at Marinup, buried fifty-three paces due south of the detention cells. Günter was kind enough to place it there for me during his visit to the site a few months ago, and even with his artificial limb I imagine that his steps will be roughly in line with your own youthful gait. I still hope that you will come to retrieve it, now more than ever.

I will attach both the birth notice for your daughter and the death notice for Alice to this letter. With her parent's consent I will also enclose Alice's journal, which conveys her feelings about you with far greater clarity than I could ever manage. Please, Erich, accept my condolences for this terrible loss. She loved you greatly, and that is often a rare thing. I am very tired myself, and suspect that I too will not be here for your eventual return. I wish you peace.

Your friend,

Johnathon Alexander

PART FOUR

PART FOUR

Twenty-five

Vinnie

The gas-lamp hissed a gentle whisper into the darkness as Vinnie, hands trembling, set the final letter down on top of the others, beside the tattered old notebook.

"You have finished?" The old man on the other side of the folding camp table looked up from his own reading.

"Yeah." Vinnie shook his head slowly, trying to regain some clarity. "Yes. I've finished."

"Good." Helen's grandfather climbed to his feet, slow and awkward. "In that case I will be packing up these papers and going to bed. It is a little past my bedtime, I am afraid."

Vinnie glanced at his watch. Ten-thirty. Time had slipped away with the daylight while the old man had been talking, telling the story of his time in the prison camp, and then setting Vinnie to reading Alice's diary and letters. A gentle breeze filtered through the night forest and one of the old pieces of paper would have flown from the pile had Vinnie not caught it.

Silently, thoughtfully, he watched the doctor gather

together the leather-covered notebook and the letters, the paper yellowing and brittle with age.

"I will see you in the morning, Vincent. Goodnight."

"Goodnight, Doctor Pieters."

There were questions to ask, things that needed to be said, but Vinnie knew this was not the time. Helen also rose from her folding chair, not quite assisting the old man up the steps into the campervan but standing close by in case she was needed. When the aluminium door had closed behind him, she turned and winked.

"Come on. I'll walk you back over to your tent with the lamp."

"Thanks."

Neither spoke as they crunched across the ball-bearing gravel towards the pine tree. Somewhere deep in the trees an owl screeched and there was a brief skitter of noise from the undergrowth. As they came nearer, two grey roos, grazing, found themselves caught in the unexpected light and looked up startled before bounding into the darkness. Vinnie and Helen listened to their crashing passage.

"It seems pretty incredible."

Helen simply nodded. "I know."

"I've got lots of questions."

"Yeah, I know that, too. He'll answer them tomorrow."

"Do you know what he wants?"

"I've got a rough idea, but that's for him to tell you, not me. Tomorrow."

"Fair enough." He wasn't satisfied, but knew that it would have to do. "You wanna stay for a while?"

In the soft glare of the lamp Helen smiled at him and shook her head.

"Not right now if you don't mind, Vinnie. I'm pretty much done in myself."

"Yeah, all right. Me too, really."

"Good." She waited a moment longer while Vinnie fished his own torch from inside the tent. "I'll see you tomorrow. Goodnight."

"Helen?"

"Yeah?"

"Did he come back?"

Another smile.

"He'll tell you in the morning, Vinnie. Sleep well."

Her footsteps faded across the gravel.

Restless, Vinnie lay dozing for hours, a sleep plagued with nightmares until eventually he woke in the tremulous light of early dawn, bathed in sweat, scars tingling and itching. With the safety of daylight growing every second, Vinnie crawled outside to light the fire and boil some water.

Sitting in the cool dawn, Vinnie sensed in himself a restlessness. The still-dark gaps between the trees seemed alive with spirits, but not malevolent. There was something, some presence, watching and drawing him to itself. He sipped at his coffee and sat, quiet and restive, growing accustomed to the feeling.

A more distinct movement at the uphill end of the clearing caught his attention. It was a large black cockatoo. Its belly and throat glowed fiery scarlet against the sable of its body. Vinnie watched it stretch its wings as though testing the morning and then emit an enormous screech – a call which echoed around the open space and off the trees – before leaping into the air.

The black wings beat against the sky, carrying the

cockatoo in one giant revolution around the clearing and then off, above the treetops, in the direction of the prison site.

Pausing only to smother the flames of his tiny campfire with the dregs of his coffee, Vinnie followed.

This early in the morning the grasslands of the abandoned camp were a hive of activity. Kangaroos grazed indolently between the concrete foundations, moving only when one patch of dewy feed was exhausted. In the scrub the scurry and bustle of other creatures marked their presence, ignorant or uncaring of Vinnie's intrusion into their world.

Sitting on the foundation of the hospital, Vinnie closed his eyes. Just for a few seconds. Immediately the sounds of the forest changed, almost imperceptibly. It was nothing Vinnie could identify, no alteration in pitch or pace, but somehow a shift occurred in the very fabric of the sound, and the familiarity, the secure, calming noise of waking forest, was suddenly and wrenchingly gone. In its place Vinnie found himself hearing the morning forest through alien ears. The rustlings became sinister, threatening, the screeches of the cockatoos cruel and mocking. With the change came the notion from deep in his brain that the very nature of the forest itself had changed, that it was now pressing in, crushing his thoughts, his belonging, his very identity. It was as if the trees and undergrowth would continue in upon him until they had choked and strangled and absorbed him back into the cycle of forest life.

Vinnie sat holding his breath, caught in the utter helplessness of being alien in such a place, and as he sat there the fences and huts of Marinup Camp Sixteen were once again erected. Searchlights probed rainy nights from atop guard towers and men huddled against the ferociously passive nature of the landscape in which they dwelled.

And then it passed as quickly as it had arrived and Vinnie opened his eyes to the world as he knew it. He breathed deeply for a few minutes, still startled by the intensity of the experience, aware that his hands were shaking and glad there was no one to witness his weakness.

The sun rose above the tree line and in the sudden warming glow Vinnie studied the wall of the forest and wondered what mysteries lay beyond it, in the living nooks and depressions and below the thick undergrowth and high in the dim greenness of the canopy.

The morning became still, and hesitantly Vinnie closed his eyes again, expecting that alien hopelessness to sweep over him once more, but this time there was only darkness and silence and the briefest stirring of the air around him as the morning breeze dropped to a whisper. Lying in a patch of eucalypt shade that fell across the crumbling foundation, Vinnie slept.

May 1947

In the late afternoons they would wheel Mathilde and the other patients out and sit them in the sun; the pale light reaching through the usually heavy overcast and bringing wan warmth into the enclosed south-western verandah. Like all the others she was tiny and emaciated, skin barely clinging to a skeleton, twig-like in its delicacy.

The hospital was a converted kastel on a west-facing slope, well outside town, its manicured gardens stretching away to a line of trees at the bottom of the property. A few miles away, the uniform conifers of the forest stood aloof, turning the valley below into a deep cleft of green, so different from that of Marinup, Erich thought.

"How is she today?"

The nurse, one of seven or eight who regularly did rounds of the wards, approached silently from behind. Her German was the same thick-accented speech that reminded him so much of Günter. Erich turned to meet her and shrugged.

"The same as yesterday, and the day before that."

He knew this nurse. Maria. She seemed to come by more regularly than the others. Erich thought she was probably a few years older than him but unlike the younger nurses this one gave the impression that she was genuinely concerned for Mathilde. And for him.

"Patience. She will improve." Her hand rested lightly on Erich's shoulder as he stood motionless, staring out the broad windows at the distant, impassive pines. The gesture didn't seem overly familiar, as some might have assumed; rather it was gently supportive.

"Yes. In time."

Erich looked away from the window and back at the girl in the chair. The familiar, fine features he knew so well still lurked clearly behind the almost translucent skin. As he watched, she breathed in sharply and coughed, the effort wracking her body and sending convulsions the length of her back and legs.

Instantly Erich was holding her hand as wave after wave spasmed through her, threatening to break the fragile body in two. Her hand in his was thin and bony, with no strength in it, and he had to be careful not to squeeze too hard.

As the coughing spasm died away her eyes opened and she fixed him with a gaze as blue as his own.

"Erich?"

"I'm here, sister."

"I had the strangest dream."

"Shh. It is all right."

Mathilde smiled, even that brief effort seeming to tax her weakened body.

"You are so good to me, brother."

"I have to be. I told you I'd come back."

"You did."

Her eyes closed and she eased back into the cushions, falling asleep again almost instantly.

"The doctor says that she is coming along. Just slowly, that is all, but she will make it."

Maria arranged the blanket around his sister's knees and legs as she spoke, tucking it well in to preserve what little warmth her body was able to generate.

"I know. It seems so long, though. And so far away."

"Far away?"

"From everything."

Maria paused in her arranging of the blanket. "You have heard from your sweetheart?"

"Bad news."

The nurse finished and stood to face him again. "The baby?"

"A girl. Born April sixth."

"But that is good news, surely?" Maria was mystified. In their previous conversations it had seemed clear to her that the only hope in this ex-soldier's life was the Australian girl and their baby. "You did not even tell me."

"There were ... complications."

"The baby?"

"No." Erich shook his head. "The girl. Alice. She died in childbirth."

"Oh." Maria's hand lifted to her mouth. "Erich, I am so sorry."

Erich simply acknowledged her sympathy with a tiny nod.

"You are all right?"

"I don't know." He shrugged. "I feel empty. Like none of it is real."

Mathilde stirred against her cushions and the two of them, conversation interrupted, prepared for another coughing fit, but it never came and the girl settled again.

"Have you told her?"

"No. None of it. She has enough to worry about as things are."

"That is true."

The two stood either side of the girl asleep in her cane chair. Maria looked at the man standing opposite her, seemingly so young and so old at the same time, and felt the most tremendous sense of loss on his behalf.

"What will you do?"

"I do not know. Wait for Mathilde to get better."

"And then?"

Another shrug. "Who knows?"

"If there is anything I can do, if you need to talk ..."

"Thank you." Erich cut her off. "I will be fine."

"All right, then." She walked towards the next patient, a few steps down the verandah, but before reaching the man she stopped and turned back to Erich.

"Erich?"

"Yes?"

"I am sure that your daughter is a beautiful little girl."
With a hesitant smile she continued her rounds.

Twenty-six

Vinnie

The sun had heated the sand, turning it into a massive white hotplate. It seared the soles of Vinnie's bare feet.

"Ow! Hot."

"Don't be such a baby." His fifteen-year-old sister pulled at his arm, impatient.

"That hurts, Kat!"

"Then stop complaining and hurry up." She hadn't wanted to bring him along in the first place, her kid brother tagging along with her. What if Adam was here? What would he think? "Get a move on."

"Hey! Katia!"

Shit. Adam. And the rest. The girl pulled her little brother close and whispered, "Listen, Vin, don't you say a word, okay? Not a *word* to anyone."

She released him roughly, leaving fingermarks on his arm.

"Hey, Katia, how you goin'?"

"Yeah, Adam, not too bad."

"Who's this?"

"This" – a vague nod in his direction was the only

indication that she was talking about him – "is my little brother, Vinnie. Dad said I had to bring him."

"G'day." The older boy stuck out his hand but pulled it away at the last second, leaving Vinnie with his own dangling in mid-air. He and Katia laughed. "Does it speak?"

"Not if he knows what's good for him."

Adam laughed again. He had straggly blonde hair, thick with salt and sand which shook out a fine cloud as his head moved.

"Got him well trained, eh? Cool. Come and siddown."

They followed the older boy across to where a group of teenagers, all around his sister's age, lounged listlessly on towels. There were a few greetings for Kat and a few curious stares at him but, apart from those, none of the others even acknowledged Vinnie's presence. He settled himself a little apart, spreading his towel carefully so as not to get it sandy. Then there was nothing to do but listen to the others talk.

"How'd you go in your exams?"

"Crap. Bloody Johnson gave me a 'D' for phys-ed."

"Serious? That must be the first D you've ever got in your life."

"It is. My dad went apeshit."

The sun was hot and the water was glistening, the deep blue of the Indian Ocean. On the horizon the holiday island of Rottnest crouched shimmering. Ignoring the sniggers directed his way from the older kids, Vinnie smeared greasy sunscreen across his arms and back.

"I'm goin' for a swim, Kat."

"Whatever." She barely looked at him. "Just be careful, all right?"

"Yeah."

291

Glad to be away from his sister's friends, Vinnie hopped across the sand until he reached the cool slush at the tideline. From up on the beach the water looked calm, but now Vinnie realised how big the surf really was. Waves curved around the end of the groin, building in the shallow water until their crests broke about twenty-five metres out then rolled all the way in to the beach, their faces torn by a legion of kids on boogie boards who skidded them all the way into the shallows.

"Cool."

Vinnie wasn't worried. He was a strong swimmer, already big for his age.

A concrete pylon about three metres high jutted from the water thirty or forty metres out. Vinnie's father had told him once that it was the remains of a shark net, or something like that. Someone had tied an old piece of rope around it and a group of boys about his own age were clambering up and leaping from the top, timing their jumps into the crests of the passing waves. He glanced back to where Kat and her friends were paying him no attention whatsoever and with a quick, deep breath he waded a few steps and dived into the foaming face of the next big wave.

After the baking heat of the sun the water stung his body, raising instant gooseflesh, and he felt himself lift out the back of the wave, gasping a quick, salty breath before ducking under the next one. Then up again, a couple of steps, another wave and the sandy bottom disappeared from under him. Two or three strong kicks under water and Vinnie was through the break, striking out for his target in measured, even strokes.

Once atop the pylon he stopped for a couple of minutes to

catch his breath. From out here the beach appeared further away than the pylon had looked from the beach. The waves drove around the old concrete with a thundering hiss that surged up and down the rounded sides, making the entire structure tremble slightly. He could see Katia and her group, a dark cluster of tiny figures against the gleaming white expanse of sand. He waved, but no one waved back.

"Come on, mate, hurry up, eh?"

The speaker was another kid clinging to the rope at his feet, impatient to climb up and leap off himself.

"Sorry."

Vinnie watched the next wave thunder towards him and, trying not to notice the dark shadows on the bottom of the bay, dived out into the blue.

Leaping from the pylon filled the hot summer afternoon. Sometimes other kids would chat, comment and joke about each other's form, sometimes one would swim out, rest for a few moments, jump off once and swim straight in again without comment to anyone. As the afternoon wound past, though, more and more of the kids headed in, until finally Vinnie found himself alone on the crumbling structure.

"Cool." There was just enough room to sit, so he settled for a few minutes, studying the beach again, looking at the families herding their children up the sand to the cold fresh-water showers beside the surf club. The lifeguards were knocking off, rolling up the red and yellow flags at either end of the patrol area and loading them onto a mini four-wheel drive. A figure on the beach caught his attention. It was Katia, waving furiously.

"Shit!" The time. He'd forgotten all about it. Kat would kill him if they missed the last bus.

He waved back and launched himself off the pylon, noticing as he did so that in the time he'd been out there the wind had come up and the waves seemed a little larger than they had on the swim out.

He swam hard, feeling the water curl around and suck at him but preoccupied with what Kat was going to say. Two big waves lifted him and slipped beneath, sliding powerfully in to the sand. Ten more strokes and then another wave. But this one kept lifting him higher and higher and by the time Vinnie realised something was wrong he found himself right at the lip of the wave as it curled to smash in upon itself.

Vinnie gasped, a quick, choking, cut-off breath, as the monstrous green behemoth hurled him down and then slammed him with enough force to knock the wind from him. He tumbled over and over in a world of salty, airless white and then felt a sharp blow in the small of his back as he hit the sandy bottom. He was sucked up again, rolling once more through the water column until finally he surfaced in the deep channel that ran parallel to the beach, the channel through which the water flinging itself onto the sand was escaping before flowing out to sea.

Gasping a mouthful of salt water, Vinnie attempted to strike out again for the beach before the next wave caught him, but the longshore rip had him now and was pulling him sideways. He tried to spin into the force, to lever himself against it, but his arms were burning, an incredible pain building in his shoulders. The more he struggled into the current, the worse it got. Briefly, in the trough between two waves, his toes brushed the sandy bottom and he scrabbled for purchase, but quickly and mercilessly he was lifted back away and along the channel.

Then he was under, struggling. The water closed over his head, almost without him being aware of actually sinking. Kicking hard, he burst to the surface, gasped a quick breath and was about to go under again when someone grabbed the back of his boardies.

Everything went grey for a few seconds and then he was out of the current, in shallow water, struggling his feet into the soft bottom and stumbling through the shallows beside his sister until both of them collapsed on the damp sand.

"Shit, Vinnie. You all right?"

Through the massive, sobbing breaths wracking his body, Vinnie managed a nod.

"You scared the hell out of me, Vin."

"Sorry."

"Look at me." She grabbed his chin and turned his head to face hers.

"Please don't ever scare me like that again, okay?"

"Okay."

The two of them sat panting for what seemed ages, until Katia eventually climbed to her feet again.

"You up to walking?" She offered a hand and pulled Vinnie up.

"Yeah."

"Good then. We've missed the bus."

"How'll we get home?"

"Walk until we find a phone. Then I'll call Dad."

"Kat?"

"Yeah, Vin?"

"Thanks. I was stuffed there."

"Whatever. You'd do the same for me."

They collected their towels and trudged through the thick

sand towards the car park. There was a public phone about four hundred metres away, so they called home and settled down to wait for their father.

August 1947

"Erich?"

"Yes?"

"Why do you not talk with me about what happened in Australia?"

Erich stopped and looked at his sister. The summer air was warm and birdcalls echoed about the garden.

"What do you want to know?"

"Whatever it is that you are not telling me. I am your sister, after all. You should talk to me."

He started walking again. With every passing week her weight on his arm was becoming appreciably heavier. She was also able to walk further each time, with less and less assistance.

"There are things I do not want to bother you with."

"Nonsense." Mathilde laughed. "You were always far too serious about yourself. What happened?"

He didn't answer and for several seconds the only sound was their footsteps crunching on the gravel driveway. A couple of hundred yards behind them, anyone watching from the verandah of the hospital would have been forgiven for thinking them to be a couple of young lovers, out for a summer stroll.

"Was it a girl?" Mathilde nudged him, her tone gently teasing, but his sudden, sharp intake of breath gave him away.

"It was, wasn't it? What was her name?"

296

"Come and sit down." Erich steered his sister towards a nearby bench.

"Is it that serious?" Mathilde kept the light-hearted tone, but something about her brother's manner was starting to alarm her. "Are you going to run back to your Australian girlfriend and leave me stranded here?"

"Don't be silly."

They settled side by side, Mathilde's arm still linked through his own.

"Her name was Alice."

Mathilde stayed quiet, not interrupting, and for over an hour Erich talked. He told her everything about his time in Marinup. About Stutt and Günter, the doctor, Guard Thomas and, of course, Alice. How they met. How they said farewell. About the baby. Only when he got to telling her about Doctor Alexander's final letter did he stop, his voice cracking.

"Why are you so upset? I will come to Australia with you. You know I will."

"No."

Mathilde dropped her arm from his and stared closely at him.

"Don't be silly, Erich. She is your lover and the mother of your child. You must go to her."

Wordlessly, Erich reached into an inside pocket and brought out a piece of much folded, once-white paper, which he handed to her.

As she read the letter, her face crumpled.

"Oh, Erich. My poor, poor brother. You loved her?"

"Yes. Of course."

She said nothing more for some time, until finally, "This changes nothing, you know."

"What do you mean?"

"Of course, you must still return to Australia. It says here that you will still be most welcome. We both will."

"Perhaps." Erich shook his head, doubt belying his words. "But perhaps not."

"You are being stupid."

"No. You will not be able to leave here for some time and that means that I will stay too."

"I can manage without you."

"Be that as it may, you are my only family left. I won't leave you again."

"Erich!" For the first time in as long as he could remember, his sister was genuinely angry. "How can you dare to tell me all of these things, and then ignore my advice, as though I have lost the capacity for intelligence? You are as arrogant as father sometimes."

"Not at all. I just know where my duty lies."

"Like you did when you went off to the war?"

"That was different."

"No. No it wasn't, brother. When you went off to fight, everyone knew it was to impress father, to make him proud of you for following in the family tradition and being honourable. Except it wasn't like that, was it? We both know that. But that is what you're doing again right now, Erich. Pretending that there's some higher cause driving you, because you're too scared or uninformed to face up to the reality of your life."

"At the moment you are the reality of my life, and that's all there is to it."

"And that baby? In Australia? The one you fathered? Are you telling me she isn't part of your responsibility? Of your family?"

"Of course, but she is fine, being loved and looked after, and you have no one left except me, so that is where my priorities must be for the moment. Later, who knows, but for now ..."

"You can be so pig-headed, do you know that?"

"I take after my sister."

The two were silent, neither making eye contact. Finally it was Mathilde who broke the quiet.

"So then, if you are not going, what will you do with yourself?"

Erich shrugged. "I do not know. Wait for you to get healthy again, I guess."

"No. Not enough. That isn't a suitable job for anyone. Waiting."

"Well, what do you want, then? Answer me?"

Mathilde rested her hand lightly on his forearm. "Erich, you know I love you more than anything else. And you know that I wouldn't have survived that camp if I hadn't known, deep inside myself, that you would come and find me. But I won't have you rescue me at the expense of your own life. I couldn't live with that."

Erich said nothing. He held his back straight and his gaze imperious as she continued.

"If you are not going to go back to Australia for this child, then that is your decision. Only you can make it and if it is what you think best, then I will support you. But Erich, I won't have you sitting around all day waiting on me. And I don't want you to be clearing rubble from building sites for the rest of your life. That's no life for anyone, especially not a strong young man with so much to offer. So you must find something, a path to follow, because it is the only way you will find happiness. That is all I am saying."

Her grip tightened on his arm, and, turning, Erich noticed pale beads of moisture on her brow and upper lip.

"You are all right?"

"I am very tired, that is all. I am not used to all this talking."

"We should head back up to the house."

"Yes."

She was slow to her feet and once back in the dim coolness of the ward she eased onto the bed, clearly exhausted, and appeared to fall asleep almost at once. Erich crept from the room, but when he reached the door her voice stopped him.

"Erich?"

He met her gaze steadily.

"Please think about what I have said. You don't know how much it hurts me to say these things to you, but there is no one else to tell you."

"Sleep now. I will be back this evening."

"Goodbye."

He closed the door as quietly as possible.

Twenty-seven

Vinnie

Vinnie lurched back into awareness with a start. The sun was higher now but a coolness in the air suggested it was still early. His skin prickled, chilled from the concrete, and the dream of that day at the beach, momentarily vivid, started fading into memory again.

The last of the grazing animals had retired into the forest; the only signs of life were a few drifting insects and a bobtail lizard, all stumps and scales, picking slowly between the hospital and mess hall foundations. Vinnie watched its sluggish progress with a kind of detachment.

Unconsciously, his right hand lifted to brush along the scar line on his face and neck. Thoughts of Katia gave way to thoughts of Helen and her grandfather and with slow realisation Vinnie knew exactly what task Doctor Pieters had for him. There was no moment of blinding clarity, no flash of inspiration, just the drifting recollection of words from an old letter, and a sudden understanding that up until this week the old man had never returned to Marinup.

The gift I spoke of in my last letter to you will remain in place at

Marinup … From the remains of the old detention cells it was a simple matter to look at the sun, compare its position with the hands on his watch and work out what direction was roughly south. *Fifty-three paces of youthful gait.* There Vinnie should find buried the doctor's final gift to the young Erich. Almost like a pirate treasure, Vinnie thought, as he counted his measured paces through the old guard's hut lines, past the camp administration building, and finally through a small clump of native shrubbery, to stop in a shaded clearing, right in the centre of the heart-shaped relief he'd noticed during his first exploration of the site.

A smile crept into his expression as Vinnie studied the shape at his feet. At its widest the heart was probably three metres across, and easily that much lengthways. It was a lot of ground to cover without any digging implements. As well, there were signs dotted around warning that this was an historic site and shouldn't be interfered with in any way. A sudden uncertainty seized him.

A rustle in the overhead trees made Vinnie look up, and he was not overly surprised to see another of the black cockatoos watching him. The creature met his eye and let out a grating screech that seemed to travel right through him.

As the bird's cry echoed away, the whole bush seemed to pause, standing silent for a time, before a heavy whipping of the air heralded the arrival of another of the giant birds. It slid out of the sky to perch in the same tree as the first. Then a third, and a fourth, and in seconds the air above the clearing was alive with the black phantoms of the forest, seemingly pouring from between trees and sky and perching in unnerving silence. After two minutes the trees were dripping with black shapes that watched silently with grave interest.

"Great."

It was like being in front of an audience and having no idea of what you were required to perform. Vinnie turned his attention back to the stone-bordered heart. Dropping to hands and knees, he edged his way around the shape, examining the mossy ground closely for even the slightest sign – some clue to an old disturbance that might indicate where to dig.

He reached the point of the heart where the two sides met in symmetrical collision, and Vinnie understood.

Using his bare hands to scrape away the surface layer of moss, he got to work with a stick, chipping the solid earth, removing at first tiny, then larger and larger, clumps of dry, reddish-brown soil, placing them carefully to one side.

As the sun climbed and the shade in the clearing disappeared, Vinnie continued chipping away and scraping the dirt aside until eventually the stick banged against something solid and hollow, slipping off with a ringing sound.

It was a box about the size of a small shoebox or large cigar tin, wrapped in rotting canvas that was torn where the stick had punctured it. It rested in the bottom of the hole, tied tightly with what looked like waxed twine or string, blackened with moisture, age and dirt.

This was it. As Vinnie lifted it from the earth a cacophony of noise erupted from the trees around him, accompanied by the threshing of hundreds of black wings against the air, as the entire flock of cockatoos lifted as one and circled above him before dispersing again into the forest.

Then Vinnie was alone in that strange, semi-silence of the daytime forest, turning the box over, examining it from all

303

angles. There was nothing to indicate its origins or its intended recipient.

Filling the hole took only a couple of minutes and then, gathering his discovery protectively to him, Vinnie set off back towards the Marinup town-site to deliver it.

July 1948

"And so this is to be our home?"

"Do you like it?"

"Yes, Erich. I like it very much."

Mathilde stepped into the tiny parlour. At this time of the afternoon the sun shone in from the west through the high garret windows and lit the sparse area in a warm yellow light.

"I know it isn't very big" – Erich looked slightly embarrassed – "but it is all I can afford at the moment."

"It is fine. It is very fine."

The stilted, formal expression reminded Erich of the same words spoken by a different girl in a different place, and something inside him quivered at the memory.

Mathilde explored the room, walking easily and unassisted. Here and there she ran her fingers across things – the rough surface of the wooden table, the back of one of the two chairs. At the mantelpiece she stopped and picked up the framed photograph, the solitary ornamentation in the room.

"This is Matilda?"

"It is." Erich came and stood beside her. "Her grandfather sent it with the letter informing me of the doctor's death."

"She is beautiful."

The infant in the picture, no more than a year old, stared into the camera with a solemn expression framed by dark, curly hair. Her skin was unmistakably pale, and even though the photograph was black and white, it left the distinct impression that the eyes looking out from under those heavy lashes were a deep, almost iridescent blue.

"Why did you not show me this before?"

Erich sighed. This was old ground. "You know that I won't change my mind."

"Yes, I do. As I have said many times, you are far too stubborn for your own good, brother."

"There are too many other considerations."

"I could come with you, now."

"I know. But now there are also my studies to consider. And Maria."

Mathilde crossed the bare floorboards and circled her arm around her brother's waist.

"There will always be a college of medicine for you to return to. There will always be Maria. I should very much like to see my niece, as you know."

"Perhaps. But not now."

"Then when?"

"Later. Come, I will show you your room."

Erich guided her out into the narrow entry passage.

"The kitchen is through here, the bathroom through that door there. I have set up my room in the attic at the top of the stairs, and yours is here."

"Have you been living in the attic all of this past year?"

"No, of course not. I wanted to save you the effort of climbing those stairs all the time."

"Erich." She stopped him, mid-stride. "You know I am better now. Cured."

"I know, it's just that ..."

"Then please don't treat me like an invalid. I've had enough of it and if people are going to keep doing so then I don't think I'll be able to bear it. I want to move on now. Just like you should."

They looked at each other for many moments, but he dropped his eyes, refusing to meet the challenge in her words, and silently followed her into the room that was to be hers. After so long in the hospital, it felt strange to have a room that belonged to her. A private space. Once again, Mathilde made a slow circumnavigation, finally sitting on the single iron-framed bed beside the far window.

"Do you like it?"

She realised how nervous her brother really was.

"Yes, Erich. It's just lovely."

And he smiled, one of his rare smiles.

"Good. I'll leave you to get settled while I go and fix dinner."

And then she was alone. Mathilde lay back and closed her eyes, listening to the noises of the house, the water clunking through pipes, and beyond to the distant sounds of the city – a child's bicycle bell, an occasional car, pedestrians passing in the street outside. The window showed a glimpse of tree-tops and blue and Mathilde breathed in the solitude, so rare and so precious after over a year in convalescence.

A knock on the front door was answered by hurried foot-steps. Maria was here. Mathilde listened to her brother's murmured tones as he greeted Maria at the door and the two disappeared back into the kitchen.

Maria, Mathilde reflected, was good for Erich. In many ways the nurse had saved him just as he had saved his sister. It had been her who had put him in touch with the professor of medicine at the university and her who took on the burden of nursing Mathilde while he did his study. And now it was Maria who, it seemed, was keeping him here – here in crumbling, post-war Germany, with its hardship and unemployment – and committing him to a life on the other side of the world from his daughter. Mathilde felt her eyes mist up, as they always did when she thought about the little girl.

"Are you awake?" A gentle knock at the bedroom door. Maria.

"Yes."

The other girl entered. "Do you like the place?"

"I do. It's a little spartan compared with what I'm used to, but I guess that is my brother for you."

"Isn't it?" Maria laughed. "God knows I try to get him to brighten the place up, but he says he likes it this way."

"Too long in that prison camp, I imagine."

The women shared a smile. Maria was still in her nurse's uniform.

"And how are you?" The clinical tone, the predictable question.

"I'm fine." Mathilde tried to stop irritation from creeping into her voice. "Just fine. Cured, remember?"

"I'm sorry." Maria laughed uncertainly. "Habit, I guess."

"That's all right. How are things at the hospital?"

"The same as ever. It seems strange without you there. You know you were our longest resident?"

"I believe it was mentioned."

"Well, everyone misses you."

"That's nice."

Maria sat on the other side of the bed, opposite Mathilde.

307

She wore a hesitant expression, as though she was about to speak but was having trouble with the words.

"Mathilde …" She stopped.

"Yes, Maria?"

"Have you talked to him about his daughter?"

Mathilde looked away, out the window to where a bird, perhaps a hawk of some sort, drifted high and distant on a warm updraft.

"I've tried. But I don't think he really listens to me."

"You know he does."

"Then why is he still here in Germany?"

"Because he loves you."

"Really? I thought it might be because he loves you." Try as she might, Mathilde couldn't keep the bitter edge from her voice. "You and his studies seem to be what he spends most of his time thinking about right now."

"Loves me?" To Mathilde's surprise, the other girl's face took on a sad, almost wistful expression. "No. All I can hope is that in time he might learn to love me, but for the moment you and that little girl in Australia are the only two who can lay claim to Erich's love." She paused for a moment, considering. "He is fond of me, certainly."

"Then why do you ask about the child?"

"Because I don't know if Erich has told you everything about it. About his" she searched for the right word – "situation."

"What do you mean? What situation?"

"It's really not my place."

"What?" Mathilde gripped the nurse's arm with a strength that belied her still frail appearance.

308

"You should ask him. Your brother has been tearing himself apart for this last year, that's really all I can tell you."

Mathilde let go her arm and the other girl rose from the bed.

"I must get back to help Erich with the dinner. It is good to see you finally at home, Mathilde."

The bedroom door closed, leaving Mathilde alone in the early evening light.

Twenty-eight

Vinnie

"How did you work out what I was going to ask of you?"

The old man turned the parcel over and over. His hands, Vinnie noticed, were shaking slightly.

"Dunno. Just kind of figured it out."

The two of them sat in silence on either side of the folding table. Helen had taken the campervan into town to pick up milk and a few other bits and pieces.

"Where was it?"

"Buried in this heart shape on the ground."

"Ah, yes. I'd forgotten them. How much like Günter."

"Them?"

"The garden beds. The Italian prisoners built several of them on the outskirts of the camp."

"Why hearts?"

The old man smiled.

"They weren't all hearts. There were also diamonds, clubs and spades."

"Cards?"

"*Ja.*" Even with the doctor's accent, it was strange to hear the occasional German words creep into the conversation. "Familiar shapes, you understand?"

"I think so."

"Was it difficult to find?"

"Not really. Not once I thought about it. And I just had this feeling."

"Hmmm."

The old man tugged absently at the string holding the canvas wrapping.

"This will need to be cut."

"I have a pocket knife in my tent. Would you like me to get it?"

"No. Not just yet." The old man shook his head. "This has waited for me for half a century now, and I am thinking that a few more minutes will make little difference. We will wait for my grand-daughter to return. She would be upset to miss out on this."

"Fair enough."

Arriving back at the clearing, the box clutched to his chest, Vinnie had had a moment of doubt. Had he done the right thing? Seeing the old man drinking tea at the table beside Helen's tent, he'd hesitated. It had been the old man who had noticed him and had offered a welcoming nod.

"Doctor?"

"Yes, Vincent?"

"Why didn't you come back earlier? You knew this was here, right?"

"I knew that it might be."

"Why then?"

"I am ill. Helen has told you that, I imagine."

"Yeah."

"Then, how do I put this? Then I am putting some ghosts to rest before I pass on. That is all, really."

"And the box?"

"I really am not sure. I did not actually think it would still be here, after all this time."

"But you still came."

"Yes, I did."

"So now what?"

"Now, Vincent, we will wait for Helen to return from the town and we will see what is in this little bundle here. But before then I have some questions to ask of you, also."

"Me?"

"Yes, if you do not mind."

"I guess not."

"You do not have to answer me, if it makes you uncomfortable."

"Okay."

"Why are you here?"

"Helen didn't tell you?"

"My grand-daughter is very good at keeping other's business to herself. It is an admirable trait, I think. She takes a little after her grandmother in that way."

"Alice?"

"*Ja.* Alice. She had an ability to listen to another's life and see right to the meaning of it, really see where that person was, what they were thinking, why they were troubled. It is a talent I have never really been able to develop, I am afraid. My wife could do it as well."

"Your wife?"

"Maria. We met after the war, when I was back in Germany."

"Oh."

"But this is not the topic. You were about to tell me what happened to you to bring you to this clearing in the middle of the bush."

"Don't really know how to start. There's not a lot to tell really. I was in an accident with my sister, she was killed, I got all this" – he gestured at his face and neck – "and I just wanted to get away from all the stares, I guess."

"Who was staring?" The old man was sitting forward.

"Everyone. You can't walk around lookin' like this and not attract attention."

"So you run away from it?"

"Nah. But sometimes you need time out, you know?"

"Are you certain you are not running away? What do your parents think of you being here."

Vinnie shrugged.

"They do not know?"

"They know I'm okay. I called them."

"But they do not know where you are? Or why you are here?"

"Nah. But that's not really their problem, is it? It's mine."

"Of course it is their problem, Vincent. They are your parents."

"You don't understand all the background. There's more to it than that."

"Then tell me."

Vinnie shook his head. "You wouldn't get it."

The old man's blue eyes burned with an old fire. "Vincent, at your age I ran away from my parents to go and fight for my country, in a war that neither of them believed in. When I

313

came back they were both dead. Do not assume that I can not understand what it is to be a young man."

"You don't understand what it's like to look like this."

"Perhaps not, but I certainly know what it means to run from your problems."

"My dad reckons it's my fault that Katia got killed."

"And was it?"

Vinnie stared at the old man. His face, trained by years of being a doctor, surrendered nothing. The silence hung in the air while Vinnie struggled for an answer. None came, and he dropped his gaze to where an ant was struggling to navigate through dead grass.

"Vincent ..." This time there was gentleness in the old man's tone. Still expectant but less confrontational. "*Was* it your fault?"

On the far edge of the clearing the campervan emerged from the tree line, bumping across the field in a cloud of red dust. Vinnie stayed silent. As the van pulled up in its customary place, Doctor Pieters reached across and gripped Vinnie's wrist.

"I think you should answer that question, Vincent. First to yourself, and then to me. Then you will know what and who you are really running from."

Vinnie stood and fled to his own tent, before Helen could come around from the driver's side.

July 1948

"So, my brother, what is it you are not telling me?"

Mathilde and Erich sat in the garden in the twilight.

"Excuse me?"

"Last night Maria came into my room and we had a discussion."

"A discussion?"

"About you and your daughter."

Mathilde was aware of the sudden tension in the way her brother was sitting.

"What did she tell you?"

"Very little."

"She had no right to say anything."

"Of course she did. Don't be pig-headed. She only suggested that I needed to talk to you. That there were things you hadn't told me."

"Even so ..."

"Don't even think about taking this out on her, Erich. The girl loves you and you should appreciate that much more than you do. Even if you don't love her back."

"This is not about love. It is about privacy."

"Do you remember me telling you once that I wouldn't have you ruin your own life on my account?"

"Vaguely."

"Well, I did."

"What of it?"

"Erich." Mathilde shook her head despairingly. "Don't you understand that if you have reasons for not going back there and you won't share them with me then of course I will assume that I am those reasons?"

"There is much more to it."

"Then for God's sake *tell me*!"

After a few moments Erich stood and walked into the house, leaving Mathilde alone in the tiny garden. She sighed as the door slammed.

As a child Erich had been aloof, detached somehow from the rest of the family, but not like this. Since returning from Australia he was so distant, so hard to reach, almost as though he viewed himself as an outsider, someone untouchable.

The door opened again and her brother re-emerged, a piece of paper in his hand.

"Do you remember our discussion in the hospital gardens?"

"Of course."

"Well, this arrived a few weeks later. At the same time as the photograph."

He thrust the page into her hands. It was in English, typed, but still difficult for her to translate. He sat and waited, watching in calm, expectant silence for twenty minutes while she struggled through unfamiliar idiom and expression.

"Do I understand this?"

"Yes." Erich nodded. "Under Australian law her grandparents became her legal parents, and after the death of Doctor Alexander they clearly re-thought their decision to welcome us back to Australia."

"But surely ..."

"There is no surely. Alice's father makes that quite clear there. They will tell her about me when she is older and allow her to make her own decision as to whether she wants me as her father or not. Until then, they believe it would be better for her and for them if I stay away."

"I thought they said you would be most welcome?"

"Doctor Alexander said that in his letter, yes."

"How can they change their minds, so?"

316

Erich shrugged. "It would not be hard. From what Günter writes, Australia is not an easy place for a former German soldier to live at the moment. There are a lot of people with bad memories of the war."

"But that is not your fault, and surely not your daughter's."

"No, but her grandparents feel that it would be better for her to grow up without the stigma of a German father. Perhaps in some years …"

"You cannot accept this, Erich."

"Mathilde, I must accept it. What can I do?"

"You can get on a boat and go back there. You are her father. You can challenge for adoption."

"No, I can't …" Her brother's voice choked slightly, his shoulders sagging in a suggestion of defeat. The gesture looked unnatural on him.

"So you will simply stay here."

"I will stay here, become a doctor, and perhaps in time I can do something good with this life of mine."

"How can you say that?" Mathilde stood, anger in her stance and in her eyes. "How can you look at that photograph in there and suggest that you have done nothing good with yourself?"

"That was not what I said."

"It was what you meant. You are such a foolish man sometimes, Erich. I hope you know that, because you make me so angry. I never met your Alice, but I am certain this is not what she wanted for her child."

"I have given up trying to work out what she would have wanted."

There was no anger in Erich's voice, just quiet resignation.

317

"Well then, what do you want?"

"Me?"

"Yes, you. If you can't decide what she would have wanted for the baby, you can at least tell me what your own feelings are."

"Maria thinks ..."

"Not Maria, *you*. What do you want for your child?"

Erich looked at the sky. "I do not know. I want her to be happy."

"Without a father? Is that possible?"

"There was a war. Many children have no fathers."

"She wasn't born in the war. I'll ask again, what do you want for her?"

Her brother's gaze met hers.

"I really do not know."

"Well, you should think about it. Because I think that all you are doing is running away, and once you can answer me that simple little question, then, my brother, perhaps you'll know what it is you're running away from."

Twenty-nine

Vinnie

Sunset at the prison camp ruins approached with a gentle rapidity that Vinnie found reassuring. Once the sun descended below the trees the whole clearing became dappled and crazed with muted shadows, moving with the faint sea breeze that stretched all this way inland to run up the escarpment and trickle through the forest. The cooling touch of it after the heat of the afternoon soothed both Vinnie's skin and mind.

Lying on his back, looking up, the sky was still blue, a shimmering vault, deepening slightly, and stained pink at the edges with the last vestige of daylight. There was a constancy to it that touched Vinnie and settled his rushing thoughts into something less chaotic.

Was it his fault? Perhaps. Could he have done anything different that night? He didn't know. His father thought so. Did he let his sister burn?

All afternoon the question had plagued him, eventually driving him from his tent and back along the prison camp trail for the second time that day, there to lie again on the foundations of the old hospital, in the growing shade, to seek some kind of peace, some kind of understanding.

When he closed his eyes the fireshadow started leaping again, and he remembered the crackle of the laughing flames and the nauseating despair that drove him down through his pain and into unconsciousness. He remembered the jolting, screaming of the ambulance, the coming to briefly and the cold slide of a needle into his arm. He saw the metal crumpled and burning like waste paper, and Katia imprisoned and burning somewhere within the brightness.

But was it his fault?

"I thought you'd be here."

Helen stood a couple of metres away, beside the thin eucalypt in whose shade he'd been resting. The hesitant manner and uncertain expression were so different from her usual confidence.

"Are you all right? Grandad told me what you talked about. And what he said."

Vinnie shrugged. "I can't work it out."

"If it was your fault?"

"Yeah."

She sat beside him, legs hugged up to her chest.

"You're the only one who can answer that particular question; you know that, don't you?"

"I guess so."

"No, Vinnie." She took him gently by his chin and turned his face to hers. "You're the only one. Not your parents, not me, not anyone but you."

"Yeah, I get that. I've had a hundred counsellors telling me the same fucking thing again and again. It's not my fault. I know."

320

"No, you don't. If you knew it, you'd believe it."

"Well, that's just great then. If I don't believe it wasn't my fault, then it must have really been my fault. Is that it?"

"Don't be a dickhead, Vinnie. You know that's not what I mean."

"Yeah." The anger drained from him as quickly as it had flared. "Yeah. I'm sorry. It's just, I feel like it's so much bullshit, you know? Having to feel like this. Not being able to work it all out."

"I don't know, I can only imagine."

"Helen?"

"Yeah?"

"When he dies, your grandfather, will you miss him?"

"Of course I will. I don't really know him all that well, but I'll miss him. He's my grandfather."

"That's the thing, you see? With Kat. I miss her – so much. It's like there's this massive hole, this part of me that's gone now, and I can't feel sorry for myself because it's probably my fault in the first place. I mean, what if I'd been a bit faster? Got out of the car when she first told me to? Or pushed myself a bit harder into the heat. I might have got her out."

"And you might have got yourself killed too, and left your parents with no one."

"At least I'd have tried."

"Vinnie …" Helen reached over again and ran a finger along the purple welt that marked his face. "You tried. Don't ever let anyone – including yourself – tell you that you didn't try. Shit, I don't think there's any way I'd be able to do this to myself. This mark on your face, this is all the proof you need that you tried."

Her finger ran along the edge of the scar, tracing across the side of his nose, the corner of his mouth, through the faint creasing below his jaw, and slowly down his neck, stopping only where the discolouration ran into the collar of his t-shirt. Vinnie felt her hand on his shoulder.

"You need to be a bit forgiving of yourself."

As the gloom deepened across the clearing, Vinnie looked out to the trees a hundred metres distant, beyond the old fence line. The spaces between the trunks were already dark and alive and he found himself listening not to the sounds of the bush but to the breathing of the girl beside him, the regular, even pulse of it against the growing night.

Finally he stood. "We oughta get back. I'm gettin' eaten alive by mozzies."

He offered her a hand, which she took without hesitation, and hoisted her back to her feet.

"Got plans for the evening?"

"You asking me out?" She offered a half-smile.

"Perhaps."

"I told you before, Vinnie, you'll have to work a lot harder than that to get a date with me. Besides, as it turns out I do have plans, and so do you."

"Yeah?"

"Yeah. There's a little matter of a parcel my grandfather wants to unwrap."

"He hasn't done it yet?"

"He wanted to wait until you could join us. Actually, he was quite insistent."

"We'd better get a move on then."

She reached out and took his hand as though it was the most natural thing in the world. In the darkness Vinnie smiled.

May 1949

The ship came around the harbour breakwater at three in the afternoon, attended by stubby tugs which churned the murky water as they shoved, nudged and whistled it into position. Standing on the wharf, Erich felt Maria take his hand. It was clammy and nervous.

"Relax, my darling. It will be fine."

"I wish I could be so confident."

"Here comes Mathilde."

His sister pushed her way through the throng of people, looking anxiously around until she spotted the tall frame of her brother. Maria was beside him and they were holding hands, she noticed. That was good. It had been a long time coming. She waved and moved towards them.

"You nearly missed the boat docking."

"I know. I'm sorry. Can you see them yet?"

The promenade decks of the liner, towering above the wharf now, were lined with hundreds of passengers, clutching children and waving to familiar faces ashore.

"No. I doubt I could recognise them."

"I wonder how long they'll be?"

With a final blast of its whistle, the tugboat gave the stern of the ship a massive shove and the great weight eased alongside the creaking timbers of the wharf. At the bow and stern sailors hurled weighted lines to waiting hands, and the heavy moorings were hauled across and made fast.

"Where will we meet them?"

"Outside the customs hall." Erich pulled nervously at the tight collar of his shirt.

"Relax." Maria fussed at him, re-straightening his tie.

The wharf was a hubbub of voices, a mixture of German,

323

French and English. Children darted between legs, grabbed at by anxious parents if they ventured too close to the narrowing gap between ship and wharf.

Then it seemed like scant minutes passed before the ship was made fully fast to the dock. Hatches and doors opened, gangways were hoisted into position, and cranes lifted pallets of luggage from the holds, depositing them on the wharf inside the fenced-off customs area.

"Come on."

Still holding Erich's hand, Maria led the way inside.

Two guards stood barring entry to the massive customs area. Between them a sign, in French and German, stated: *No Entry: Passengers Only*.

"How long until people start getting off?" Mathilde asked one of the guards.

"First-class passengers should be through in half an hour or so, second and third class sometime after that."

The three stood watching as, at first, a trickle of people, then a flood started to pour through the wide double doors. Erich found himself surrounded by a sea of smiling faces, tears, hugs and kisses. All the while he craned his neck, peering through into the densely packed hall, searching for some hint of a familiar face, some feature that he might recognise.

After forty-five minutes the crowd began to thin out a little as departing passengers left the terminal, arm in arm with friends and relatives, hauling steamer cases.

"Are you certain this was the right ship?" Maria squeezed his hand, vestiges of concern on her face.

"Yes." It was Mathilde who answered her. "They are probably just held up inside. There are still people coming through. I imagine they travelled third class, didn't they?"

"I don't know." Erich spoke without stopping his search for a second. "Probably."

"Do you think they could have come past without us realising it? Perhaps they have gone to find a hotel."

"I would not have thought so. The arrangements in the telegram were quite specific."

"We'll wait a little longer."

For another five minutes they stood, jostled less and less by the now rapidly dissipating crowd.

"I need to go to the toilet. Wait here for me." Mathilde started away.

"I'll come with you." Maria dropped Erich's hand, delivered a quick, reassuring kiss to his cheek which Erich barely even noticed, and followed.

Erich checked his watch again. Fifty-five minutes. A bead of sweat escaped from his hairline and tickled its way down his face, making him wipe at it irritably.

Then there they were.

Alice's parents were younger than he'd imagined them. Her father, tall, dark-suited and grey at the temples. And her mother – at a glance Erich realised that he could not have failed to recognise her. The same long dark hair, tied back. The same cheekbones and nose. They hadn't recognised him, of course, as they stood gripping their bags, surrounded by a babble of Germanic and Gallic voices. Between them, clutching their hands, a three-year-old girl with dark curly hair and a serious expression stared wide-eyed at all the activity and the strangeness.

Erich just stood and looked, then Alice's father noticed him staring and caught his eye.

"Erich?" The man's voice was high with uncertainty, his

Australian accent, with its elongated vowels, ringing foreign in the emptying terminal.

Erich stepped forward. "Mr Andrews?"

Seconds passed. Finally Erich offered his hand. The other man seemed to hesitate for a second before taking it in an iron grasp.

"Call me Peter. This is my wife, Lynn."

"How do you do?" After so long speaking only German, Erich was surprised at how different and tentative the English words felt in his mouth.

"Hello." The woman smiled, and it was Alice's smile.

Erich found himself only vaguely aware of them or his sister and fiancé, who had approached silently from behind and stood waiting. All he was really conscious of were the big blue eyes that watched him, eyes that mirrored the hesitancy and anxiousness in his own.

"And this is Matilda." Peter Andrews crouched beside his grand-daughter and put a reassuring arm around her shoulders. "Tilly, this is Erich, your daddy, who we've been talking about. Do you remember?"

Erich too crouched down to the same level as the little girl, who continued to regard him from within the protective curve of her grandfather's arm. He was barely breathing, and was only dimly aware of the other man saying again, "Tilly? Your daddy. Remember?"

Hesitant, terrified, longing, Erich stretches an arm out across the gap between them, offering a hand which hangs for an eternity, regarded with considered seriousness, until in a moment of sudden decision the little girl reaches towards him and takes a finger, just one, in her own tenuous grip. The contact sends a jolt up Erich's arm.

Then the little girl smiles at him, and her smile is that of her mother, and Erich is back in a dim-lit, prison camp hospital on a rainy afternoon.

And he's smiling back at her.

Thirty

Vinnie

Vinnie, Helen and her grandfather sat on three sides of the table, the parcel, still wrapped in the canvas, between them, the only sound the gentle hiss of gas from the lamp. The old man reached out and picked it up, turning it thoughtfully one more time.

"It almost seems a shame to open it now."

"Why, Grandad?"

"After all these years it is like opening a grave. I am starting to wonder if perhaps there are things which are best left consigned to history."

Helen looked at the old man, worried. This was a different man from the one she had come to know over the last few days.

"I could take it back and replace it for you, if you'd like."

"No, Vincent." The old man smiled. "I don't think that will be necessary."

Placing the bundle back down, Erich Pieters pushed it across to his grand-daughter.

"You should open this."

"I couldn't."

"Of course you can. You are my grand-daughter. Whatever is in there will soon belong to you in any case."

"Are you sure?"

"Of course."

Picking up the pocket knife, Helen began to slice though the twine around the package. Even after so long in the ground, it was tough and it took several seconds of concerted effort to saw through it. Finally, it fell away and she was able to peel back the outer layers of the heavy, waterproofed canvas.

Inside was a tin box, tarnished slightly with age, but overall little the worse for wear after its fifty or so years underground. The canvas wrappings had done their work well.

"*Mien Gott!*" The old man's voice was barely a whisper. "This is something I never thought I would see again."

There were tears glistening in his old eyes as Erich reached out with shaking hands and pulled the tin towards himself.

"What is it?" Helen and Vinnie peered at the dull metallic sheen on the surface of the tin as the old man turned it to the light.

"A relic. A piece of history. Just … there."

In the dim cast of light from the lantern, words shimmered on the lid of the tin, finely engraved letters that swam into the old man's vision as they had once before, many years earlier.

To my darling husband on the occasion of his graduation. With fondest love, Emmaline.

With shaking hands he opened the tin and an envelope fell from it onto the table. Ignoring it, the old doctor pulled from a padded slot one of the scalpels. The surgical knife,

329

with its stainless steel shaft and perfectly balanced mother of pearl handle, seemed untouched by the passage of time. In the light from the gas lamp it gleamed with an internal iridescence that swept the old man back into the past. He smiled.

"Who would have thought ..." The old man's voice trailed off and his eyes closed, and for a few seconds the night gave way to a summer day, deep in the forest, with sun slanting down in thick beams between the jarrahs. A young German prisoner stopped his chopping and looked up, between the thick canopy of green, fixing his gaze on the tiny slivers of blue beyond and making a promise to himself, a promise about a girl who was at that moment only a few kilometres away, working with her grandfather in a prison camp hospital. And the young soldier smiled.

"Grandad? Are you all right?"

Helen touched her grandfather lightly on the shoulder and the old man's eyes opened again, watery with memory. He was smiling.

"*Ja, Ja*. I am fine."

He replaced the scalpel in its slot, and pushed the entire box towards his granddaughter.

"You should take this."

"I couldn't."

"Of course you must. It belonged to your great-grand-father."

"But ..."

"Shh." The doctor held up a finger. "I will hear no argument. They are of little use to me now."

Helen said nothing more, only gathered the tin to herself, running a finger lightly across the words on the lid.

330

"And you, Vincent, must open this."

The envelope was made of thick white paper and felt heavy and creamy to touch. On the front was written in elegant copperplate handwriting: *Private Erich Pieters. Afrika Korps. Personal.*

"Are you sure?"

"My eyes are not what they used to be. I am afraid I would have difficulty making out the writing. And besides" – the old man held Vinnie's gaze with his own – "this letter was written to a troubled young man. Not to a retired doctor. I imagine it will be far more appropriate that you read it to me."

Using the knife, Vinnie sliced carefully along the top of the envelope and extracted from it several sheets of the same creamy white paper, folded neatly. The elegant handwriting was easy to read.

Perth, January 25th, 1947
Dear Erich,
So, my friend, you have managed to return to Marinup. I hope you do not mind me causing you the inconvenience of coming all the way back here, but it seemed to me that you might find the trip rewarding. While of course, I have no way to predict when you will finally receive this little gift, I hope it finds you in happy times.

I imagine that the campsite is somewhat changed from how you remember it. By the time I left, some months ago now, they were dismantling the camp around me day by day and already there was a strange desolation about the place, but at the same time an unusual feeling of re-birth, as though things were returning to the way they were meant to be. This is important, I think, and it is why I have asked Günter to bury this gift here for

331

you to find – I believe it will be important for you to see this place in a different light.

I have already written to you in Germany, earlier this week, conveying my feeling about Alice and the situation she has found herself in. I imagine that by the time you read this letter the two of you and your child will be well and truly reunited. I believe this because I am certain that you feel the same way for her as she clearly does for you, and I know you well enough to be confident that you will do the right thing by both her and the baby. I will not pretend that this will not pose a whole new set of challenges for the two of you, for you will be bringing this baby up together in a world vastly different from the one that both I and your parents inhabited. My hope for you both is that you are able to see your way to doing this bravely, honestly, and by facing up directly to the many difficulties with which you will be confronted. I pray that despite all of this you will both be able to see the good in what you have created.

Because it is a good thing – don't forget that. All suffering in life must serve a purpose. The only time that suffering is point-less is if we as people allow it to become so. This is perhaps the one thing that I have learned in my many years as a medical practitioner. If we allow suffering to become meaningless, then it will almost definitely remain so, and this is how faith and compassion die. If we utilise the experience of difficulty, how-ever, we can turn ourselves into the people we are truly destined to become.

Never forget this, Erich, because your experiences through the war have at times been terrible, but the true pity will be if you fail to make anything of them for yourself, if you fail to let yourself be governed in a positive way by the loss of your parents and your compulsory separation from my grand-daughter. Likewise, if she surrenders to the hopelessness she so often feels at the moment, then and only then will her suffering win out over hope. And it is important to me, and to the world, that this baby of yours be born and grow with hope, Erich. I am sure you understand that.

I am also certain that you will recognise the gift that I am leaving for you. My hope is that it will assist you along a career path for which I still believe you demonstrate an amazing aptitude and talent. I would like to think that at some point down the track you will use these scalpels and remember me as your friend, and as someone who admires you deeply. After the trouble that these scalpels caused for you, I feel it is appropriate that you have them – an example, perhaps, of drawing out the positives from our suffering?

Farewell then, my friend. I would be surprised if I am still walking this earth when you read this letter, but you should know that if it is at all possible I will be watching over you, and Alice, and your family.

I wish you peace and happiness.

Your friend

Doctor Johnathon Alexander

As Vinnie read the final words, and the doctor's name, a deep silence descended across the clearing. Helen sniffed a little and wiped at her eyes, but otherwise the stillness of the night was absolute.

The three people sat, each alone in the bush night, each exploring the words from the past in their own context. Eventually, it was Vinnie who stood and stepped away from the table.

"I might head back over to my own camp, if that's all right."

"Of course. Thank you, Vincent."

The stars above the clearing seemed closer than before, more bright and intense. There was no moon and the ink-vault of the heavens stretched overhead in perfect harmony. At his campsite Vinnie crawled into his tent and lay on his sleeping bag, but knew immediately that he would be unable to sleep, so he crept out again and put a match to the fire, which was still kindled from that morning.

The words of the long-dead doctor rang in his mind, echoing through the years, speaking to him from somewhere beyond his experience. Vinnie watched the flames and lifted his gaze to the leaping shadows that surrounded him. Their ethereal dance was no longer threatening, no longer gleefully evil. Suddenly the fireshadow was nothing more than light. Harmless, dissipating patches of light and darkness.

Vinnie was barely aware of the light in the campervan flicking off and the crunch of Helen's footsteps towards him through the night.

"Hey there."

She eased into the circle of light and down beside him.

"Hi."

He felt her weight on his shoulder as she slipped her arm though his, hugging it to herself and leaning into him.

"Thanks, Vinnie."

"No worries."

They sat like that through the night, not speaking, barely moving, each aware of the other only by their body warmth, by the gentle heave of one another's breathing, the occasional intake of breath and the infrequent throwing of more wood into the fire. Sometime in the small hours a full moon climbed slowly over the northern tree-line and bathed the clearing in bright silver, every detail clear in monochrome. Finally, when the eastern horizon was glowing with the first signs of dawn, Vinnie stirred to his feet.

"You okay?"

"Yeah."

"Can I ask a favour?"

"Sure."

"You wanna help me get the tent down?"

"You going somewhere?"

"I thought I might take you up on your offer of a lift home, if it's still open."

"Course it is."

An early morning breeze trembled through the branches of the pine tree above. The forest stood aloof, passively observant, its unseen depths reflecting the passage of many lives past and many yet to come. And later, as the final plumes of dust settled in the wake of the departing camper-van and the old burned-down townsite relaxed again into uneasy quietude, a single black cockatoo wheeled twice in the warm breeze, high above, before gliding effortlessly away towards its home.

Acknowledgments

While the events and characters of this story are fictional, there is a very real context behind the story of Erich Pieters. During the Second World War large numbers of German and Italian prisoners worked in the farms and forests of South-West W.A. and indeed across Australia. It was their labour that supplied Perth with fuel and food and in many cases after the war these prisoners became stalwarts of the Western Australian German and Italian communities. The remains of the Marinup townsite and POW Camp 16 still stand in the jarrah forest just outside Dwellingup and I have tried to reproduce both them and the details of camp life as accurately as possible. As with any work of fiction, however, imagination has also played a large part, and any errors or inaccuracies are mine.

The Marinup area is a strange place, quiet, peaceful and oddly haunted, and I would recommend people visit this unique part of our nation's cultural heritage.

In writing this book, I am indebted to an enormous number of people: Mr Ernie Pollis, local historian and expert on the Marinup camp, generously shared his time, his formidable knowledge and his resources with me to help me develop the story of Erich. My family and colleagues at Trinity College, Perth, have as always proved to be supportive critics in the best sense of the words. Lucy Leonhardt, given the unenviable task of pointing out the weaknesses and inaccuracies in the manuscript, managed to do so in the nicest possible way. Leonie Tyle, my editor, continued to have faith in and encouraged my writing, and the team at UQP did the same.

And finally I thank Imogen, my best friend, my best critic and the other half of me, for all this and more.

If you are interested in learning more about the Marinup campsite, I can recommend reading Rosemary Johnston's unpublished thesis *Marinup POW Camp* which is available in the Battye Library in Perth. For a more general background, *Behind Barbed Wire: Internment in Australia during World War II* by Margaret Bevage and *Stalag Australia* by Barbara Winter both proved extremely useful. Colleen Camarda's book *I Loved an Italian Prisoner of War* provided me with a more personal perspective of the issues of love and internment. Information on the German wartime experience and the assassination attempt on Hitler's life came from a wide range of sources; however, Laurence Rees' *The Nazi's – A Warning from History*, Ron Rosenbaum's excellent *Explaining Hitler*, the *Penguin Historical Atlas of the Third Reich* (edited by Richard Overy) and Ian Westwell's *Hitler's Third Reich – The Journey from Victory to Defeat* proved to be constant sources of reference.

OTHER

UQP

Titles by
Anthony Eaton

a new kind of dreaming

"You want to hear a story?"

"Eh?"

"This town, it's full of stories. Some Aboriginal, some white, some Malay and Indonesian. All sorts of different ideas. I reckon you might need to hear one of them."

When the court sent Jamie Riley to Port Barren, he hadn't expected much – thought he'd just serve his time and get out. He hadn't counted on being drawn into the town's murky past, into a web of secrets, lies and murder which might well cost him much more than just his freedom.

This is the story of a boy's journey to reveal a buried secret, and of a town too scared of its past to face its future.

It's a story for anyone who dreams ...

The story of Jamie becomes an almost archetypal quest, and the landscape of the town and the desert take on a magical, almost spiritual, quality which adds another dimension to a well-told and beautifully written tale.

Australian Bookseller & Publisher

Eaton subtly mixes cultures and stories and tells a rattling good yarn.

Newsletter Australian Centre for Youth Literature

The Darkness

The Darkness comes for all of us eventually …

In the small coastal town of Isolation Bay, a shadow hangs over the lives of Rohan Peters and his mother Eileen. Bound together by small town superstition, their lives are dominated by fear.

Into this setting comes Rachel, a girl on the run from her own dark history. As Rohan and Rachel struggle to build a friendship amidst the paranoia of Isolation Bay, their pasts come crashing down on them in an event that will change both of their lives forever.

A fine study of a young man's emotional journey and an exciting read that would probably make an effective movie.

Viewpoint

A vivid tale of the wild days of our history and how no one can escape the past.

Reading Time

Nathan Nuttboard Hits the Beach

A few days at the beach, camping with your family. Sounds like a good time, right?

Maybe, but don't forget to factor in:

the motorbike riding bogan

an older sister in love

a tent which is suffering a spiritual crisis

a surfer named Gnarly who's idea of fun involves exfoliating sparkplugs!

For **Nathan Nuttboard**, this could be an interesting few days.

> *This is a fun read with lots of laughs and just enough adventure to keep you on your toes. The boys will love it.*
>
> Goodreading
>
> *An easy-to-read, humorous book that evokes instant memories of family holidays and captures the language of young people.*
>
> Primary Focus Fiction